THE 7 HABITS OF HIGHLY EFFECTIVE REAPERS

THE GRIM REAPER CHRONICLES

BOOK ONE

C.A. KENNEDY

THE 7 HABITS OF HIGHLY EFFECTIVE REAPERS

ISBN: 978-1-963705-16-4

Published in the United States of America by Harbor Lane Books, LLC.

www.harborlanebooks.com

A forward from actor and musician, Johnny Depp—
Okay, not really. He doesn't even know I exist...yet...anyway.

Actually, this is my dedication page, and I'm dedicating this book to my dad. I would never have let him read this book because of the language and sex, but I know he would have still been proud of his daughter for writing a story and getting it published.

For you, Dad—I miss you every day.

CHAPTER 1

October 4:

Someone is killing witches, but it really isn't my concern. Above my pay grade, if you will. My job is to collect their souls, get them to the ferry, and let Management sort it out on the other side.

This latest one isn't too happy about her untimely death, though. She skips over the shock and denial part of grief, briefly focuses on the second stage of pain and guilt, then launches right into Stage Three with anger and bargaining. All of this occurs before I've even had my lunch.

I glance at my watch. It's 12:15 and the next ferry leaves at 2:00. We still have plenty of time, but this isn't how I envisioned spending the earlier part of my day.

It's warm for October in Boston. I'm too hot in my leather jacket, but here we are, sitting on a park bench in the sun. You would think as a demon with a job designation of Grim Reaper, Level 7, the heat wouldn't bother me, but I've always preferred the cold.

I adjust my Ray-Bans. "We really need to get a move on, Carol."

I study her, wondering why she's resisting the inevitable. She has short hair that's mostly gray and is wearing a matching yellow shirt and pants. I didn't ask, but from her appearance, I'm guessing she was out for a morning walk when someone abducted and murdered her. That's what exercise and trying to take care of your health will get you.

Dead.

I try to remember what the information from the file I received on my iPad said about her.

Name: Carol Taylor

Date of Birth (DOB): 4/11 (65)

Date of Death (DOD): 10/04

Time of Death (TOD): 10:48 a.m.

Species: Witch

Marital status: Divorced

Something about two living children and—

Shit.

I can't recall enough of the pertinent information about her to cajole her into willingly accompanying me to the ferry. If there is family waiting for her on the other side, I didn't read far enough along to see it.

"I told you, I'm not going." She stares straight ahead. She won't even look at me.

"Well, that's just silly. You have to go." I try to reason with her. "I'm sure you've got family there who are eager to see you."

"Only my grandmother. I lived with her until I was sixteen." She still won't look in my direction.

"Well, there you go. That's great. I'm sure she'll be happy to see you again." *Problem solved.*

"She drank too much, and she liked to hit me with a

coat hanger. I hated her." She finally turns to face me. "Do you have a name?"

It's Aiden Finn, but I'm not telling her that. I hate my first name. "It's Finn." I vaguely wonder if she's going to lodge a complaint against me with Management, but I've followed almost everything by the book. I lean my elbows back on the park bench, studying her. "What's this about, Carol?"

The 7 Habits of Highly Effective Reapers: Grim Reaper Training 101: *Use Their Given Name to Connect with Your Charge.*

"I can't leave Tommy." She crosses her arms. "He'll be all alone. I can't do it."

Tommy? I kick myself again for not reading her entire file. She's divorced, so he's not her husband. Son? Boyfriend?

"Your son?" I make a guess.

She scowls at me and makes a *pfft* noise with her lips. "My son and daughter couldn't care less about me. I haven't seen them in years."

Then who is Tommy? I furrow my brow, waiting for her to tell me.

"My cat." She starts to cry. "He's the only one who truly loves me. I got him as a kitten."

Of course, it's a cat. She's a witch. They almost all have a familiar of some kind or are big animal lovers. I try not to roll my eyes as she continues to cry.

I reach into the inner pocket of my jacket and pull out a cloth handkerchief. I hand it to her. "I'm sure someone will take care of him."

"How? No one knows I'm—" She waves the handkerchief in her hand like a flag.

There's that word again. Dead.

She has a point. I reaped the soul of another murdered witch two weeks ago, and I overheard an Angel of Death mention reaping another one last week. Authorities have only found one body so far. Since Carol's body is in an abandoned warehouse off Addison Street, it will take weeks, if not months, before someone finds her.

I could tip off the police...

Not your problem, Finn.

But I do need to get her on the ferry. I glance at my watch again. "I'll take care of him."

Her eyes widen. "You'll take his soul, too, so he can go with me?"

I'm not sure if her expression indicates surprise or horror. I, however, am shocked her mind went there.

"What? No, nothing like that." For one thing, that would involve a ton of paperwork and pet reaps are a whole different department. "I'll find him a home." I lie because that's what demons do. What I'm actually planning is to take him to the pound or an animal shelter. I mean, I'm not heartless. I wouldn't leave him in the apartment to die—would I?

"How would you do that? No one can see you." She waves the hand holding the handkerchief again, this time toward all the people in the park.

She found this out earlier when we were on the sidewalk and someone walked through her. I had to explain she's incorporeal, so we're both invisible at the moment. Everything appears normal to us, but to anyone looking our way, all they see is an empty park bench. Since it's situated in the broiling sun, no one is stupid enough to want to sit here. Except for us, apparently. The sun is directly overhead. It really is hot.

"I'll make myself visible, get your cat, and find him a good home."

"Promise?"

Crap. I might lie, but I don't break promises. Before I know what I'm doing, I make a promise to her. "I'll pick him up this evening." *I can't believe I'm doing this.*

She's relieved, I think. She gives me details and information about the cat. Food, toys, and where his carrier is. She also tells me where to find a spare key. In truth, I don't need one, I could literally go straight through the door without opening it, but I can only do that in Grim Reaper mode and, like it is right now, Management can track exactly where I am. I'm not sure what they would think about me helping a soul out with their cat. Probably that I'm going soft.

I frown. I certainly don't need anyone in Management to think that. I'll need to make myself visible so I'm not tracked, but it also means someone could see me going into Carol's place and identify me. This could make me a potential murder suspect.

Figure it out later, Finn. You've got a job to do.

"Okay, that's settled." It's not settled at all, but I need to turn my attention back to the matter at hand, which is getting Carol to the ferry on time.

"Can we go now?" I ask her hopefully.

She's reluctant, but she finally nods. We get up off the bench and start walking.

I breathe a sigh of relief. I've managed to get her past the depression of Stage Four. She's moving nicely into Stage Five—acceptance. I'll still have to deal with the cat later on, but my day is looking up. I may even have time for lunch.

Every religion has its own belief system about how the afterlife works, and it's not my place to tell someone whether their belief is right or wrong. The part I do get to explain, however, is their journey into the afterlife begins with a ferry ride across the River Styx.

The river connects Earth to the Underworld and the whole thing is really in another realm, but Management likes to have an order to things, so we access this realm by going underground. Since I'm currently assigned to the Boston area, I normally use Portal 127, which is elevator C in the Promenade Building. It also houses the law offices of Walters, Sheraton, and Welch from floors 1 through 20, Regional Management from floors 21 to 24, and Upper Management on floor 25.

I push the button for the elevator and we wait. As usual, I look out of place here. I check my reflection in the steel doors of the elevator. Black, unruly hair in need of a trim, black leather jacket, black T-shirt, blue jeans, and black biker boots. I'm over three thousand years old, but from my reflection, you would assume I'm a human in my early thirties.

Standing next to Carol and me is an older man, or rather, his soul is with us. His body is most likely at the hospital since he's wearing a hospital gown. He's accompanied by an Angel of Death. I can't recall his name, but it's something like Raymond, Richard, or maybe Randy. We contradict each other. His hair is sandy brown and cut neatly above his collar. He's wearing a brown suit and tie, white dress shirt, brown pants, and tan dress shoes, one of which is untied, but I'm not going to mention it to him. We may both work for Management doing the same thing, but we work in different divisions. The angels dislike us almost as much as we demons hate them.

He raises his eyebrows in greeting out of politeness, but his eyes have a wary look. I get that from angels a lot.

The doors open. I usher Carol in. She hasn't told me she's a witch, but it's in her file. Not that it matters, though, because as a Grim Reaper, I can see what humans might call a second aura whenever I observe a person—or any creature, for that matter. Hers is purple, indicating she's a witch. The old man's is yellow, telling me he is human, and Raymond, Richard, or Randy has a blue second aura, so if I didn't know him, I would still have the ability to tell he's an angel. My second aura, by the way, is black. No surprise there at all.

I wait for what's-his-name to push the button for the basement, but he doesn't, so I lean across and press it for him. We all stand in silence.

I have prepared Carol for what happens next, but when the doors open and we step out into what at first glance looks like an underground cave, I can see the fear in the old man's eyes as we go past him. The Angel of Death forgot to tell his Charge he wasn't depositing him at the entranceway to the bowels of Hell. Carol turns back as the poor guy begins to wail, but I usher her forward. We head down the hill to the dock and get in line.

At the end of the dock is an old ferryboat. It reminds me of the ones you see at Long Wharf that shuttle people back and forth from Boston Harbor to places like Salem and Cape Cod. As usual, there's also a dense fog hanging out over the river, obscuring any hint of what passengers may find on the other side.

I reach into my pocket and bring out an obul.

"For the fare." I hand the coin to Carol. "You'll need it to pay the ferryman, so he'll take you across the river."

She glances down, then folds her fingers over it. "You will keep your promise, won't you?"

"Yes," I promise her again. I'm still wondering why I agreed to find a home for her cat, but I did.

She finally relaxes as we wait while the five souls ahead of us drop their coins into the slot and walk through the turnstile. This is my drop-off point. I don't go any farther. I show Carol where to put the coin and my job is done.

She drops the coin into the slot and places her hand on the turnstile, but before I realize what she's doing, she turns around and launches herself at me. "Thank you!" She gives me a hug and a kiss on the cheek.

Behind me, a couple of demons snicker. I'm going to hear about this for weeks if they tell the others.

Shit.

She finally releases me. She gives a broad smile and a wave, then goes through the turnstile.

I don't wait to see if Carol makes it down to the ferry. I turn and head back up the hill toward the elevator. Two younger demons burst out laughing when I pass by them, but then they recognize me. The stare I give them stops them in their tracks. Good. I've scared them.

"Sorry," one of them mumbles. At least he has the good sense to gaze down in submission.

Yeah, that's right, you better look away. I was doing this before you were even a devil's spawn. Don't mess with me.

I get into the elevator and hit the button for the lobby. A glance at my watch tells me if I hurry, I should have enough time to grab lunch before my next reap at 4:00. After that, I have to go pick up a cat.

My second reap for the day goes off without a hitch. He's a fifty-seven-year-old banker named Marvin. This Charge is human. I make a point to scan his entire file on my iPhone ahead of time in case he pulls a Carol on me, but Marvin's already resigned himself to his fate. He tells me he thought he had indigestion from lunch after eating a burger and onion rings, but a couple of hours later, he passed from a massive coronary event while sitting at his desk. His secretary found him.

Marvin is firmly in Stage Five of grief. Other than telling me about the indigestion, he has little to say except he'll miss his wife and kids.

I get Marvin squared away. I'm done for the day, except I now have the cat to pick up. I'll take him home with me for the night. Tomorrow, I'll see if I can call in a favor with somebody to help me find him a home.

Carol's apartment block is a nondescript brownstone with white window frames. Typical for the Beacon Hill area. It's near the intersection of Joy and Myrtle Street. Overall, it's not a bad location. You can easily travel by foot to shop or eat. I'm not sure how much of that I would do at the moment if I were a witch, but the people I pass on the sidewalk are oblivious. They have no idea a killer is out there walking amongst them.

I casually wait at the apartment building entrance until someone enters the security door, then trail in behind them. There are only three floors and no elevator. Carol's apartment is on the next floor up. I take the steps, two at a time. As I reach the landing, a lovely vision of long, cascading ringlets of copper hair and piercing blue eyes, which seem to see straight through me, assaults my senses. I do love redheads. She makes me think of autumn and blue skies.

Too flowery, Finn.

Let's try that again.

I reach the second floor to find a red-headed woman with bright blue eyes staring at me as she stands in front of the door to apartment 201 with a key in her hand.

Better.

Carol's apartment, 202, is directly across the hall. I hesitate. I don't really need to have anyone see me enter Carol's apartment. She is, after all, lying dead in a vacant warehouse. But it will seem strange if I turn around now and go back down the stairs. That could make this woman remember me more.

Besides, we're both standing frozen in our spots, staring at each other already. Me, looking undecided, and her, watching me nervously like she wonders if I'm going to push my way into her apartment when she opens the door. She's got the prettiest purple second aura I have ever seen. She's a witch.

I give her a smile and raise my eyebrows in greeting as I approach the door to 202. I move slowly but deliberately so I don't frighten her.

"Hi," I say as casually as I can while I reach up to the ledge of the doorframe. My fingers touch the spare key Carol told me about earlier. "I'm here for the cat."

Nope, that didn't sound strange at all.

Her brow creases as she turns to watch me. She pushes a strand of red hair behind her ear. "I didn't know Carol was out of town."

"Uh, yeah." I can't help but continue to stare into her blue eyes. They're mesmerizing. I could get lost in those eyes.

Get a grip, Finn.

"Family emergency. Her son," I lie. I clear the errant

thoughts floating around in my head, but before I can stop myself— "I'm her nephew, Finn."

What the hell? Where did that come from?

"I'm Chloe." She smiles shyly. Shifting her purse on her shoulder, she sticks her hand out in a gesture to shake mine.

She has a nice, firm handshake. Up close, she's about three inches shorter than I am. She's wearing a gray fluffy cardigan that's too big over a green button-up shirt. She also has on a pair of black dress pants and what women typically refer to as sensible shoes. It's an odd combination and I can't help but think she's dressed way too old for someone so young. I'm guessing she's maybe twenty-four or twenty-five.

I glance down. I'm still holding her hand and acting like an idiot. "Sorry." I let go.

"It's strange Carol didn't ask me to watch him. I usually feed Tommy when she goes out of town," she informs me. I get the feeling she is checking me out. I wonder if maybe she's a little affected by me, too.

Shut this down, Finn.

"It was sudden. I guess she didn't want to bother you." I want to continue talking to her, but I motion to the door behind me. "I guess I better see about Tommy."

"Of course." She gives me another shy smile. "Nice to meet you, Finn."

"You, too."

I put the key in the lock. Opening the door, I give her a nod before stepping inside. I don't need to, but I turn on the light. Demons have excellent vision in the dark. Out of habit from trying to appear human, I reach over and switch it on, anyway.

The apartment has an older woman's feel to it, but also

has a Bohemian vibe going on. Carol has used a lot of pinks, greens, and yellows in her color scheme. Apparently, she also embraced her inner witch. Nearby is a goddess statue posing on an end table next to the couch, and a Green Man plaque hangs on the wall next to a small flat screen television. Beneath it is a bookshelf with a stag statue and ceramic bell, along with a few books on witchcraft stacked on top of each other. I recognize a couple of other witchy decor items scattered about, like a throw pillow with an embroidered triquetra on the couch and a sandstone coaster next to the goddess statue with a triple moon on it.

Carol went walking this morning without her purse or phone. Both sit on a worn-out brown recliner covered in black cat hair. The material is frayed at the top. I suspect Tommy uses the chair to sharpen his claws.

Peering around uneasily, as if I expect someone to catch me, I open the purse.

Her billfold contains her driver's license, an insurance card, sixty dollars, and a few credit cards. I could order parts for my bike with the cards, but at some point, a police detective will investigate Carol's murder. With all the technology they have these days, they could easily trace the credit card purchases. I leave the cards and take the cash. It's not like Carol has a need for it anymore. I don't either, but old habits die hard.

Out of the corner of my eye, something moves. A large cat with long, black hair and green eyes stares at me from the doorway to what I'm guessing is the kitchen.

Tommy, I presume.

Humans have long associated witches with black cats, and black cats with the devil. This amuses me because cats hate devils and demons the same way we hate them.

Tommy hisses at me and runs off.

Crap. It didn't occur to me that to get Tommy into a carrier, I would have to pick him up and handle him.

I follow him into the kitchen and turn on the light. Tommy sits under the kitchen table, watching me. On the floor, at the end of the kitchen cabinets, are two empty food bowls and a half empty water bowl sitting on a white plastic mat with blue paw prints all over it. In the corner is a litter box. By the smell, I suspect Tommy recently used it.

I need to find the laundry room since I've been told the carrier is on a shelf above the wash machine. *Why did I promise to do this?*

I'm in the process of retrieving the carrier when it occurs to me, I could leave the cat here for a while. Let him get to know me. This place isn't too bad. I could even stay here.

Stop kidding yourself, Finn.

Okay, it has nothing to do with the cat. I would like to see the woman across the hall again. Find out if she is seeing anyone, and if not, ask her if she would like to get a coffee or maybe grab a drink with me.

I shake my head. I don't know where that thought came from. Today, I have promised one witch I would find a home for her cat, and now I want to ask another witch out on a date. What is wrong with me? I may lie, but I don't make promises and I don't do dates.

Yet, here we are.

I take the carrier to the kitchen and set it on the table. Opening the little metal door, I bend down on one knee so I can get closer to this cat. Yellow eyes glare at me, and Tommy makes a yowling noise in his throat.

"Yeah, yeah, I'm a demon. You're a cat. Get over it."

We study each other. Tommy doesn't move and neither

do I. After a moment, I reach my hand out. This isn't as hard as I thought—

A paw with tiny razors on the end reaches out, shredding the top of my hand.

"Fuck!" I raise up, banging my head hard into the bottom of the kitchen table. My eyes turn black. For a few seconds, I want to murder this cat.

It's only a cat. Get a grip.

And—I'm back under control. The black recedes and the whites of my eyes reappear, but my hand is bleeding. Drops of it are dripping onto the vinyl floor. I get up and go to the sink, leaving a line of black blood droplets along the way. I run cool water over three long, deep scratch marks.

Ripping a paper towel off the towel holder, I pat down the top of my hand. The scratches will heal fast. In about an hour, there won't be any evidence of a wound. I get a few more paper towels to wipe up the trail of blood I made before it dries.

Tommy runs off to the living room.

Maybe I need a net? I shrug the idea off for the moment. I consider leaving him in the apartment, at least until tomorrow. I'll show up at the same time. Perhaps I'll get lucky and get to see the neighbor again.

This is a bad idea, but I blame it on the cat.

I find the cat food, fill the bowls, refresh the water, and, after much debate, clean the litter box. Tommy is hiding out somewhere when I go back into the living room. I let him stay hidden. I shut off the light before leaving the apartment.

Round one goes to the cat. He gets to stay in his home for another day, and I may get the opportunity to see Chloe again tomorrow. Maybe it's a win for both of us.

I'm still trying to process the day's events in my mind when I arrive at the entrance of the Echelon, the building where I live off of Sudbury Street. They advertise themselves as luxury condominiums with a panoramic view of the bay, but you can forget about trying to purchase the penthouse on the forty-fifth floor because it's mine. I invested and reinvested my ill-gotten gains from years ago. Now, I can buy almost anything I want. I bought it for the close proximity to the city and historic areas along with the stunning views—and because I find solitude up here away from everyone and everything.

I get off the elevator and step out into the foyer. The cash I left in an envelope next to an antique vase on the round mahogany table to my right is no longer there. It appears the housekeeper has been in while I was gone. The gray marble floors are all clean and shiny again.

I go through the double doors of the foyer, venturing farther into the apartment. Walking across the gray wooden floor to the living room, it's clean, too. I toss my jacket over a contemporary style chair, which matches the contemporary style couch. Both—gray.

So much gray.

I sometimes regret giving the interior designer carte blanche with the decorating. At the time, I found her a pleasant distraction. We had some fun times together. I said neutral colors when she asked me about the color scheme. This is how things ended up.

Heading over to the bar table, I pour myself two generous fingers of Irish whiskey from a crystal decanter. Picking up the remote, I turn on the television, but my attention goes to the window instead. There's darkness on the ground below, but from my vantage point, I can see the last of the orange and yellow as the sun slowly sinks below the horizon. How many sunsets have I seen in my lifetime?

I'm lost in my own thoughts when I become vaguely aware the news has come on. I don't pay much attention until I catch the words *body found* and then *Quincy Shores.* Reaching for the remote, I turn up the sound as a perky blonde reporter from the side of the road gives the few details the police have released to the public. At this point, I know more than they do.

Digging into my pocket, I pull out my iPhone. I tap on the app with the Grim Reaper holding a scythe on it and begin swiping left.

Yes, the tech department has a macabre sense of humor. I can still recall the days when crows and ravens delivered scrolls with the names of the Charges we were to reap. At some point, it became letters magically appearing in our mailboxes, next came telegrams, then phone calls with messages left on answering machines, pagers with numbers for us to call to talk to a messenger service, emails (which didn't work out too well because they all kept going into spam folders), and now we have apps. The birds with scrolls thing was weird, but mostly it's always been about Grim Reapers and Angels of Death blending in with the other species on Earth.

It takes quite a few swipes to find the file I want, but I finally work my way back to my Charge from about two weeks ago.

Name: Valerie Burns
Date of Birth (DOB): 3/29 (32)
Date of Death (DOD): 9/20
Time of Death (TOD): 1:42 p.m.
Species: Witch

Marital status: Single
Reception Committee:
Fern Burns (mother)
Nell Reynolds (grandmother)

That reap was a rough one. Several things went wrong. We usually receive the files at least twenty-four hours before a reap is to occur, but for some reason hers didn't appear until the morning of her DOD and I didn't get a notification until mid-morning. The location the app gave me was a mile marker.

I was late, so when I arrived, Valerie was gone. She had wandered off further into the woods. To track her, I had to go directly to the scene where she died. Some demons get off on visiting the scenes of murders as soon as they happen, but I'm not one of them.

When I found her body, her hands were bound. She had been stabbed repeatedly and her heart removed. The killer, who is most likely a wannabe devil worshiper, even painted a symbol on her forehead with her blood. The police are going to have a field day with that one.

The news moves on to a story about a family of five who died in a house fire. Luckily, those weren't mine. I don't like multiple reaps, especially when they involve children. Management normally likes to save time, so they often assign them all to one Grim Reaper. This makes it like herding cats. Sometimes, if it's something big, like an apartment complex fire or a multiple car accident, they'll send help, and I'll end up working with multiple Grim Reapers or Angels of Death.

Those are fun. Not.

At least, I've somehow managed to avoid getting assigned to one of those lately. Those are seriously the worst. When we're all forced to work together, it always turns into an issue about who has jurisdiction. The angels act like (or as if) they have the final authority, even if there is a senior Grim Reaper on the scene who outranks them. Something about moral superiority, I guess.

The angels want everyone to believe the only souls they handle are the ones going to Heaven, but the truth is, Management wants us all to remain neutral. They assign our Charges randomly, so we never know what type of soul we'll get. We're two divisions doing the same thing, but the way it was explained to me is that it's like baseball. There's a National League and an American League, but they both play the same game. That's just the way it is.

This reminds me, there's a game on tonight. The Red Sox are playing the Yankees. If I hurry, I should have just enough time to fix myself something to eat before it starts.

I wander into the kitchen, ignoring the pale gray cabinets and open the stainless-steel refrigerator, which I guess is a gray color, too, isn't it?

What part of your body were you thinking with when you approved all of this, Finn?

My attention turns to more pressing matters. What do I want to eat?

I have a private chef who comes in to fix five meals to carry me through the weeknights. Half the time, I end up eating takeout instead, but tonight I simply want to heat something up and watch the game. I choose a container marked *Chicken Alfredo* and stick it into the microwave.

As a demon, I don't have to eat often. We can go a year or more without food, but we lose body mass and get weak when we do. The problem is, we're a lot like pack animals. If a demon senses another demon is vulnerable, they'll turn on them in a minute. This is why I eat regularly, exercise, and spar in the gym a couple of times a week, either boxing or martial arts. I'm old, but the few younger demons who have ever tried to challenge me have only done it once.

I dump the chicken alfredo out of the heated bowl onto a plate, pour myself a glass of Seghesio Zinfandel, and return to the living room. The game is about to get underway. I take a sip of my wine, then settle onto the couch with my dinner just in time for the first pitch.

CHAPTER 2

October 5:

I'm not even out of bed yet and my day is a total disaster. Sometime during the night, my schedule changed. When I awoke at 7:30 this morning, I found a notification on my iPad informing me my entire schedule is scuttled. Now, I've got a 9:15 on I-90. This is the same thing that happened on the day of the Valerie Burns reap.

I guess I jinxed myself when I mentioned multiple reaps last night because as I look at my schedule, there are multiple Charges with their times of death scattered minutes apart. There's also a nice large red special advisory banner across the top alerting me to the addition of two Angels of Death and two other Grim Reapers. I've done this long enough to know we're dealing with one messy multi-vehicle car accident.

The rain hammers the windows while I lay in bed studying the files. Without checking the weather app, I already know the temperature dropped from yesterday. I'm dreading today and it hasn't even started yet.

Getting out of bed, I pad into the bathroom to shower,

but first I brush my teeth. I inspect the stubble on my face, consider whether I should shave, and decide to skip it. Stepping into the shower, I turn the faucet handle almost all the way to the left. The water is not quite to the point of scalding, although it is painful to the skin—exactly the way I like it.

Some demons loathe water and never bathe. Spend time stuck in a room with a demon who hasn't bathed in over a thousand years and it will give you a good idea of what Hell smells like. Humans worry about the fire and brimstone, but it's the stench they should fear. Thankfully, I've only made the visit twice.

I would like to linger longer in the shower, but I don't have the time. Stepping out onto the gray bath mat, I grab a big, fluffy gray towel to dry off with before heading back to the bedroom to dress.

Rain and the cooler temperatures are going to make the outdoors miserable. The big decision is what to wear. I settle on jeans and a green and black flannel shirt with a black T-shirt underneath. I strap my knife holster around my ankle before pulling on a pair of waterproof boots to complete my outfit. From my appearance, you would probably assume I'm a construction worker, which should work in my favor if I have to make myself visible. After a final check in the mirror, I grab my phone, watch, billfold, and black raincoat.

I'm almost ready to face the day, but first, I need my caffeine and sugar fix. I stop at the closest Dunks, which is only a block away from the Echelon. A large black coffee and a cruller in hand, it's time to head toward my destination. Vehicle accidents are the only reaps we try to make it to before they happen. Remember what I said about who has jurisdiction? The Death Squad is like one of those police shows where all the cops show up at once and start arguing about who's in charge.

Okay, we don't call ourselves that. I made it up.

I arrive at 9:05 a.m. because I'm a GR7. If I arrive any earlier, it automatically puts me over everyone else because of my rank. Some demons want this. They like ordering angels around, but I'm not one of them. I want to do my job and get out of there. If I'm last to arrive, the pissing contest is over, and someone else has already sorted the details out.

As expected, I'm the last of the five to arrive, so I'm in the clear. Two Grim Reapers and two Angels of Death are all standing on top of the same hill near the highway. Doing it this way keeps everyone out of the way of the accident but gives us an unobstructed view of what is about to happen.

I stroll up to the two demons standing about fifty feet from the angels. I recognize one of them. Her name is Roz. She's prepared for the weather with rain boots and a black rain slicker. She's got the hood pulled completely up, but the rain is dripping off it onto her forehead. I can tell from the sour expression on her face, she doesn't like this weather at all. I haven't seen her in a while and her appearance is a little different. Last time, she had long braids, but even with the hood, I can see her hair is cut short. It's now a golden honey color.

Her dark eyes show she recognizes me. "Finn." She greets me with a fist bump. She gestures to the other demon. He has on a Red Sox baseball cap and a thin windbreaker. With this weather, he's a little underdressed for the occasion. I get the sense he's young for a demon. Maybe a few hundred years or so.

"This is Tyler. He's a GR2," she tells me.

"What's up?" He holds out his clenched hand for a fist bump the same way Roz did.

I ignore him. "What have we got?" I ask Roz. She knows I'm not talking about the accident itself. We have ten minutes to go. She's a GR4 and is almost always early. I'm hoping she's in charge.

She rolls her eyes and points. "The kid over there arrived first. He's an AoD1."

My eyes drift over to the two angels. I recognize the younger one as the Angel of Death I overheard the other day talking about his Charge, the murdered witch. I didn't realize he was a Level 1. Management rarely gives those types of assignments to a newbie. No wonder he was so freaked out that day.

He has dark hair a few shades lighter than mine. I don't recognize the other angel at all. He's probably much older than his appearance indicates, but as a human, he appears in his late twenties or early thirties. He's got the typical angel thing going on, meaning he's pretty boy handsome. I'm sure if he smiles, he'll have perfectly straight, shiny white teeth. He reminds me of a male underwear model. He's all wavy blond hair and chiseled good looks. I bet he has the personality to match.

I frown. Roz realizes the same thing I do. Since the younger, inexperienced angel arrived first, Blondie has seniority. He's on point.

"Do you know him?" I ask Roz.

She shakes her head.

This could get interesting, then.

The two of them watch us as we watch them. The younger one is asking the older one some questions, and Blondie's getting annoyed. They share an umbrella, but the younger one is only partially under it. I don't think angels are required to dress alike, but most of them do. Both have on light brown pants, tan trench coats, and dark brown wingtip shoes. They are going to have fun going down this hill when it's time to locate their Charges.

"Should we—" Roz waves her hand toward them.

I shake my head. Let them come to us.

What we should do is walk over, introduce ourselves, and let them know we're team players. Something about the way Blondie stands there watching us pisses me off, though, and I don't want to give him the satisfaction of acknowledging he's in charge first.

Yes, it's a power play. I should have arrived earlier. Bite me.

I glance at my watch. We have five minutes to go. It takes him another thirty seconds to realize we're not coming to him, so he finally gives in. The pair walk over to us.

Roz suppresses a smile.

"Morning," Blondie says, trying to sound cordial but failing. He stares down his nose at us. "Looks like the gang's all here." Since he has the umbrella, it puts us facing him and forces the AoD1 to stand next to us. We all end up in a row in front of him like he's lining up his ducks. Nice power move.

"Four minutes to go." He glances at his watch. "Let's do a few quick introductions, then we can coordinate our positions."

Roz shoots me a sideways glance.

I know, Roz. I know.

"Wallace, AoD5." He establishes himself in charge.

"Nelson. AoD1," the other angel says. He's obviously

nervous around us demons. Up close, he looks like he's in high school.

"Smith. GR2." Tyler chomps his peppermint gum. Maybe it's my imagination, but I can smell weed. I suspect Tyler is high.

"Henson. GR4." Roz is next, all businesslike.

Wallace smirks. He not only knows he's in charge, he also believes he outranks all of us.

"Finn." I keep my face blank but stare him dead in the eyes. "GR7."

And there it is. The realization of who I am. For a second, there's a hint of fear on his face.

Yes, I'm the one who beat his superior to within an inch of his life. Yes, I would have killed him, too, but there wasn't a piece of silver or iron in sight.

I did some serious time in Hell for that little indiscretion.

"Fudge," Wallace says, since angels can't swear. "Aiden Finn." He stares at me as if I've suddenly grown a set of horns, but I'm not that type of demon.

Nelson glances at Wallace. He's lost, but I can bet Wallace will fill him in later.

Roz stares down at the ground and tries to hide her grin.

"Whoa," Tyler mumbles. Out of the corner of my eye, I see him lean forward from his place in line to take a peek at me.

I've thrown Wallace off his game, but he works quickly to compose himself. We have about a minute. Six adults and three children are about to lose their lives, but we don't know how. This is all part of the Grand Plan. We're not allowed to interfere with their deaths, even if we want to try.

Angels aren't supposed to take the attitude of being mightier than thou, but Wallace does something unexpected. He benches me. He gives me the job of herding the cats, or rather, keeping all the Charges in one place as they are brought to the side of the road. This job belongs to the new kid, but this is a pissing contest. It's his way of putting me in my place.

Whatever.

Ten seconds to go. We're now all standing in a row at the top of the hill, waiting for things to begin.

Roz nudges me. "Fifty says the pickup truck causes it," she whispers.

She motions at a white truck with a ladder sticking out the back of an open tailgate about a fourth of a mile up the road.

I study the scene quickly. A semi is in the middle lane, a small tan car in the right lane ahead of it, and a white SUV in front of the truck. Roz's pickup truck is weaving a bit, but they aren't leaving their lane.

I shake my head. "Small tan car." I keep my voice low enough so she's the only one to hear me.

We wait.

Almost as if on cue, the driver of the small tan car realizes they are in the approaching exit lane. The car veers in front of the SUV and hits the gas, but the SUV driver thinks they are about to rear-end the car, so they slam on the brakes. We watch as the SUV hydroplanes and the driver loses control. The semi slams into it, and a black BMW hits the back of the semi and spins, clipping the pickup truck. The pickup truck goes sideways, then T-bones a gray sports car. This causes the sports car to travel out of its lane and hit a work van. The work van then careens into the divider wall. The small tan car continues merrily on its way, the driver unaware of the mayhem they caused.

"Lucky." Roz slaps a twenty into my palm before starting down the hill. "I owe you thirty." She should know by now—I always win.

I take my time going down the hill and get the satisfaction of watching Wallace and his doppelganger get their fancy shoes muddy as they reach the bottom. Everyone gets busy while I stand around twiddling my thumbs. Actually, I have my hands in my coat pockets since it's still pouring down rain, so there's no thumb twiddling. I pull the zipper on the front up as far as it can go because the rain is getting the collar of my shirt wet. I can deal with the cold, but my jeans are getting soaked since I'm not moving around much. A large raindrop drips off the hood of my coat and hits me on the nose. Yep, I'm edging closer to a state of complete misery out here.

The problem with vehicle accidents is each soul is on their own timetable and everything goes on all at once. We not only have the souls who haven't figured out what has happened to them yet, there are also the living getting out of their cars, running up to help. Sometimes, the souls don't know how to get out of their vehicle, but we can't approach them because of all the people. Sometimes, the people start CPR, and we have to wait it out. It's total chaos.

Roz brings me Charge Number One. He's the driver of the BMW.

She doesn't roll her eyes, but her exasperated expression tells me she wants to. "Bob," she says. She walks away, shaking her head.

"Do you know how much that car costs?" he sputters. "I told her I don't want someone from the city towing it. You need to get someone from the BMW dealership to come and get it."

"I'll get right on that," I reply, and now I'm the one trying not to roll my eyes.

Bob is a definite Stage One in the Five Stages of Grief—Denial. He's wearing an expensive gray business suit like a CEO might wear and has the personality to match. He doesn't like finding out he can't have his cellphone with him. He doesn't like having to stand on the side of the road. There's a lot of stuff Bob doesn't like, and I get to hear all about it.

Tyler brings Charges Number Two and Three to me. They were in the sports car. "Sam and his daughter, Jill," he tells me. Sam is Stage One. Jill has skipped Stage One and gone straight into Stage Two. She's angry because she finally has a boyfriend and now, she suspects her best friend will end up with him. She blames everything on her father. At the moment, she's unhappy because she still has braces and life is totally unfair.

Nelson is extremely nervous when he brings me two of the children from the SUV. "Victor and Sarah." His hands shake as he motions to his Charges. "This is rough."

I nod because I don't know what to say. He wanders away, shell-shocked. Wallace should have prepared him a little better.

I'm having to do more than stand around now because some of the Charges want to wander back out to their vehicle. Plus, I'm also having lots of questions thrown at me.

"What is my wife going to do?" *I have no clue.*

"Am I going to Hell?" *If you have to ask—*

"How long do we have to stand here?" *How should I know?*

"Why do we have to stand here?" *Because I said so.*

"Can I borrow your phone to call my attorney? I'm suing all of you." *No, Bob, for the third time, you can't. Fuck off.*

More Charges are slowly brought over to my spot. Thankfully, the rain lets up and finally stops. Roz brings her last Charge from the pickup truck and Nelson brings a man and another child from the SUV. Tyler brings his, then after a while, Wallace comes over with his Charge from the van.

"Okay, folks, we're ready to go," Wallace announces. He begins explaining to the group how everything works. He sounds like a tour guide.

I tune out what he's saying because something doesn't sit right with me. Wallace didn't fill me in on who was handling which Charge after he designated me as the Watcher, but I did give the files a once-over this morning. I pull out my iPhone and quickly scan through them. Six adults and three kids. Except as I glance around, there are six adults and four kids.

I nudge Roz. I point to the numbers on the screen. "Count's off."

Her eyes widen. She takes my phone and scans through the files, stopping on the family from the SUV. One adult and two children. *Victor, 37. Sarah, 8. Rick, 6.* The father stands a few feet from my left with his three kids in front of him.

"What's your children's names?" I ask as quietly as possible while Wallace drones on about the group's journey into the afterlife. It's clear he's not paying attention to what is happening.

"Sarah, Rick, and Junior."

"Junior?"

"My oldest son is Victor. We call him Junior."

Roz still has my phone. She peers up at me. "Finn, he's a Yo-Yo." We both stare at the boy.

Shit. My attention turns toward the SUV. The engine is on fire. If the kid re-enters his body while he's still in the vehicle, he's going to have third-degree burns if Rescue doesn't get to him in time. If he doesn't re-enter his body, he's in limbo because he's not on the manifest.

"Let it go, Finn," Roz warns me. "We don't need the trouble."

"What's going on?" Nelson realizes something is up with his Charges.

"The kid's a Yo-Yo." Roz gestures toward the oldest boy.

"What's a Yo-Yo?" he asks.

"A round tripper," I reply. "He was supposed to return to his body."

"That's not right. I verified all their names," he argues.

"This one is Victor Junior," I tell him.

"What's going on?" Wallace pushes his way through the Charges. He scowls at me.

"This one's not supposed to be here." I motion to the boy. "He's on a round trip."

"Impossible." He takes out his own phone, silently studying the screen. The color drains from his face. He turns around to stare at the SUV, then looks back at me. "Weren't you keeping count?"

"I was the Watcher, remember? It wasn't my job," I remind him. "The boy needs to go back."

The color drains from Nelson's face and he looks like he's about to throw up. He waits for Wallace to offer him guidance, but the lead angel is too busy scrolling through his files, mumbling to himself. Meanwhile, the engine fire spreads.

"He needs to go back," I repeat.

"Well, it's too late for that to happen," Wallace snaps at me. "You need to do your job. Get everyone together and let's go. Upper Management will have to sort it out."

I glance at Roz.

"Finn, don't." She grabs at my arm, but I pull away from her.

Before I change my mind, I head toward the SUV.

Wallace blocks me. "Where do you think you're going?"

"To save him."

"No, you're not. It's too late."

"It's not." I move forward again.

He blocks me again and gets up in my face. "I said no." He gives me a small shove backward. I shove him back. Hard. He rushes toward me, but I make myself visible before he can react. He tries to block me, but he's unprepared and his arm goes straight through me. The Charges step out of the way as I push past him, running toward the SUV. To my surprise, Tyler follows.

When we reach the SUV, the interior is full of smoke and flames are about to engulf the entire engine. Fire and Rescue haven't realized the boy is inside because they're concentrating on the larger fire—the trailer of the semi.

I wipe my hand across the driver's side window and peer inside. The boy is lying in the backseat. The rear passenger door is bent, but if we can pry it open, we can get him out.

"What do we do?" Tyler asks from behind me.

"Pull."

I grab hold of the mangled door. The heat is intense. We only have about a minute or two before the fire spreads inside. The metal cuts through my hand, but I'll worry about it later. Demons are stronger than humans, but we don't have super strength. I can't pull it open by myself. When Tyler jumps in and we pull on it together, it gives way enough for one of us to get inside. I motion to Tyler.

"Fuck," he says under his breath.

"Hurry," I tell him as he inches inside.

"Seatbelt's stuck."

I reach down into my boot and grab my *Gerber Ghoststrike* from its holster. It's got a nice, sharp blade, perfect for things like stuck seatbelts and bar fights. I doubt Wallace would approve if he knew I'm carrying a weapon. He's lucky I didn't use it on him.

"Whoa," Tyler says as I hand the knife to him. "Nice." He cuts through the material, then passes it back to me.

He scoops up the boy, backing out through the opening. He hands Junior off to me, and we move away from the SUV. I lay him on the wet pavement, then place my hands at the center of his chest. I count the chest pushes up to thirty in my head, give two rescue breaths, then start the count again.

Junior and his father join us. They both stare down at his body. The father appears lost. It's clear he doesn't know what to do.

I glance up at them. "It's not his time."

The father nods, but he looks to me for guidance.

"You need to tell him it's okay. He needs to go back."

Victor Senior stays silent, but he finally gets it together. "It's okay, son. You need to go back," he parrots.

"How?" Victor Junior looks up at him in confusion.

"Close your eyes," I interrupt, directing his attention to me. "You'll see a bright white light. All you have to do is step back through it."

Victor Junior peers up once more at his father, then closes his eyes. He goes from a solid form to a translucent one before fading away. I remove my hands from his chest. The boy opens his eyes and coughs.

Rescue notices us around the boy on the ground. A couple of paramedics rush over. I stand and move out of their way so they can work.

Tyler and I take a few more steps back.

"Thank you." The father gives us both a smile.

I nod.

"Dude, that was intense," Tyler says as we watch the paramedics work with the boy. Victor Junior most likely won't remember a thing. If he does, it will seem like a weird dream.

A glance to the side of the road tells me Wallace, Roz, Nelson, and the Charges have left us behind. Not a good sign. Tyler hasn't seen *intense* yet, but I'm afraid he will soon.

"Come on, let's go." I take a breath.

I've disobeyed a direct order—again.

Jack, our supervisor, stands waiting outside the elevator when Tyler and I bring Victor down to the Underground. By his expression, it's a fair bet Wallace has already filed a formal complaint with DR and Jack is not happy about it.

Jack and I grew up together, but I'm a couple of years older. If I hadn't gotten myself into trouble back in 79 A.D., I would most likely outrank him by now. Then again—maybe not. Jack has a ruthless streak in him. He will climb over bodies to get to the top. As it is, he's moved up the chain and although I've kept my GR7 designation, he's gotten a few promotions, making him a GR10, and my current boss.

Although I would never admit it to his face, he's one of the few demons I wouldn't want to get in an actual fight with because I suspect he could kick my ass. He's a good four inches taller than me, tanned, athletic, and if he was human instead of a Grim Reaper, he probably would have ended up as a general in the military. Jack even has the crew cut, so he looks the part.

Usually, we get along fine, but I can tell by the way he's clenching his jaw and the bulging vein on his forehead—he's super pissed.

He waves us over, away from Victor. "What the fuck did you two do?" he asks through clenched teeth.

"We didn't do anything," I reply. Tyler is about to owe me a huge favor, and one day I'll collect. "I told Tyler to help me. He's got nothing to do with this."

Tyler shoots me a questioning look but remains silent.

Jack narrows his eyes, studying Tyler. "Get the Charge on the ferry." He puts his hand up to stop me. "You stay here."

"Later, man." Tyler bobs his head at me, then goes back and collects Victor. They head down the hill toward the dock.

"Okay, Finn, what the hell happened?" he asks once Tyler is out of earshot.

I give him an abbreviated version of the events. "Wallace shouldn't have sent Nelson in to handle a multiple car accident by himself. He wasn't ready for it." I sidestep the fact I disobeyed a direct order. "If anything, they should write Nelson up for his mistake."

He rubs the back of his neck. "Yes, but it's the angels we're talking about here, and he's their problem, not mine.

Plus, that's not what I'm talking about, and you know it. I don't get why you're always so hung up on doing the right thing. That's what got you into so much trouble the last time."

I know. I know. At least I didn't completely lose my temper this time, so there's that. "How bad is it?"

"Well, the angels are probably going to consider a life was saved, so no harm done, but we'll have to see. You know how they are." He curls his lips in disgust. "At least they didn't suspend you, so that's a plus."

"When is the hearing?"

"Thursday. They haven't set a time yet, so I guess you'll get the information in your brief when they do. Whenever it is, I'll see you then."

He moves over to the elevator and presses the button. The doors open. He steps inside. "And Finn, one more thing. From now on, when someone gives you an order, you follow it. Understood?"

He doesn't wait for me to respond. The doors close and he's gone.

I'm ready for this day to end, but I still have Tommy to deal with before I can go home. It's 3:45 when I arrive at Carol's apartment building. My heart skips a beat when I get to the second floor. A woman stands in front of 201. She's wearing a blue hooded raincoat and green nursing scrubs. When she turns to face me, however, it's a blonde instead of Chloe. She's got a purple second aura, too. Another witch.

"I've got mace," she informs me before I can say anything. She puts her hand on top of her purse.

I raise my hands. "Just here to feed the cat."

She scowls at me. "How's Carol's son?" No introduction from this witch.

"About the same."

I fish the key to 202 out of my pocket and let myself into Carol's apartment before she can ask me any more questions. It's been a hell of a day. I want to get this over with and go home.

Tommy has strewn almost an entire roll of toilet paper from the bathroom all across the living room floor. It's shredded into hundreds of tiny pieces.

Damn cat.

CHAPTER 3

October 6:

Despite my misadventure yesterday, my Wednesday is like any other day. For a Grim Reaper, that is. I have two reaps and, for a change, no problem with either of them. My workday ends by 6:30.

I'd decided earlier in the day I would stake out, I mean, wait around Carol's apartment to see if I could catch another glimpse of Chloe. I reach the apartment complex a little after 7:00. It's about the same time I saw her the first time, so I'm taking a chance that this is when she typically gets home from work.

As I reach the top step on the second floor, I'm rewarded with the sight of copper hair in front of apartment 201. Her appearance takes my breath away. Before I can say or do anything, an apple rolls across the floor, heading in my direction. *Weird.* I catch it with my hand before it can continue rolling down the steps.

I stand, watching as Chloe attempts to hang on to multiple grocery bags, her purse, and the key to her apartment, all while trying to open the door. She has dropped one bag already and is trying not to drop the second. She mutters something under her breath as she drops her keys instead.

"Let me help," I offer, coming to her side.

She's not paying attention to her surroundings, and I startle her. Embarrassed by her predicament, a deep crimson creeps into her cheeks when she sees me. I pick up her keys and take the bag that's about to fall. Unlocking the door, I open it for her.

"Thank you," she says as I take a step back, allowing her to enter the apartment.

I bend down to retrieve the rest of her spilled groceries. Five more apples are scattered across the floor, and a head of lettuce has made its way over to the baseboard.

She hasn't come back to the door yet. I hesitate whether to follow her into the apartment but decide to take a chance. The apartment layout is identical to Carol's, but it's in reverse. The entrance to the kitchen sits on the left instead of the right. I find Chloe there, untangling herself from the grocery bags and her purse, all of which are on top of the kitchen counter in one big pile.

"I guess I'm one of those people who would rather die trying than have to make two separate trips up the stairs with a bunch of groceries," she tells me as she takes the groceries out of one of the bags.

I raise an eyebrow. That's one death I don't believe I've ever actually seen. "Where do you want—" I lift up the ones I'm holding.

She waves her hand at the counter. "Anywhere is fine." She takes more items out of the grocery bag and sets them to one side.

"Do you need help?" I suspect she will say no, but it gives me a chance to stay with her a little longer.

"No, I've got it. Thanks." She studies me as she removes a loaf of French bread from the bag directly in front of her. "How's Carol's son?"

"What?" Her question catches me off guard. I quickly try to remember what I told her the first time we met. Right, I'm Carol's nephew.

"You said he had been in an accident," she replies. "I thought she might have mentioned how he was doing when she called to check on Tommy."

Of course. Carol would call to check on Tommy while she was away. "She didn't have time to go into any details about what was going on. It sounds like she might be away for a while, though."

As in, she's not coming back—ever.

"It surprised me she went to see him." Chloe moves around the kitchen, putting items into the cabinets and the refrigerator. "After the way she's always talked about him, I assumed they weren't close."

"Yeah, it's the same with her daughter, too." Sell the lie. I'm glad I paid attention when Carol told me about her family.

"I didn't know she had any other family." I'm not sure if she's talking about me as Carol's nephew or if she means Carol's daughter.

"She doesn't," I reply and hope this covers both. I can't take my eyes off this woman. She's so graceful, moving from one side of the kitchen to the other.

"Your mother isn't still living?" she asks. "Or are you related to Carol through your father's side of the family?"

The nephew thing again. "Both of my parents are dead." This is the truth. Both of my parents were fallen angels. That's why I'm a demon, but also have the Grim Reaper skills. I never knew either of them. I don't even know who they were. “My mother’s side,” I add, and suddenly I feel bad lying to her.

“Oh, I’m sorry.” Her gaze softens at the mention of my parents. In truth, I haven’t given them a thought in years.

“It happened a long time ago.” *Thousands and thousands of years ago.*

She reaches out to take one of the grocery bags from me, and I belatedly discover I’m still holding them. “Well, I’m glad Carol has you to help her out.” The soft smile returns.

I nod. I have no reason to stay now. “Well, I should probably see about Tommy.” I point my thumb over my shoulder toward the living room.

I want to ask her out, but I hesitate. I’m not sure why. I mean, I’m a demon—right? I’m a badass, master-of-my-universe demon. I take what I want. Women practically throw themselves at me every single day and night. I’ve bought women drinks before and ended up back at their place before the order even made it to the table. Although, if I’m honest, that lost its appeal several decades ago.

It suddenly occurs to me, I’ve never actually asked a woman out on a date. Maybe that’s the problem?

“Oh, okay. Well, thank you.” She appears confused. A small V forms between her eyebrows. She takes the second bag from me. “I appreciate the help.”

“No problem.” I turn to go. I hesitate again. I close my eyes. *Ask her, Finn.*

I turn back around.

“Would you—” we both say in unison.

“You first.” Her cheeks go a soft pink.

“Go out with me?” I get the words out, then hold my breath.

“Have dinner with me?” She bites her lip. Motioning to the food on the counter, she rambles on, “I’m making spaghetti. Andrea, my roommate, is working the night shift. I hate to eat alone."

"Sure," I reply.

I believe she's relieved I've said yes, but then her cheeks turn entirely red. I wish I knew what she was thinking.

"Good." She motions at the remaining items on the counter. "I should probably get started, then."

"I'll feed Tommy and come back."

We continue staring at each other.

She comes to her senses first. "Okay." She laughs nervously.

"Okay." I give her a lopsided grin and retreat a couple of steps. "I'll be—right back." She's still smiling as I turn and head toward the door.

Going across the hall, I let myself into Carol's apartment. I walk by the refrigerator. A bill for the garbage collection under a magnet on the door catches my attention. It's a few days overdue. It occurs to me there are probably other bills accumulating in Carol's mailbox. I'll need to figure out where the mailboxes in the apartment complex are located. If I'm going to sell the story that she is out of town, I'll have to collect the mail and keep her bills paid.

Plus, I'm going to have to purchase cat food and kitty litter, I realize as I scoop the litter box and put the remnants into a used plastic bag from the drugstore. Thankfully, Carol accumulated a large stash of plastic bags, which I found inside a single plastic bag under the kitchen sink. Is this woman across the hall worth all this trouble? I drop the bag with the scooped litter into the garbage can. It smells terrible. The trash needs to go out, too.

What are you doing, Finn?

I have no logic to explain my actions. If I didn't know better, I would say Carol put a spell on me. Witch souls can't do that—can they?

I go through Carol's purse until I find her keys. There's one for a mailbox on the key ring. I remove it and stick it into my pocket. I'll find the mailbox later and get the mail tonight before I leave. Or if I get lucky—in the morning.

Don't go there.

This woman across the hall is different. I don't know why, but I don't want dinner to turn into a one-night stand. Is that what this attraction is all about? Maybe I just need to get laid. It has been a while. I push the thought out of my mind.

Tommy appears as I ponder my reaction to Chloe. He gives me his usual glare of disdain before settling in to eat his food. I watch him eat for a moment before switching off the kitchen light. I lock the apartment door behind me, then head back across the hall.

Chloe didn't lock the door while I was gone, so I let myself back in. I take off my jacket, laying it over one of the chairs in the living room. Unlike Carol's apartment, there's nothing obvious to indicate the two women who live here are witches. The configuration of the room is similar, however. Tan couch and coffee table here, television on a stand sitting there. Instead of a recliner, they have two Queen Anne chairs with embroidered seat covers and a small antique table in between the two with an oriental vase sitting on top of it. Contemporary meets Victorian. It's odd, but it works.

I note Chloe has put on some smooth jazz for music. It's playing through a soundbar near the television where she's docked her phone. Dinner is cooking and it smells delicious. I follow the scent back into the kitchen. She's set the kitchen table and placed a pair of candles on it. It's—romantic. There's a weird little flutter in my stomach. It's unsettling. I'm on my first real date. Well, I think it's a date, although perhaps she just didn't want to eat alone.

There are candles, Finn. It's a date.

I tear my eyes away from them to watch Chloe standing at the kitchen counter. She's chopping garlic, and there's already meat cooking on the stove. She has on a white apron, but she's changed into a pair of cream-colored pants and a blue top. The outfit is more fashionable than what I've seen her in before. It's more like something a woman her age should wear. She's pulled her hair up, exposing her neck. I imagine myself coming up behind her to kiss it, but she's holding a knife. *Bad idea, Finn.*

I roll my eyes, shaking the image of her stabbing me out of my mind. "Is there anything I can do to help?" Her mincing abilities with the knife are amazing.

She pushes a strand of hair behind her ear. "Yes, stir the meat, please." She points to the stovetop.

A cast-iron skillet containing ground beef sits simmering over an open flame.

Fuck!

Not much can hurt or kill a demon, but iron is one of them. I can't touch the handle without getting a severe and painful burn. I glance over to make sure she's not watching. Sliding a kitchen towel off the counter, I use it to hold the handle while I stir the meat with a wooden spoon. A couple of seconds later, she sets an oven glove down next to me.

Well, yes, I guess that would work, too.

She gives me a big smile before returning to her mincing and chopping. She brings the garlic over, adding it to a large pot of spaghetti sauce as it's about to come to a boil. “I cheated a little and used canned tomatoes. The ones at the store didn’t seem like they were fresh,” she confesses as she stirs in the garlic. She adds in some minced basil and a pinch of oregano. “Hopefully, it will taste okay.” She takes over cooking the meat.

“Smells wonderful.” I move out of her way.

“There’s wine in the fridge if you want some. The wine-glasses are in the cabinet on the left. There’s a corkscrew in the drawer.” She waves her hand in different directions.

Opening the refrigerator, I locate a bottle of Cabernet Franc on the bottom shelf. I open the wrong cabinet door, but she’s busy draining the meat and doesn’t notice. I find the wineglasses behind the next door and the corkscrew in the drawer. Peeling the foil off the top of the bottle, I pick up the corkscrew and press the point into the cork.

“So, Finn, what do you do when you’re not pet-sitting cats?” She adds the meat to the spaghetti sauce.

“I’m a process server and I do skip tracing.” I tell the cover story I’ve created for questions like this. If anyone ever calls to check up on me, the law firm will confirm I do contract work for them. Since I served subpoenas for extra pay back when times were lean, and I’ve done some debt collecting, I understand how it all works if someone asks. We do occasionally receive a small stipend for the soul reaping, but Management is out of touch with the cost of living, so a demon’s got to do what a demon’s got to do. Luckily, I have my investments, so my pay isn’t an issue any longer.

“What about you?” I pour the wine into the two glasses, then hand one to her. The kitchen is small. It doesn’t leave much space between us. I lean back against the counter where I can study her better. She is stunning, but I get the feeling she doesn't know it or subconsciously tries to hide it.

"I work at the museum. I mostly do inventory in the back, but I occasionally help set up exhibits and I assist the chief curator." She takes a sip. "I was studying to become a historian, but my grandmother got sick, so I ended up dropping out to take care of her. I'm hoping to take a couple of night classes in January." She's rambling, and I suspect she's as nervous about our dinner date as I am. She takes a big gulp of wine this time before setting the wineglass down. Moving back to the stove, she stirs the sauce again and adds the spaghetti noodles to the boiling water.

"What made you want to become a historian?" I wonder what she would do if she knew I could give her a play-by-play of the last three thousand years.

"The past has always fascinated me." Opening the cabinet door, she takes out a colander and places it in the sink. "Can you imagine living back in the Victorian times or even earlier? The clothes, the music. Even the way they talked back then." Her face lights up. "I love learning about all of it. I find the research fascinating."

I smile. Now I know who owns the Victorian chairs. Of course, if she knew how things were in the past, she probably wouldn't think so highly of it. Take, for instance, The Black Death of 1348 in England. I was stuck in London almost that entire year. Work was almost nonstop from autumn all the way through until December of the following year. It's funny how history books downplay events like that for stories about kings, queens, and the fights between countries.

Chloe moves on to talking about the music and literature from different time periods. I can hear the passion in her voice. If the candles weren't enough of a hint, I can confirm she's quite the romantic. She reminds me of one of those girl-next-door types you used to see in old Hollywood movies. I should have expected it, I guess, but I hadn't thought any farther ahead than simply seeing her again. I've never done the romance thing. Where would I begin?

She finishes preparing dinner, then fills two plates with the spaghetti noodles and sauce before adding a piece of French bread to the side of each plate and carrying them to the table. I follow with the wineglasses and bottle of wine.

She motions where I should sit. As she starts to sit down herself, she realizes she's still wearing the apron. I take a seat while she heads back into the kitchen.

When she returns, the apron is gone. The blue shirt she wears has a row of buttons in front, and either she accidentally missed a button or perhaps she intentionally has her shirt open a little lower than I would expect. Either way, I'm treated to a nice view of some freckled cleavage and a suggestive hint of lace from her tan bra peeking out. I suppress a smile by taking a drink of my wine.

Eyes up, Finn. Don't ogle the girl.

I concentrate on my meal instead. She can cook, and she does it well.

The food is fantastic. "This is really good."

She beams at me appreciatively from over the table. She pushes a wayward strand of hair off her face. "I'm glad you like it." The pink returns to her cheeks. I'm beginning to suspect it happens whenever she's embarrassed or nervous.

I try to think of something else to say. We end up sitting in awkward silence.

"I heard you met my roommate," she pipes up.

At first, I don't know what she means, but then I realize she's talking about our meeting in the hall the other night.

"I did." I twirl some noodles onto my fork. "She seems nice."

Chloe bursts out laughing. I glance up in surprise. "Liar." She grins at me.

I say nothing for a moment, then grin back at her. "Okay, she's terrifying. I was trying to be kind."

We both laugh, and just like that, the ice is broken. I find myself relaxing.

"She thinks you're trouble. You know, one of those bad boy biker types." She tears off a piece of her bread. "She told me I should stay away from you."

"I do have a bike," I respond. "What did you tell her?"

"I told her I like bad boys." She pops the bread into her mouth, slowly licking the butter from her fingers. Suddenly, I find I can't take my eyes off her mouth.

She wants you, Finn.

I shift uncomfortably in my chair and glance away. I want her, too, but I remind myself of my plan to take things slowly.

"Have you two known each other long?" I change the subject.

Seriously? Dude! After she just—

I concentrate on what she's saying as I work to shut down the little voice in my head.

"Since high school. My grandmother brought me here to live after my parents died. She sent me to a private school, but since I was there on a scholarship and my family didn't come from old money, I never fit in. The other students teased me a lot until Andrea stepped in. I guess we're both kind of misfits. We've been best friends ever since."

The conversation shifts to movies we've seen and books we've read. We find we have similar tastes in both. We also enjoy some of the same music. I imagine it's the sort of things humans discuss when they go out on first dates. For the first time in a long time, I'm enjoying talking to someone. We continue to stay at the table long after we're done eating. Before I know it, we've finished almost the entire bottle of wine.

Chloe yawns. "Sorry, I rarely stay up late during the week—or drink this much wine." Her eyebrows raise as she picks up the bottle and discovers it's nearly empty. She measures out the last of the wine between our two glasses.

I glance at my watch. It's almost midnight. "I had no idea it was this late." Since she's yawning, I hope I haven't overstayed my welcome.

Have we sat here for almost four hours? I don't know where the time went. She doesn't, either. We get up from the table and carry our plates back to the kitchen. I help her wash the pots and pans, then we load everything into the dishwasher. It's oddly domestic, and strangely, I like it.

Back in the living room, I grab my jacket and start to put it on. I don't want to come across as overeager, but I want to ask her out again. I straighten my collar as I consider what to say.

"Would you maybe like to get dinner or something with me on Saturday?" For some reason, my voice cracks at the end. It comes out sounding like I'm a seventeen-year-old boy asking a girl to the prom.

Smooth, Finn.

"I don't think so," she replies a little too quickly.

Not the answer I was expecting. I thought tonight had gone well. Maybe she really didn't want to eat by herself, after all.

"Okay," I say slowly. I don't know where to go from here. "I guess this is goodbye, then."

She turns red again. "I'm sorry. That's not what I meant." She shakes her head and mumbles, "Stupid," under her breath. "What I meant was, I don't think I'll have time for dinner on Saturday. The museum is hosting a benefit that night. I have to work." She hesitates. "We can bring a plus one, though, if you would like to come."

I'm oddly relieved she hasn't turned me down flat, but this could mean meeting coworkers and friends. Isn't that the kind of thing people do after they've become a couple? I'm certainly not ready for anything like that. I need to play this cool.

"I'd like that." The words fly out of my mouth with no hesitation whatsoever. I don't even pause before giving her an answer.

You're an idiot, Finn. You know that?

"Great!" Her face lights up. "Give me your phone. I'll put my number in so you can text me. I have to be there early to help set everything up, but I'll put you on the guest list and send you the information. It's suit and tie. I hope that's okay."

I'm not sure how she got all those words out in one breath.

I unlock my phone, silently handing it to her. "No, it's fine," I lie. I hate wearing ties and suits. Having spent time in both the Victorian and Edwardian eras, I hate any occasion that forces me to have to dress up. In my opinion, those were the worst times for men's fashion, ever—except for maybe disco suits in the 1970s.

"There." She starts to hand me back my phone. Her eyes focus in on my Grim Reaper app. "That's cute. What type of app is it?"

I take the phone from her before she tries to open it.

"Just a silly game." I shrug nonchalantly, quickly shoving the phone back into my pocket.

"Neat. I like the one where you decorate living rooms and stuff."

I have no clue what she's talking about, but I nod.

Neither of us says anything. It goes back to feeling awkward. My nights with women don't usually end like this. Normally, clothes are already coming off. It doesn't matter where we end up, either. In bed, on a table, the couch, or against a wall.

"I guess I better go." I shake the image of what I would like to do with Chloe in any one of those locations out of my mind. I give her a smile. "Thanks for dinner. That was nice."

She smiles, too. "Thanks for joining me."

I'm back to nodding again. Lots of nodding. It's time to go. "Goodnight."

I move to turn toward the door when Chloe half lunges and half falls into me. Her move is totally unexpected and extremely uncoordinated. I believe her plan was to kiss me, but she ends up knocking me into the door with such force, my head bangs into the wood. Our lips and teeth smash into each other. I fully expect to taste the metallic flavor of blood in my mouth, but as I test them with my tongue, my lips feel okay.

I've had women throw themselves at me before, but never quite like this. It's charming. Painful, but charming. I end up catching her by the forearms as she attempts to regain her footing.

"Oh my God. I'm so sorry." Her face goes bright red. She starts to pull away from me, but I'm still holding her. I decide I can't let this moment pass. Instead of releasing her, I move my hands to the side of her face, angling her head where my lips slant over hers. It's a tender kiss at first, but then her lips part, and I can't stop myself. My tongue finds its way through.

As the kiss intensifies, she makes a small mewing noise in the back of her throat. Her arms twine around my neck and she's returning the kiss, our tongues mingling together. She may not have the experience most of the women I've been with do, but she's imitating my moves and eager to learn. It's such a simple act, but it stirs something deep inside me that I haven't felt in—well, forever. I struggle to hold myself in check as my resolve about taking things slow begins to weaken.

When she finally pulls away from me, we're both breathless.

"Do you want to stay?" She catches me off guard again.

Yes!

The image of the things I want to do to her intensifies and I suspect she's more than willing to let me do them. *She asked you, Finn. What are you waiting for? Carpe diem!*

From the back of my brain, though, another little voice won't shut up. It's louder than the one controlling the lower part of my anatomy right now. She's not like the other women I've been with, it reminds me again. I need to take things slow.

"I want to," I force myself to say. "I have an early morning, though. It sounds like you do, too." I run my thumb along her cheek. "I should go."

"Okay," she replies wistfully. She takes a step back so I can open the door.

"Saturday," I tell her.

"Saturday." One more nod.

I give her a chaste kiss and get myself out of there before I change my mind.

CHAPTER 4

October 7:

I only have one reap on my schedule for today, and it's an early one. My app informs me I do indeed have a disciplinary hearing with Management this afternoon, though. Since they've assigned me a Charge for this morning, I assume this hearing is only going to result in a slap on the wrist along with another write-up in my file. I have done what I thought was the right thing to do in the past, however, and ended up paying dearly for it. In other words, I'm not exactly sure how this hearing will play out.

Since it's the angels I'm appearing in front of, I start the morning by dressing to impress. I stray from my preference of blue jeans and a T-shirt. Instead, I go with black pants, black shirt, and a black sports jacket. I want Jack to believe I'm taking the hearing seriously after our little talk yesterday—even if I suspect it's an enormous waste of everyone's time.

I scroll through the information on my app. My reap begins at 9:35 this morning. If I plan it right, I only need to make one trip to the Promenade Building today. I check over my Charge's file to make sure I'm not overlooking anything.

Name: Duke Craton

DOB: 3/12 (24)

DOD: 10/7

TOD: 9:35/10:15 a.m. - final departure 12:05 a.m.

Species: Human

Marital status: Single

Reception Committee:

Floyd Craton (father)

Barbara Craton (grandmother)

Duke is a twenty-four-year-old construction worker who fell off the roof at a construction site earlier this morning but was still hanging in there when they transported him to the hospital. He has a few internal injuries the doctors don't know about yet, so I meet up with him shortly after they bring him into the emergency room. He's another one of those round trips, like Victor Junior was yesterday, but he also has an actual time of death noted in his file, so he's with me and then he's not, and then he's with me again before going back into his body one more time before he departs completely.

This is why Roz referred to the one yesterday as a Yo-Yo. Unfortunately, this Yo-Yo is about to have his string cut.

Since I still have about thirty minutes before Duke's true TOD, I sneak off to the break room to grab a cup of coffee while I wait. I'm in full Grim Reaper mode, but unlike my Charges, I can pick things up and move them around even when I'm invisible. Once I hold the item in my hand, it becomes invisible, too. In a little while, someone is probably going to wonder who emptied the coffee pot and ate the last doughnut from the box sitting on the counter, but they'll never know it was me.

I return to my post outside the emergency room and enjoy my coffee and jelly-filled pastry. I didn't consider the powdered sugar on the doughnut, though. It's all over the front of my black shirt.

Fuck.

Duke comes through the doors of the operating room for his last time while I'm trying to brush the white powdery mess off myself. I think I'm making it worse.

He stares at my shirt. I can tell he wants to say something, but he's still recovering from the series of round trips he was on, so he doesn't question me when the first stop we make is into the men's restroom. I wet a towel, running it down the entire length of the front of my shirt while he stands next to the hand dryers. It gets rid of the powdered sugar. Now, I just have to hope it's okay when it dries, although I'm having my doubts.

We leave the restroom, and I steer us toward the exit doors of the emergency room.

Oddly, we walk right past Chloe's roommate as we're about to go out. She's wearing blue scrubs with small teddy bears on them. I realize she's a nurse here. The badge on her lanyard tells me her name is Andrea Scott. Seeing her makes me want to see Chloe again, but I suspect she might find it a bit too stalkerish if she gets home and finds me waiting for her. Of course, if my timing is right, we could accidentally bump into each other in the hall again. Maybe I'll get lucky and get to see her tonight—if they don't haul me away in shackles after my hearing, that is.

A demon can hope.

If Duke discusses his first few hours in the afterlife with any of the other passengers on the ferry, he'll discover it hasn't been exactly by the book. Technically, I'm supposed to get him to the ferry as soon as possible, however, there's no rule saying I've got to do it right away.

It's all good as long as I get him there by departure time.

My shirt is now dry, but as I suspected, it has white powdered sugar smudges all over the front of it. Instead of traveling all the way back to my place to change, I'll save time by stopping somewhere to buy a shirt.

I know we'll pass by *Drinkwater's* on the way to the Promenade Building, so we end up there. It's a high-end men's clothing boutique. The salesclerk is right on top of me as soon as I enter the store. This is also about the time Duke starts asking me a bunch of questions. He has some opinions about which shirt I should buy, too.

"Not that one. The other one." He points.

"This one?" I've tried on three now.

"Yeah, that one fits you better."

"You think so?"

"Definitely."

"What about the color?"

"Dude, come on—they're all black." He shakes his head at me. He wanders off to the tie section while I debate between the dark dark black and the dark black.

Since I'm visible but Duke is not, the over-attentive salesclerk backs off as soon as I begin talking to myself, but I like the fit and color of each shirt, so I make his day. I buy them both. I keep the dark dark black one I have on and arrange for him to ship the other one to my place.

Our next stop is the dry cleaners, so I can drop off my old shirt.

Duke is already in Stage Five. I can tell he's bored. "They

must pay you by the hour," he says as we come out of the dry cleaners.

And I thought I was the sarcastic one.

I narrow my eyes. "Come on. Let's go."

I'm tempted to take him the long way to the Promenade Building, but I am getting close on my time. As it is, I drop him off shortly before the ferry departs.

It's a little before 1:00 as I return to the lobby. Since I'm going to the twenty-third floor into angel territory, Security has to escort me upstairs. I sign in, then wait for the guy behind the desk to check my photo and signature on my driver's license. He sees me almost every single day but chooses today to act like he doesn't recognize me. He studies me for a moment before waving his hand to the left and tells me to take a seat. His attention returns to whatever it is he's staring at on his phone. Even though he's human, I can't help but think he fits right in around this place.

The seating area he's directed me to is like the setup you might find in a doctor's office. Uncomfortable wooden framed chairs with ugly brown back covers and even uglier brown and orange seat cushions. It appears Nelson is waiting for the same security guard I am. He glances up as I take a seat against the wall directly across from him. Sitting in this position is good because it allows me to keep an eye on everything going on around me. It's another one of those old habits I seem to have picked up from somewhere over my many years. This one, I suspect, is from my time spent in Tombstone during the 1880s.

To keep my mind off the hearing, I watch while a steady stream of Grim Reapers and Angels of Death enter the building, get on the elevator with their Charges, then return a few minutes later without them. Bored, my attention shifts back to the lobby itself.

Several groups of the same type of chairs Nelson and I are sitting in are scattered around in small clusters. Although now that I think about it, I've rarely seen anyone use them. Usually, I don't even notice they're here, nor do I pay attention to the dreadful contemporary paintings made of lines and squiggles they've hung as artwork on the cream-colored walls. I study the one on the wall to my right. The painting is worse up close than it is from a distance. Having spent some time in France in the summer of 1890, I've always preferred landscapes. I may or may not have a Van Gogh painting of a wheat field in the village of Auvers-sur-Oise hanging in my study.

My glance shifts over to Nelson. He's miserable. I should probably feel sorry for him, but I don't. Okay, maybe I do a little. I've been through these inquiries a few times. I'm dreading it, too. I broke a rule again, but the kid is all right because of me, so what are they going to do? Of course, the angel side of Management is handling this because of Nelson and Wallace, so it could mean I'm in more trouble than I think I am.

I try to take my mind off this possibility by asking Nelson about the murdered witch I overheard him talking about. He's already nervous sitting next to me, so I don't think he's going to answer, but he finally tells me what happened.

"I got sick when I saw it. The body, I mean," he says. "I've never seen anything like it." He goes on to describe how many times the killer had stabbed her. He also mentions he noticed her heart was missing. It's gory stuff. "After I got sick. I had to clean it up. You know, DNA and stuff." This part, he didn't need to tell me. I almost tell him as long as he's in Angel of Death mode, his DNA isn't an issue, but I don't. Instead, I ask him whether he saw a symbol of some kind. He gives me a strange look. "Yeah, on the forehead. What does it mean?"

"I don't know." I shrug. "What did it look like?"

He describes it as a circle with triangles and another circle in the middle. His eyes narrow. "Why are you asking?"

"Just curious." I give him my best evil demon smile to stop him from asking me anything else. It works. We sit in silence for a few more minutes until the security guard arrives.

"Finn and Nelson?"

We both get up and follow him to elevator A.

Unlike the elevator I usually take, music is playing as we step inside. I didn't know that was a thing anymore. The security guard presses the button, taking us up to the twenty-third floor. Overhead, a garbled instrumental version of *Walking on Sunshine* plays from a speaker.

I swear it's the longest elevator ride of my life.

A brown-haired angel behind the counter in the reception area stands to greet us as we get off the elevator. I haven't seen her before, but I've only been on this floor once. She's wearing a white, no-nonsense dress with high ruffles around the neck. She's attractive in an angelic sort of way. She escorts us down the hall to a room on the left. Batting her baby blues, she motions inside and tells us to take a seat.

We enter a room painted in soft shades of blue. I spot a coffee machine in the corner. Next to it is a full bowl of fruit. Looks like the angels up here have it made. The waiting rooms in Lower Management have dirty tan walls and a funny smell. We consider ourselves lucky if we can even find a place to sit.

Tyler and Roz are already in the room, but there's no sign of Wallace. Nelson fixes himself a cup of coffee while I take the seat next to Roz.

"They're talking to Wallace now." Roz tilts her head toward a closed door across the hallway.

"Who's our rep?" I ask.

"Corsun." She makes a face.

The two have bad blood between them. I don't know why, but I do know she doesn't like him. I've known Corsun for years. Demons aren't all that social, but he's the closest thing I have to a friend. We go way back, and by that, I mean about fifteen hundred years or so. We may or may not have pillaged a few villages back in the day. I can say we've definitely fought in more than one bar fight together.

Corsun works as an attorney for Walters, Sheraton, and Welch. He also serves as our demon counsel when there's a hearing like the one today.

Tyler leans around Roz to stare at me. "So, how much trouble are we in?" He's wearing black dress pants, a white shirt, and a thin black tie. He's also got on black shoes, but no socks. His outfit makes me wonder if he moonlights as a server in a restaurant.

"Hopefully, not much. When they ask, tell them I told you to help me," I remind him.

Roz shoots me a glance, like she thinks I've lost my mind. I shrug. Like I said before, he'll owe me a favor one day. I have every intention of collecting, so there's no reason we should both go down for this.

We all glance up as the door across the hall opens. Wallace comes out. He stops, glares at me, then stomps off down the corridor without a word.

In the room across from us, I catch sight of Jack and Corsun sitting across from each other on opposite sides of a conference table. A young male angel with brown skin and light brown eyes comes out of the room, blocking my view. He gestures at Roz, indicating it's her turn, then gives Nelson a sympathetic look. No doubt the two know each other.

Roz glances back at me, but I can't read her expression. She follows the angel across the hall and the door closes behind them.

I have no idea what Roz will tell them. Demons usually stick together, but you never know. We'll sell each other out in a heartbeat if we feel it may help us get ahead or out of trouble, and we'll never blink an eye. If they promise her something, it could go either way.

The room becomes quiet. Tyler leans his head back against the wall and closes his eyes. Nelson keeps shifting around in his chair. He gets up from his seat and helps himself to another cup of coffee. Instead of sitting back down, he remains standing.

He stares at me with the cup of coffee in his hand. "Did you actually try to kill your supervisor one time?" The question comes out of nowhere.

Did he seriously ask me that? I frown at him.

Tyler's head pops up. He turns to stare at me, waiting to see how I respond.

Should I answer him?

"I did," I finally reply. I wonder where he's going with this. This is common knowledge in the demon world, but I've never had an angel question me about it before.

"Wallace said you served time in Hell after it happened." Nelson takes a sip of his coffee. He's almost flippant about it. He acts like we're casually discussing the weather instead of my life. He's either really stupid for thinking it's okay to press a demon for information when he's the only angel in the room, or he has a little false bravado in him since we're up here in angel territory. I suspect it's a bit of both. I would tell him exactly what I think of him and Wallace, but the kid hasn't been into the hearing yet. It would probably make things worse. I decide I'll play along a little.

"Also true." I try to keep the annoyed look off my face. I did one whole year, but time moves differently down there. It felt more like a hundred. I don't mention this to him, though.

"Why?"

"Why what?"

Nelson stares at me over the cup of coffee. "Why did you do it?"

And now he's about to piss me off. He either knows something or thinks he knows something. There's a tone to his voice. I'm guessing his questions are leading up to whatever it is.

"What have you heard?" I fold my arms across my chest.

Nelson shrugs. "He made you mad, so you tried to kill him. That you're hot-headed."

Me, hot-headed? Only when provoked—which is what's about to happen here if he keeps pressing me on the matter.

"Sounds about right." I won't make it easy for him. I'm curious to see how badly he wants to know.

Before he can ask anything else, however, the door to the conference room opens again. That didn't take long. Roz glances in my direction. She gives me a one-shoulder shrug. The male angel is with her, so she can't say anything.

He peers into the room where we are. "Nelson, you can go on in." He motions for Roz to follow him. She purses her lips, but I can't read her expression. It either went extremely well or it went incredibly bad. They head down the hall.

Nelson sets his cup of coffee on the counter, wipes his hands on his pants, then takes a deep breath. He avoids glancing in my direction as he goes past me. If Corsun gets to question him, he'll tear him apart. I try not to appear too smug.

"And then there were two," Tyler murmurs after the door to the conference room closes. He gets up and wanders around the room. "I appreciate you taking the heat on this." He fiddles with the stack of coffee cups. "You know, I grew up hearing stories about you."

Hearing stories? And now, I feel old. Ancient even. I'm not sure how to respond. I make a *hmm* noise, hoping he'll change the subject.

"You're practically a legend."

I raise an eyebrow. I've been called many things, but a legend isn't one of them.

"Don't believe everything you hear." Part of me would like to know what he's heard, but I'm not about to ask. I glance at my watch. It's almost 3:30.

It's an hour later when Tyler goes into the hearing, and almost 5:00 when I'm finally ushered into the room. Tyler gives me a thumbs-up as we pass each other. I take the seat next to Corsun. Across from me are Jack and two angels. The female one on the left is about my height with reddish hair bluntly cut to her shoulders. Her crisp white shirt is adorned with a bow, a look that makes her appear almost matronly. If I didn't know she was an angel, I would assume she was in her mid-forties and maybe a schoolteacher. I can't remember her name, but she's the equivalent of Jack in the angel division.

The male angel sitting on the right is more of a conundrum to me. The way Muriel and Jack defer to him makes me suspect he's Upper Management. He's dressed all in white, his suit tailored to perfection. It's most likely Italian and expensive. His hair is dark with a touch of silver near the temples. His amber eyes have a steeliness to them. It doesn't quite gel with his angel persona. Even Jack appears to find him intimidating.

"Finn." Jack stands, reaching out across the table to shake my hand. Demons don't do the handshake thing, so this is obviously for the angel's benefit.

"Jack." I try to sound casual.

"This is Muriel." He waves his hand first to his left, then his right. "And Mr. Fitz."

"Hello, Finn," Muriel extends her hand. It feels like ice in mine. I'm sure my hand feels like it's scalding hers. It's one of those opposite energy things.

Mr. Fitz also shakes my hand, but unlike Muriel, who only met my eyes for a second, he continues to keep eye contact with me. He is definitely Upper Management.

Jack is in all black, like I am. Only he's gone a step further with a full suit, including a tie, vest, and pocket square. He's about four inches taller than Muriel and a few inches taller than Mr. Fitz.

"So, Finn," Jack starts. He tents his fingers in front of him. "Couple of things to discuss here." This is for the angel's benefit, because Jack normally gets straight to the point, and it usually involves a lot of swearing. "We understand you've waived a formal 812 disciplinary hearing, so this is simply an informal hearing about some miscommunication which occurred between you and the Angel of Death on point the other day."

"Wallace," Muriel supplies.

Miscommunication? Is that what we're calling it? I stare at Corsun. I wasn't aware I waived my formal hearing. He's been busy. He slides a piece of paper over to me, then hands me a pen. It's a waiver form. There's a small X where he wants me to sign. I open my mouth to say something, but his expression stops me. I swallow, choosing my words carefully. "Yes, things were happening quickly. There's a possibility we had some miscommunication."

I saved the kid because the angel didn't want to do his damn job.

"And?" Jack motions with his eyes toward Mr. Fitz. He wants me to make this matter go away. I scowl. His eyes narrow. Message received.

I turn first to Mr. Fitz, then to Muriel. "I apologize for the confusion."

Muriel appears satisfied with my apology. "I'm glad we could clear this up."

Just like that? This hearing is total bullshit. I'm pissed. I try to keep my expression blank. "Anything else?" I ask Jack.

"Well, actually." Mr. Fitz leans forward in his chair before Jack can reply. "You had a conversation with one of our AoDs earlier today."

Shit. Nelson told them I asked about the witch's death.

"About?" I act like I don't know what he's talking about.

"He said you asked about one of his Charges from a few weeks ago. I believe it was a witch." He studies me. "We were wondering why."

I'm not sure if telling them I've noticed a pattern is in

my best interest or not. "I had a similar one the other day," I say instead. I keep my explanation vague. "I guess it made me curious because I overheard him mentioning his to someone in the ferry line."

"I see," he replies. He motions to Muriel. "You'll need to speak with him. Nelson, is it?" He leans back in his chair. "I'm sure I don't have to remind you about the privacy rules."

"No, of course not." I try to sound contrite. "I apologize for that as well." I'm hoping this will satisfy him.

He slides a white business card across the table. "If anything else comes up on this, we'd appreciate it if you could report it to me or Jack."

"Downstairs will look into it on our end," Jack offers. His expression shows he doesn't like how Mr. Fitz has taken over the discussion.

"What do you think is going on?" I pick up the card from the table. I already know there's a serial killer, but I'm not sure how far down the rabbit hole Management has gone or why they would have any interest in it.

Muriel purses her lips. "It's not our place to say."

The three exchange glances. I wonder what they're not telling me. Jack begins straightening the papers in front of him while Muriel taps around on her notebook.

Finally, Mr. Fitz stands, indicating the hearing is over. "Nice to meet you, Finn." He doesn't offer to shake my hand again.

"Same," I reply.

Jack gets up and motions for Corsun and I to follow him out into the hallway. He doesn't say a word as he leads us back to the elevators. Since it's after 6:00, the place is mostly deserted.

"Well, we dodged a big one back there," Jack mutters,

finally breaking his silence. He pushes the button for the elevator. "Muriel would have liked to take things further, but Mr. Fitz didn't want to press the matter." He lowers his voice. "You shoved an angel?" He sounds mad, but there's a trace of amusement in his voice.

I know better than to reply.

"Well, stay clear of Wallace. He appears to have it in for you." He shakes his head. "And, Finn, don't bring up any of this witch business again, either. Keep your focus on doing your job."

I remain silent.

The elevator doors mercifully slide open.

"Forgot my coat," Jack says before we can enter the elevator. "Go on, we'll talk tomorrow."

Corsun and I step into the elevator. The tension leaves my body as the elevator descends. It went much better than I hoped.

"Drinks?" Corsun asks. "You look like you could use one."

"Sounds good."

"You're buying," he says as we return to the lobby.

I would expect no less.

By the time our rideshare arrives, Corsun has decided we should celebrate our victory, not only with drinks, but a full dinner. I'm not sure it's an actual win. I had to apologize to the angels, and now I've got another write-up in my file. I guess I shouldn't complain, though. I mean, I will—but I probably shouldn't.

On our way to the restaurant, Corsun fills me in on the other interviews. Apparently, Roz and Tyler developed amnesia, and Nelson couldn't keep his story straight. Without collaboration from the others for Wallace, Management simply wanted to make the entire matter go away.

"Jack's right. Wallace won't be happy with the outcome, so watch your back," Corsun warns me.

We arrive at the restaurant to find *Del Frisco's* packed, but Corsun whispers something to the hostess. She giggles and her face flushes bright red. A mere two minutes later, we walk past the others who are waiting. She escorts us straight to our table. It's got a stunning view of the harbor. I raise an eyebrow as we take our seats.

"I told her what I could do for her later." He gives me a broad, knowing smile. He loosens his tie, studying the wine list. "If you're interested, she's got a sister who will fu—" He stops as the server arrives at the table.

"Bottle of champagne?" Corsun asks.

"Beer," I reply.

"Fat Tire and a vodka martini with a twist of lemon," he tells the server. He's quiet until she leaves. "I know I said you were buying, but this is on me, by the way." Slipping out of his jacket, he puts it on the back of his chair. "Well, it's going on my expense account, so it's actually on Management. What I'm saying is—get whatever you want."

Corsun always lives life to excess and I'm always the more reserved one. Since we've both got dark hair, brown eyes, and are about the same height and build, we occasionally get mistaken for brothers, but our personalities are nothing alike. The few times he has led me astray involve some stories I would rather forget. Our escapades go way, way, way back.

The conversation returns to the hearing, then shifts to

work, Corsun's hatred for Management, and finally to sports and whether the Red Sox can go all the way to the playoffs. By the time we've made our way through a couple of appetizers and dinner arrives, Corsun is on his third martini. He orders a fourth.

"You've got a weird moral compass for a demon." He points his finger at me as we enjoy our meal. I suspect I'll have to pour him into a taxi or order an Uber for him when we leave. I've always been able to drink him under the table. Then again, I'm nursing my first beer while a second full one sits in front of me. I loathe feeling out of control.

"How do you mean?" I ask.

He cuts a bite-sized piece of meat off his sixteen-ounce steak, then stabs it with his fork. "I've seen you lie, cheat, and steal, but when it comes to being a Grim Reaper, you're all about doing the right thing." He emphasizes his point by holding the fork in the air before sticking it into his mouth. "I've seen angels cut more corners than you do."

"That's interesting. How so?" They've cooked my steak to perfection, but I'm questioning the green beans. They've got a hard crunch when I bite into them.

Corsun glances around. He leans over his plate, lowering his voice. "Fudging the TODs when they're late to the ferry. I've even heard a few will let you grease their palms to change a DOD."

"Why would they want to change a Date of Death?" I'm not entirely sure he knows what he's talking about, but it sounds like something Corsun would know. He's the type of attorney who gives the profession a bad name. If I ever got brought up on charges in the human court system, I would want him by my side there, too.

He rubs his fingers together. "Money, my friend." He laughs. "Say a company is going to merge with another company and nobody knows the CEO is going to have a heart attack on the eighth, but the sale won't happen until after the tenth. Move the date one way or another and you can short a stock or keep the price going up until the merger is complete. Whichever way works the best."

Why have I never heard of this? I guess that's what happens when you become a pariah in the demon community. You miss out on the office gossip. "You say Angels of Death are doing this?"

"Well, demons mostly, but yeah, I know a few." He cuts another piece off his steak. "All I'm saying is some of those angels aren't as high and mighty as they want you to think they are. Some of them are real pieces of work." He stops, perhaps realizing he's told me too much. He sets down his knife and reaches for his drink. "Let's just say some of those halos are more than a little tarnished."

In reality, most angels don't have halos, or wings, either. Halos are an optical illusion, although the thing about angels earning their wings is true. Takes millennia for it to happen, from what I've heard. I've yet to meet a single angel who has earned them, but then, we don't travel in the same social circles, either so—

"I thought the moment someone dies is predetermined from the moment they are born. There's a Book of Life or something," I reply. I take a bite of mashed potatoes. They are quite good.

"Not anymore. These days, it's all done through the computer system Management uses. The book is digital now."

He moves on from the subject of angels. Our conversation shifts again to more benign subjects like all the rain we've been having and what some of the demons we hung out with in the old old days are doing now. Sometimes, I wonder what life might have been like if I hadn't gotten the Grim Reaper designation at birth. Would I have ended up an attorney like Corsun or doing something in politics? Probably in prison. The thought sobers me. I finish the rest of my second beer as Corsun settles the tab.

"Awfully early to call it a night," he says as we stand out under the awning of the restaurant. It's pouring down rain again. "We could visit a club until Veronica gets off her shift." He glances behind him. "Or is her name Valerie? Maybe she's the sister." He ponders this as I hail him a cab. He gets in and slides over, thinking I'm getting in, too. "Doesn't matter. I'll give you first choice. They'll both give you a good time. Trust me." He peers up at me expectantly.

"I've got an early morning," I offer as an excuse. "Thank Management for dinner." I shut the door to the cab, watching as it pulls out into traffic. Glancing down at my watch, I note the time. It's later than I thought. I suspect I've missed my window to see Chloe, but I still need to stop by and visit Tommy. I wonder again if something is wrong with me. I gave up a night of sowing my wild oats for feeding a cat and scooping a litter box.

I frown.

It's probably best not to tell Corsun. *Or anyone else.*

CHAPTER 5

October 9:

Friday is one long day of reaps with me impatiently waiting for Saturday to arrive. Chloe and I exchange a few text messages throughout the day, but it's mostly about the museum benefit. She tells me she's working late into the night to help put the finishing touches on everything, so I won't get to see her at all until the next day.

Saturday morning finally rolls around. From the moment I wake, I count down the hours until tonight. By the end of the day, I'm practically shoving my Charge through the turnstile to get them onboard. Once that's done, I rush home, take a quick shower, get dressed, and I'm out the door.

It's 8:10 when I pull into the parking deck of the museum. I prefer riding my bike over driving cars, but in a moment of weakness caused by Corsun spurring me on, I splurged and bought myself a black McLaren 675LT. It's my choice of transportation for this evening. I take a quick glance in the rearview mirror to make sure my tie is on straight. Getting out of the car, I hand my keys off to the valet.

"Nice car," the valet remarks as he gives me my ticket.

I know. "Thanks."

I check my reflection in the glass one more time to make sure I'm presentable before entering the museum. My choice of attire for the night includes a pair of black leather Berluti shoes, a black linen shirt, black dress pants, and a black jacket and tie.

A young woman sits at a table inside the door. Her black and orange name tag reads, "Hello, My Name is Denise." She stares at me with bedroom eyes, giving me a coquettish smile as she asks for my name. Once she locates it, she welcomes me to the museum. She offers me a brochure with a picture of the front of the building on it. Our hands briefly touch as I take it from her. She responds with a blush. Leaning forward, she whispers, "I get off at ten."

I give a polite smile, but don't comment on the invitation.

"Hello, My Name is Patrick," an older volunteer with gray hair, signals me forward to another line. For some reason, there's a lot of security in place for a charity event. I wait a while to pass through a metal detector before I'm completely inside the lobby of the museum. Do people actually try to come in with weapons to steal stuff from here?

Following the flow of the crowd, I walk through the lobby, past a life-size model of a T-Rex, go down a long hallway, then through a set of double doors before finally entering a large conference room. They've gone all out to decorate it for tonight's event. Orange and black balloons are everywhere, giving it a Halloween vibe. *Odd.*

Glancing at the brochure, I note a new display opens to

the public on Monday. It appears the "Friends of the Museum" are receiving an advanced preview tonight. I swipe a glass of champagne from the tray of a passing server as I begin my search for Chloe. With her long, curly mane of red hair, she's easy to find. Wearing a vintage style emerald dress with a V-neckline along with a pair of black high heels, it's the first time I've seen her in clothing that accentuates her figure instead of trying to hide it. The sight of her takes my breath away. I stop for a moment, simply admiring her.

Apparently, I'm not the only one whose attention she has tonight. It appears she's in a serious conversation with a man. Tall. Sandy brown hair. Chiseled jaw. Expensive tailor-made suit. Attractive for a hedge fund manager type.

He reaches out to touch her arm. His hand lingers there. At first, I assume he's simply one of those touchy-feely types, but as their conversation continues, their body language suggests they're overly familiar with each other. He runs his thumb over her skin, and my grip around the stem of the champagne flute tightens. It snaps in two beneath my fingers.

What the hell am I watching?

I'm not sure if I'm more upset by how I'm reacting to what I'm seeing, or if it's the appearance of an intimate connection between the two. Either way, I don't like it.

I watch as their conversation continues. She shakes her head and turns to walk away, but he grabs her by the wrist to stop her. She stares down at his hand. He lets go and takes a step back. He raises his hands up in surrender.

And I've seen enough of whatever this is.

I finish off the rest of the champagne and set the broken flute pieces on the tray of another passing server. By the time I make it through the crowd to where she's standing, the man has disappeared.

"Finn, you made it!" Chloe smiles, but there's a look of concern in her eyes. She glances over my shoulder uneasily, as if she expects the man to come back.

"I did." I study her. "Everything all right?"

An expression passes over her face. She's—worried? Embarrassed?

She waves her hand. "A little misunderstanding." She brushes it off. "What do you think?" She diverts my attention by motioning around the room. It's early, but a bunch of people are already standing around talking to each other as they drink champagne and pillage hors d'oeuvres off the servers' trays. From all indications, the evening is a huge success.

"Big turnout," I reply.

"Want to take a sneak peek at the exhibit?" She grins at me conspiratorially. "We've got about thirty minutes before they open it for the guests, but we can take a quick tour."

"Sure." I probably should have read the brochure. I have no idea what the exhibit is, but I'm happy to see it because she's excited to show it to me.

She leads me back down the hallway I initially came from, then out into the main part of the museum. I'm in front of the T-Rex again. I have to admit, it's kind of fun to see something older than I am for once—even if that something is now extinct.

We walk a little farther until we end up in an area currently blocked off to the public by a red velvet rope. After making sure no one else is watching, she unhooks it. She quickly refastens it once we're on the other side.

The area we've entered is one large open space. In the center are several small glass display cases sitting on black pedestals, while up against the side walls are a series of bigger open displays set up like miniature stages. Each stage depicts a scene from history. There are also paintings hanging along the wall in the back.

Above us, a large sign reads, 'The Occult: A Study Throughout the Ages.'

I try to disguise my smile. I wonder for a moment if she's giving me a subtle hint about what she is or that she knows what I am.

She reaches out to take my hand. "What do you think?"

"Impressive." *It really is.*

She leads me over to the first large display on the right. It's a replica of Medium Mina Crandon's seance room, which was on 10 Lime Street, here in Boston. The plaque in front of us tells the story of how the medium rose to fame during the early 1920s and how Houdini was determined to prove she was a fraud. I bite my tongue to keep from letting it slip that all the Grim Reapers in the area were keeping up with the story when it happened because we thought the whole thing was so funny.

I also have to stop myself from telling her I saw Houdini perform one time. That was back when Lower Management had me based here because of the Spanish Flu. I wonder what Chloe would think if she knew I've lived here on four separate occasions. Once in the 1800s, twice in the 1900s, and now again for the last five years in the 2000s.

"This is one of the displays I helped set up," she tells me proudly. She points to the three paneled Chinese screens, the crystal ball, and the mannequins around the table with outfits from the original time period. "Most of the time, I only do the inventory in the back, but the investigation was going on, so the museum shifted the staff around while they were dealing with all of it. I got asked to help out in here." She gestures around the room.

"Investigation?" I'm not sure what she's talking about.

"The museum break-in last month. You mean, you didn't hear about it?" Her eyebrows raise in surprise. She lowers her voice. "It was all over the news. They downplayed it to the press, but several of the items for the exhibit disappeared out of the loading dock area. That's why we have extra security tonight."

"What type of items?"

She shrugs. "Small stuff mostly, but it was all quite valuable. A set of French Tarot cards from 1750, a silver blade from a vampire hunter's kit, a few old scrolls from Biella written in 1250. Things like that." She ticks off the items on her fingers.

"And this happened back in September?"

"Right around Labor Day. We all had to take polygraphs. The police even questioned all of us." Her eyes get big as she tells me, "They still haven't found out who did it, but they cleared everyone who works here."

We move on, stopping to study a smaller display of stone effigies and voodoo dolls, but my mind is fixating on the silver blade. I'm finding it rather curious that someone stole it around the same time the murders of the witches started, especially since they were all stabbed to death and had symbols painted on them. It's almost like they're trying to perform a ritual of some sort. I'd like to ask Chloe more questions about the blade, but it might make me seem overly interested, and not in a good way.

We continue walking until we end up in front of the paintings. The first is a watercolor featuring a depiction of the Salem Witch Trials. Next is a folk art painting of

Halloween ghosts and pumpkins, and finally a painting by Salvator Rosa from the 1600s. It's of a man holding a cross up to ward off a demon, or maybe it's the devil. I work hard to hide my feelings on that last one.

Demons. We're always so misunderstood.

We turn, and I find myself standing in front of one of the smaller displays under glass. It contains three old scrolls, two rolled and tied with twine, and a third one open with its writing on display. I'm a little rusty when it comes to remembering ancient languages, but I'm guessing it predates Latin. I look closer. Beneath the writing are three symbols sketched with brownish red ink. I've seen symbols like this before. In fact, they look strangely similar to the ones I saw on the foreheads of the two murdered witches.

"What do those symbols mean?" I point to the scroll.

"Those came in the other day as replacements for the ones that were stolen. They haven't finished the translations on them yet." She reads the display information to check. "One of our historians was doing research on them. The museum borrowed books from the college library to help with the research, but the library needed them back before she finished."

I try to sound casual. "Interesting. What books were they?"

She rattles off three titles. "I only know that because I was the one who picked them up from the library." She studies me. "So, do you believe in all of this?" She waves her hand around the exhibit. "Seances, witches, devils—"

And demons.

"Of course." I give her a smile. "It's a fascinating subject." I suspect she's mostly curious about my stance on witches. I wonder how she'd feel knowing I'm a demon.

We continue our tour while she points out the areas where she helped with the displays. The last large display is a replica of the Salem Witch Trials. It's a mannequin of Thomas Newton pointing his finger at two young women sitting on a wooden bench. Thankfully, I was nowhere near Boston during those times. I did, however, know a couple of demons back then who were accused of practicing witchcraft. It didn't end well for them. Those were some strange times.

We stand staring at the display, both lost in our own thoughts. I feel her gaze shift from it to me. I look up.

"Thanks for coming," she says softly.

"Thanks for inviting me."

She leans in to kiss me, and it catches me off guard once again. It's a quick kiss, but she misses my lips entirely. She ends up planting it on my chin.

She rolls her eyes. "Well, I guess I win the prize for worst kisser."

She moves away from me, but I catch her hand, bringing her back. I'd like to do more, but it's a public place, so I give her a soft kiss, then squeeze her hand. "Doesn't seem too bad to me."

She gives me a bashful smile, biting her bottom lip. We stand staring at each other like two lovesick puppies.

"We better get out of here. They'll want to open the exhibit soon." She breaks the spell.

Maybe it wasn't Carol after all. Maybe Chloe's the one who bewitched you, Finn.

If she is, I don't think I'd mind it one bit.

We make it back to the other side of the little red rope with about five minutes to spare. The museum patrons are gathering around for the dedication. At the appointed time, the museum director gives a brief speech introducing the museum staff. When he calls out Chloe's name, she smiles at me, takes a deep breath, then walks up to join the others.

Once the exhibit is officially open, I stand off to the side to wait while Chloe and the others answer questions about it.

"Finn?" A familiar voice rises from the chatter behind me.

I turn to find Corsun standing a few feet away with an attractive auburn-haired woman hanging on his arm. She's human and a good bit older than the women I usually see him with, some of whom are often barely legal. By her expensive Chanel dress and string of South Sea pearls, I suspect it's the money attracting him to this one. Although Corsun occasionally pursues married women, from the way she's got her arm entwined around his, I'm guessing she's either a lonely, wealthy widow or recently divorced.

"Here for the exhibit?" I ask because I can't come up with anything better to say. He's as surprised to see me as I am to see him.

"Dottie wanted to see it." He tilts his head at his companion. "Dottie, this is Finn. He does contract work for us." He sells my cover story to her. "What are you doing here?" He knows how much I hate to wear a suit and tie.

"Well, I'm—"

"I'm back." Chloe arrives by my side, breathless. She interrupts before I can make up a convincing story or try to explain.

Corsun arches an eyebrow. He and I have gone through a lot together over the years, but I rarely share my personal life with him—or anyone else, for that matter. There's seriously no honor amongst demons. Even now, he's giving Chloe the once-over from head to toe. I narrow my eyes at him as a warning to back off.

"Chloe, this is Corsun, one of the attorneys from the law office I work for." I repeat the lie. "And this is Dottie." I'm uncertain how else to introduce her. The two give a friendly bob of the head to each other.

"Enchanté." Corsun takes hold of Chloe's hand. He pauses, and for a moment I think he's about to kiss it.

Back off, bro. I send him another look.

A slight twitch of his lips shows he's more amused than threatened.

"Nice to meet you both," Chloe replies as he continues to hold her hand. She's not quite sure what to make of him. "What do you think of the exhibit?"

"We haven't made it in yet. We ran into Finn first," Corsun tells her.

"You're one of the staff members they introduced, aren't you? I believe I've seen you here at one of these before," Dottie says. The two begin talking about other museum events Dottie has attended while Corsun goes back and forth from staring at Chloe to watching me. She isn't at all like the other women he's seen me with in the past. I can tell he's trying hard to figure out what we're doing here together—or rather, what I'm doing with someone like her.

"Dottie and I are going out for drinks after this," Corsun says as the women continue to talk. "You and Chloe should join us."

Yeah, that's not happening. "We'd love to, but Chloe has had a long day. Looks like the crowd is thinning." I motion toward the exhibit, hoping to distract him.

"Oh, yes. I believe it is." Dottie pats his arm. "Corsun,

dear, we should get in there. I do so want to see the Medium Crandon display."

"Of course." Corsun bows as if her every wish is his command. When he wants to, he can certainly play the charmer. He doesn't even bother to hide the smirk on his face as his attention shifts back to me and Chloe, though. He's letting me know this isn't over. We're going to have a long discussion soon about why I'm here with her. "Delighted to meet you, Chloe."

"You, too," she says. We watch as the two wander over to join the line for the exhibit. "They seem nice."

"Mmm." I don't know if I would call Corsun nice, but at least he was on his best behavior tonight.

"I guess I'm finished for the evening. I'll go get my purse and jacket from the back."

"I'll wait here."

"I had Andrea drop me off. I was wondering if you could give me a ride home."

"Certainly." I forgot we arrived separately. "I'd be happy to."

She starts to walk away, then, as if she's remembered something, she turns back. "Oh, by the way, Andrea's working tonight. All. Night." She bats her eyes at me and gives me a suggestive smile. Her hips even carry a little extra sway to them as she sashays away. If I'm not mistaken, she's propositioned me again.

Well played, Chloe. Well played.

The parking lot is still full of vehicles as we leave the museum. I give my ticket to the valet. In a few minutes, he's back with my car. I stuff a generous tip in his hand, then shoo him away. I want to do the gentlemanly thing by opening the door for Chloe. She gives me a strange look as she gets in. She's either caught off guard that I opened the door for her, or maybe she's surprised to see the car I'm driving. I'm not sure. I close the door, grinning as I go around to the driver's side and climb in.

"Nice car." She studies the touchscreen on the dashboard.

"Thank you." I beam at her, the stupid grin still on my face, and I know I must look like an idiot. I'm probably acting like one, too. I focus on adjusting the heat to distract myself. It's gotten a lot colder since I first arrived.

Since she likes jazz, I find the jazz station for her. That settled, it only takes a few minutes to get through the line out of the parking lot, and we're on the road. Traffic is light for a Saturday night. It won't take long to get back to her apartment building.

We're both quiet. Too quiet. I should start a conversation, but what do I say? Do I ask her why she told me her roommate was out? Maybe I should stick to a safer topic, like the traffic or the weather. This dating thing is hard.

"Corsun seems nice," Chloe says out of nowhere. "Have you known each other long?"

"Yes, it's been quite a few years now." *Hundreds and hundreds of years.*

"And Dottie?"

"I only met her tonight."

"Oh."

We become silent again. I'm relieved when I pull the car into the garage at her apartment building. I take the visitor's parking space closest to the door. Chloe glances over at me. She hasn't said more than a few sentences since she got in my car. She gives me a puzzled look. I wait for her to say something, but she doesn't.

I get out to open her car door, but she's already climbing out on her own when I get to her side. I lock the car with the remote, then follow her through the security gate. We go up the stairs in silence. Has she changed her mind about how she wants this evening to end and doesn't know how to tell me? Or perhaps, I completely misread her comment earlier at the museum.

Standing outside the apartment door, she digs into her purse for her apartment key. "Do you want to come in?" She gives me a nervous smile and I wish I knew what she was thinking.

"Sure." I try to sound casual. My voice comes out high-pitched at the end. Like I'm a teenager on their first date. With her in the vintage dress and me wearing a tie, it does look like we're coming home from the prom.

I can't explain it, but as she unlocks the door, I realize I've never wanted a woman as much as I want her right now. Earlier, it seemed like a done deal. But at the moment, I can't read her at all.

I follow her into the apartment like an eager puppy.

"Want a drink?" She sets her purse on the couch and slips out of her coat.

"Sure," I say again.

"Red or white?"

I'm on edge now. Maybe I should tell her I need both. "White." My vocabulary skills are reduced to one-syllable words.

The little V between her eyebrows comes back. She disappears into the kitchen.

Since Chloe is on a whole other level than the women I usually find myself attracted to, I'm feeling completely out of my depth. I'm not sure what to do with myself, either. Should I sit? Should I stand? Maybe I should casually lean against something. I can't decide.

Taking off my jacket gives me something to do. I drape it over one of the Queen Anne chairs, loosen my tie, then undo the top button of my shirt. It relaxes me a little simply by doing that.

Chloe returns with two wineglasses filled with white wine all the way to the top. A little sloshes over as she hands one to me. She takes a sip from the one she's holding. Now, we're both standing in the middle of the living room like we don't know what to do with ourselves. She hasn't asked me to sit. Perhaps, she's giving me a nightcap before sending me on my way.

She stares at me, and her cheeks turn pink. She bites her lip.

Or, maybe she's not.

She takes another drink of wine. One big gulp this time. Half of it disappears. I suspect it's an attempt to steady her nerves.

"Andrea asked me again what I'm doing with you," she says.

"I don't think she likes me."

"No, she does not." She puts a hand to her mouth as she tries not to giggle. "She wants to know why someone like you would be interested in someone like me." Her smile fades. She stares down into her wineglass like she's embarrassed.

"What do you mean?" This throws me off a bit. It's true, she's not the type I'm usually interested in, but she's the complete package. She's smart. She's pretty. She's more genuine than anyone I've ever met. Yet, somehow, she doesn't realize it.

"Well, I'm me." The blush returns. She touches the rim of her wineglass with her finger. "And you—" She waves her hand at me. "—are completely out of my league."

I don't understand. I reach over to take her wineglass from her. Setting it down with mine on the table between the two chairs, I take her hands in mine. "Chloe, you've got it backwards. You're the one who's out of my league. I'm simply in awe of you."

She gazes into my eyes, then leans forward, capturing my lips with hers. She's taking the initiative again. I guess the third time's the charm. It starts as a soft kiss but becomes something more. Her lips part. My tongue finds the entrance into her mouth. She moans as our kiss intensifies, her tongue entwining with mine. Holding her by the nape of her neck, I pull her closer. She places both hands on my chest, but one hand starts moving downward. She runs her hand over my shirt, continuing lower until her fingers brush up against the front of my pants.

Whoa! Wasn't expecting that. Desire bursts through my body. I want her. Here. Now.

On the floor? No, not like that.

On the couch? No, you need to do this right.

I pull back, gazing into her eyes. We're both panting. She wants this, too.

"Bed?" I'm back to one-syllable words.

"Bed." She grins, taking me by the hand.

She leads me out of the living room and down a hallway before stopping at a bedroom on the left. Letting go of my hand, she walks over to a bedside table and turns on the lamp. Her bedroom is almost smaller than my closet. The word *cozy* comes to mind. The walls are pale green with most of the furnishings in white. A twin bed takes up most of the room. It has a light wooden headboard made of maple with several large fluffy pillows leaning up against it. A floral duvet with a soft green background covers the bed.

There's also a small wooden table underneath the window. It barely fits into the space. A miniature cauldron, along with a single gray feather and two red candles, adorn the top. Chloe's altar. I suppress a smile. I wonder if or when she's going to tell me she's a witch. Once again, I wonder how she would react if she were to discover I'm a demon. *Let's not go there tonight, Finn.* For now, I guess, we're both keeping secrets.

Chloe walks back to me. She presses her lips together as her fingers go around my tie. They fumble as she tries to undo the knot. To help her out and save time, I pull it over my head, dropping it to the floor. She gives me a pleased look.

Next are the buttons on my shirt. I'm tempted to just rip my shirt open, but with a determined look, her fingers fly over each one, making quick work of them. My anticipation builds. She wants this as much as I do. When she finishes, she yanks the shirttails out of my pants, then pushes the shirt off my arms.

"Cuff links." I manage two one-syllable words this time. I hold my arms up, giving her access to my wrists. She removes them both, setting them on the bedside table. I use the moment to quickly remove my socks and shoes, then take out my phone, my billfold, and the foil pack I slipped into my pocket earlier in the evening before I left my place. I don't want to spawn any small demons, although for a brief second, I contemplate what our children would look like. With our DNA, it would make them half demon, half witch. I shudder. What a scary thought.

She blushes as I put the foil pack close to the bed. "Guess I haven't been much of a challenge, have I?"

"You challenge me in every way, Chloe," I tell her truthfully. "I've never met anyone like you." I remove my shirt. I attempt to toss it toward a chair in the corner, but it misses by a foot. *Real smooth, Finn.*

"Turn around." I want to get her out of the dress before she finishes undressing me.

She obediently turns. Standing behind her, I run my hand across her soft pale skin as I move her hair to one side. She leans her head to the side. I kiss her neck and shoulder as I reach to unzip her dress. She tenses.

I stop. "What's wrong?" I turn her around by the shoulders so I can see her face.

"Nothing. Nothing." She shakes her head. "I'm a little nervous. That's all." She reaches behind her back and finishes unzipping her dress. She pushes the material off her shoulders. Moving slowly, she does a little shimmy, pushing the dress down until it falls in a puddle to the floor. She's wearing a matching silk bra and panties underneath. They're the same green color as the dress. My breath catches as I see the swell of her breasts under the green lace. Her body is exquisite.

She places one hand on my shoulder as she removes each black high-heeled shoe. When she's done, she winds her hands around my neck. Tilting her head, she nips at my bottom lip. The sensation goes straight through me, traveling downward.

Her lips part, crushing into mine. She reaches behind to undo her bra. Taking a small step backward, she removes it. With a shy smile, she lets it drop to the floor.

Seeing her this way is everything I imagined and more. I pull her to the bed and quickly push back the comforter. Together, we tumble down onto the soft white sheets.

"Chloe, you are so beautiful." My voice comes out oddly

husky. I move onto my hands and knees, shifting until I'm directly above her. Our bodies touch and I feel the warmth of her exposed flesh.

I kiss her again, long and hard this time. A low moan escapes her lips as she kisses me back. Her hips arch up against me. She reaches out, grasping the sheets. I move one hand down to her right breast, massaging the soft skin there as I run my thumb over her nipple again and again. It grows beneath my touch. Taking my time, I leave a trail of kisses from her mouth, down her neck, and onto her other breast. She brings her hands up, twisting her fingers in my hair, pulling gently.

Fuck, that feels so good.

I tease her nipple with my tongue, moving over it with my mouth. Her body bows beneath me as she lets out another low moan. I move to the other breast.

"Oh, please," she whimpers. She grinds her hips against me.

I raise my gaze to meet hers. "Tell me what you want."

"You. I want you." She shoves her hips upward again.

"You do, huh?"

"I do." Her eyes fill with need.

My hand travels down her body, across her stomach to her hips. As my fingers rub against the silk of her panties, she pushes up to meet my palm. Moaning, she writhes beneath my hand as I slide it underneath the material. She's hot, wet, and ready. I wasn't expecting that quite so soon.

"Oh, baby. I want you, too."

"Please, Finn."

I drag her panties down and off. She's naked now. I stop, taking a moment to appreciate her beauty. How did I get so lucky?

Her eyes meet mine. She gives me a nervous smile. Reaching down, I undo my belt and pants. I slide out of them and my underwear, sending them to the floor. I grab the foil pack off the bedside table and tear it open.

My entire body quivers in anticipation as I kneel between her legs. Cupping her hips to lift them, I'd planned to go slow, but I can't hold back. I sink into her, deep and hard. She cries out as if in pain. Her body arches against mine like a bow, her hips jerking beneath me.

Damn.

She's a virgin.

Not anymore, she isn't. Finn, what the hell have you done?

Sweat forms on my back. I fight the urge to move, afraid I'll hurt her again.

"Fuck, Chloe."

I shake my head, trying to clear it. My body hovers over hers, lost somewhere between frustration and the need for completion. Why the fuck didn't she tell me?

"I'm so sorry, baby." My eyes lock with hers. A lone tear pools in the corner of her eye. It softly spills over onto her cheek.

Shit. Shit. Shit.

Muscles trembling, I brace my arms. I try to move as gently as I can, wanting to slip out of her without hurting her more.

She lets out a breath. As I start to move away, her hips move upward to meet mine, drawing me back inside her.

"Chloe, don't—"

She looks up at me with determination, then gives me a small, defiant smile. Her hands move to my hips, stopping me.

"I don't want to hurt you again."

"You won't." She arches her hips, pulling me back, and —my focus is lost.

"Fuck." I can't hold back any longer.

I bury my face in her hair. She cries out a garbled version of my name and we both let go.

She. Is. Mine.

I'm totally spent. Chloe sighs. She raises her hand and strokes it along my back. We stay like that for a moment, lost in each other. Her heart beats fast and hard beneath me. I catch my breath. Pushing myself up with my elbows, I give her a soft kiss before gently moving away from her to roll over onto my back. Removing the condom, I discard it in the trash can beside the bed. She curls up next to me with her head on my shoulder, her hand resting on my chest. That was everything I hoped for and more. Except, I hurt her. I'll never forgive myself for that. I can't fathom why she didn't tell me.

"That was incredible." She peeks up at me through tousled red hair. "Are you mad at me?"

"What?" I turn my head to glance at her. "Why would I be mad?"

"Because I didn't tell you."

I twirl a strand of red hair around my finger. "No, I'm not mad, but you should have told me. We would have done it differently."

"You mean there's another way to do it?" She turns red and giggles. "Can we try it?"

I raise an eyebrow. She wants to do it again? "I think you've had enough for one night." She doesn't realize how sore she's going to feel in the morning. Plus, I stupidly only brought one condom. *Idiot.*

She runs her fingers across my chest. "Will you stay and spend the night with me?"

In the back of my mind, I know I shouldn't. I don't want to leave her, though. I nod, pulling her closer. She sighs again, settling into my arms.

Relaxed and tired, we both fall asleep.

CHAPTER 6

October 10:

I wake and wonder where I am. It takes a moment before the events from last night come flooding back to me. I'm in Chloe's apartment—in her bed. Yes, we went there. It wasn't a dream.

I turn my head on the pillow. She's facing me, sound asleep. There's a serene expression on her face. I can't help but stare as she softly breathes in and out. I watch as her eyelids flutter and her lips part. The little V forms between her brows, then she licks her lips with the tip of her tongue. I'm getting hard simply watching her.

I consider waking her up, but still no condom. Plus, I'm sure after last night, she's going to be sore. The last thing I ever wanted to do was hurt her. I shake my head at the thought. She should have told me. But even so, I'm glad I was her first.

And there's that damn grin on my face again. I can't shake it. I turn my head to stare at the ceiling. This is what I wanted, right?

Don't get me wrong, last night was incredible. It's what

I've been wanting since the first time I ever laid eyes on her. Yet, last night I felt something I have never felt before and now the feeling is returning. I'm not sure what to make of it. I'm almost scared to say it, but if I didn't know better, I would say I was happy. Content, even.

I'm continuing to ponder these unknown feelings and what they mean when I notice the daylight coming in through a slit in the curtains. *What time is it?* I have a reap scheduled for 10:45 this morning. Carefully sitting up so I don't wake her, I check the clock on Chloe's nightstand. It's 10:10. I have way overslept.

Shit. Shit. Shit.

I can't remember exactly what the location is, but I suspect I won't make it on time. I slip out of bed, trying to remain quiet as I collect my clothes off the floor. I get my underwear and pants on. Where is my other sock? From the bed, Chloe giggles. She's watching me while I frantically search for it. Smiling, she points. It's peeking out from underneath her dress on the floor.

"Do you have to go?" she asks. "I thought I could make you breakfast."

"As much as I would like to stay, I have to work."

She slides over, so I can sit next to her on the bed. I start putting on my socks and shoes.

"You could call in sick," she suggests.

I wish it was an option, but Grim Reapers don't get sick days. "I'd like to, but I don't think I could get away with that." Bending down to put my other shoe on, I freeze as her hand touches me. I know what she's doing. I hold my breath as her fingers trace one of the scars crisscrossing my back. She doesn't ask, but I can tell from her silence she's wondering.

"Happened a long time ago." I get up from the bed, then

lean down to kiss her. "I'm going to be late. I've got to go." I quickly pull on my shirt. She watches as I button it up.

It feels like I should say something about last night.

It was amazing.

The best I've ever had.

I think I'm falling in love with you.

I shut that last thought down real fast. I barely know her. She barely knows me. Demons don't fall in love. And yet—

"Last night was..." I have no clue how to finish the sentence.

"For me, too." She shyly smiles up at me.

Grabbing my watch off the bedside table, I put it on. I stick the rest of my things into the pockets of my pants. I pause as I catch sight of myself in the dresser mirror. My pants and shirt are wrinkled. It's obvious from my hair what I've been up to. Yes, I'm doing the walk of shame.

I run my hand through my hair before opening the door. "I'll talk to you later."

"Bye."

"Bye." I don't want to leave, but I do.

I stop to take one last look at her before shutting the bedroom door behind me. I walk down the hall. Andrea stands near the kitchen with a cup of coffee in her hand. She's wearing green scrubs with pink ice cream cones on them. I hunt around for my jacket. Her eyes narrow as she watches me. Without saying a word, she points to where it lays over the back of one of the Queen Anne chairs.

I grab it. "Thanks." I give her a nod.

She doesn't reply, but I feel her eyes follow me as I head toward the front door.

"If you hurt her, I'll end you." Her words echo out into the hall.

A shiver runs through me. I don't doubt for one moment she would.

~

It's 11:05 when I pull into a parking space in front of the Sunnydale Assisted Living Community. There's an ambulance parked near the door. My Charge today is eighty-seven-year-old Arnold Schlowsky. Heart attack.

I stay in the car for a moment, watching the entrance. People are coming in and out of the building, all oblivious to the fact someone inside has passed away. Since I drove, I can't go into Grim Reaper mode while anyone is present. I also can't simply stroll into an assisted living facility and wander around, so I'm forced to sit and wait. Finally, a family of five gets out of a minivan, heading toward the door. If I time it right, it will appear I'm with them and no one will question me about why I'm there.

I file in with them and no one is the wiser. They don't even realize I've attached myself to their party. When I spot a restroom, I break away from my newfound family. Glancing at my watch, I'm now twenty-five minutes late.

The invisibility part is simple. If the mind can believe it, the body can achieve it.

The 7 Habits of Highly Effective Reapers: Grim Reaper Training 101: *How to Turn Invisible.*

Walking through doors and walls, though, is a little more complex. Stepping through a solid object feels like I'm getting stung by thousands of bees. Having someone walk through me, though, is the worst. With perfect timing, an orderly goes by right as I step out into the hall. I flinch as his thick arm passes through my torso. I don't know how demons who like to take possession of a body do it. Maybe that's why they're so cranky all the time. I shake off the weird feeling and head toward the Purple Wing and Room 107.

It takes me a minute to find the right room. When I do, I discover the ambulance driver and two nurses are standing around the recently departed, Arnold Schlowsky. He went peacefully, it would seem. His body sits in a chair. At first glance, you'd think he was taking a nap. Unfortunately, his soul is nowhere around.

Crap.

To track him, I'll have to touch him. Touching the deceased is the least pleasant part of my job.

The driver and the nurses are blocking me, though. Possession is not my thing and I'm not that type of demon, anyway, so I can either wait for an opening, or I can try to hunt him down without the tracking. I step back out into the hall, taking another glance around. I didn't sense him back in the direction I came from, so I head the other way.

The hallway comes out at a nurse's station. There's another long hallway to the left, double doors straight ahead, and an open space to the right.

Shit.

It's like a maze. I'm never going to find him. I turn to go back toward his room to start over, but then I hear shouting and applauding coming from the area to the right. I move around the nurse's station to get a better look. There's more shouting, then some swearing. A group of elderly men are all sitting around watching television. Since they canceled last night's game because of the weather, the Red Sox have a doubleheader.

As I come around to stand in front of them, I find Arnold sitting in a faded blue recliner watching the game. He doesn't see me, but I'm almost directly in front of him. The other men don't know I'm present, but there's no reason he can't tell I'm here. I'm puzzled at first, but then when I make a slight movement, I catch a subtle change in his expression. I get it. He knows I'm watching him, but he's ignoring me.

"It's time to go, Arnold."

"Artie," he replies, his eyes glued to the television. "You're late."

"I got stuck in traffic," I lie.

He snorts. "Looks to me like you've overslept." He wiggles his finger at my wrinkled clothes. He turns his attention back to the television.

I give Artie a reprieve through this inning and start watching the game myself. A runner steals second and the other player on base makes it to third. Another pitch, but the ball is outside of the strike zone. The Red Sox shortstop is about to walk. We watch in silence as the bases become loaded. The first baseman is up next. He keeps fouling the ball until he finally pops one up. It's a fly ball out to center field, and it's caught for the third out. The Yankees are ahead. The score is 2 to 1 as it goes to a commercial break.

"Damn." Artie hits his fist against the armrest.

I raise an eyebrow, trying not to grin. "Come on, Artie, it's time to go." I tap on my watch for emphasis.

"Oh, you're late getting here, but now you're in a hurry." He turns his full attention to me. "Where's your wings?"

"My what?"

"You're one of those guardian angels or something, aren't you?" He moves his finger up and down. "Shouldn't you have wings?"

"I believe you mean Angel of Death."

"You don't look like an angel."

"I'm not an angel. I'm a—" I stop myself. "It doesn't matter. It's time to go."

He rolls his eyes at me. With a grumpy sigh, he hauls himself to his feet. As we walk by the other men, he can't help himself. He waves his hand in front of one of them, sticking his tongue out.

He shoots one old guy the bird. "Never could stand him," he says as we start down the hall. "He cheats at cards."

We walk back down the hallway I just came from. The police and two people from the coroner's office have arrived. I try to keep us walking, but Artie stops to watch.

"Trust me, you don't want to hang around here, Artie," I tell him as he stares into his room. One of the police officers walks out, going straight through him. Artie stares at me in surprise. He holds up his hand, studying it. From his perspective, his appearance is the same as it was when he was alive. He catches on quickly, though. He reaches out his hand, sticking it through the wall. Grinning back at me, he takes a deep breath, holds it, then steps through the sheetrock.

Fuck.

I follow, and now we're both standing in his room. Artie watches the proceedings with great interest. I don't know if he's in Stage One and in total denial, or if he's moved on to acceptance in Stage Five. He's handling his passing like it's no big deal. It's almost worrisome. We watch as the remaining officer fills out a report while the two from the coroner's office prepare to move Artie's remains onto a gurney.

"Not much dignity in dying, is there?" He makes a face as they lift his body. He turns from the scene like he's seen enough, then goes to his dresser. It's an old one. Tiger oak with an attached beveled mirror on top. I watch as he tries to remove a photo tucked into the frame of the mirror. Unable to touch the photograph, his hand goes through the mirror and the frame. He tries again, and once more after that.

Finally, he turns, staring at me. "I want the photo to go with me."

I shake my head. "That's not the way it works, Artie."

"I'm wearing the clothes I had on, aren't I?" He reaches for the tan shirt under his brown cardigan. He pulls it away from his chest. "If they're coming with me, a photo should be able to come with me, too." He turns his attention back to the photo and tries once more to pick it up.

I begin to explain that his clothes are an illusion. The ones he wore are still on his body, but I can tell he's not going to listen to me, so I let it drop. "Artie, seriously, we need to go."

He folds his arms. "Not without the photo."

How do I keep getting these Charges? Assignments are random, so the Universe must have something against me.

"What's so special about the photo?" I rub the bridge of my nose with my fingers. My patience is wearing thin.

He doesn't want to tell me. We stare at each other, waiting to see who will give up first.

He lets out a frustrated sigh. "She was my first love. Okay?" His lips form a thin line. "Now, will you help me?"

"I'm sure you'll get to see her on the other side," I counter. I recall nothing on his manifest about anyone expecting him except for his parents, but Management can sort it out once he's on the ferry.

"No, I won't get to see her over there." He waves his hands around in the air. "She's still alive. She's married.

Forty-two years. She has four children and three grandchildren." He sighs. "She's the one that got away. I'll always regret not telling her how I felt when I had the chance. It's my biggest regret." He makes one more attempt at taking the photo. "This is all I have left of her."

I say nothing as I study him. Allowing Charges to carry items aboard the ferry is against the rules. I don't need to get in trouble again so soon after the last incident, but it's a minor infraction if Management finds out.

"Okay, but if you get caught, you leave my name out of it, all right?" I reach over, taking the photo off the mirror. "Promise?" I ask as he tries to reach for it. I hold it back away from him.

"Yeah, yeah." He scowls at me. "I promise."

I hand it to him and he's all smiles.

"Remember, don't let anyone see it," I remind him when we're back in the hall. I motion to the cardigan he's wearing. "Put it in your pocket. When they ask you if you have anything to declare, tell them no."

"Got it. Thanks." He holds the photo up, giving it a kiss before stuffing it into his pocket.

I bow my head, motioning toward the door. "Now, let's go."

There's no one around outside, so once we reach the car, I make myself visible. Opening the door for him, I help him inside. I never use my own transportation, so I'm breaking another rule, but this one is my own.

"Being a guardian angel must pay well," Artie says as he peers around. He tries to run his hand over the dash.

"I'm not—" I start to tell him again but give up.

Pulling out of the parking lot, I head for the Promenade Building.

Artie settles into his seat. "Hey, can we listen to the game?"

~

It's after 2:00 when I get home. I've gotten Artie on the ferry. My work is done for the day. I remove my jacket. It's picked up that odd scent assisted living and nursing homes always have in them. The shirt smells, too. The housekeeper will run it through the laundry, but the jacket and pants need dry cleaning. As I strip out of the rest of my clothes to take a shower, I realize I've left my tie at Chloe's place.

I catch myself smiling at the thought of her. Last night was—

I still don't have words for it. I've never felt anything like it in my life, which for me is a long, long time. I want to see her again, but I don't know how the whole dating thing works. I ponder this as I squeeze a little shampoo into the palm of my hand, then run it through my hair. I've got to go over to the apartment building tonight to feed Tommy. Is it too soon to call on Chloe? Call on her? Does anyone even use that term anymore? I have no clue.

I keep thinking about what Artie said about the woman in the photo and having regrets about not taking a chance to tell her how he felt. I never thought I would have those kinds of feelings for anyone, especially a witch. I mean, I'm a demon. Love's not one of the emotions we feel—is it? I wonder about this again.

I step out of the shower and grab a towel to dry off. Catching my image in the mirror, I run my hand over my chin. I haven't shaved since yesterday morning, so I've accumulated about a day and a half of growth on my face. I wonder if Chloe likes beards?

Stop it, Finn.

I decide against the beard. I shave before wandering back into the bedroom to dress. A few minutes later, I'm in jeans and a black long-sleeved T-shirt. I'm not going anywhere for a few hours, so I go with socks, but no shoes. I pad into the kitchen to find something to eat.

Since I ate with Corsun on Wednesday and at Chloe's on Thursday, there's still two containers left in the refrigerator. I take out the one marked roast beef. Inside, I find cuts of meat, mashed potatoes, and tiny carrots. I'm not crazy about cooked carrots, but I didn't eat breakfast so it will have to do. I stick it into the microwave and notice I've left my phone in the bedroom. While the food heats, I retrieve it. I have a text message. It's from Chloe. My heart skips a beat.

Hope you weren't too late this morning. I think I have something of yours.

Below the message is a picture of my tie.

I grin as I carry the phone back to the kitchen, considering how to reply. Should I try for charming or witty? Maybe I should make a joke, so I don't come across as too serious. But I am serious about her. This is hard.

I remove the food from the microwave and take a seat on one of the stools in front of the island. As I start to eat, I stare at my phone. I begin to type. Stop. Backspace and start again. After a few more attempts, I give up. I set the phone to the side.

As I finish my lunch, it comes to me.

Stopping by later to take care of Tommy. See you then?

I stare at the words. It's not charming or witty at all, but it doesn't make me appear desperate, either. My thumb hovers over the little arrow. Holding my breath, I hit send.

And now, I wait.

As the afternoon progresses, I become uneasy. I haven't heard from Chloe since she sent the text earlier in the day. My phone states it delivered my message, so she got my text. I'm not sure why she hasn't responded. I wait until a little before 7:00, then head to the apartment building, unsure of what I'll do when I arrive.

There's the sound of laughter as I climb up the stairs. Reaching the top, I see Chloe, Andrea, and two men coming out of Chloe's apartment. I recognize one of the men as the guy from the museum. Both men are human. *Interesting.* All four are dressed like they're on their way to somewhere fancy. It only takes me a couple of seconds to realize it's a double date.

Chloe's eyes widen when she sees me. Her face goes pale. "Finn." Her voice hitches.

"Chloe." Somehow, I keep my voice neutral, even through my confusion.

The guy looks from her to me, then puts his arm around her waist. He pulls her closer as if to show he's staking his territory.

Too late for that, bro. I've already planted my flag there.

"Who are you?" he demands.

Well, it would appear I'm the other guy. The one who screwed your girlfriend. Trust me, it's news to me, too.

I ignore him, studying Chloe instead. She won't make eye contact with me. I can't read her expression. Is she embarrassed? No, it's more than that. She's genuinely horrified. She stares down at the floor.

What the fuck, Chloe?

"He's our neighbor's nephew." Andrea breaks the silence. She shoots me a warning look, daring me to say otherwise. "She's out of town, so he's watching her cat."

I suspect he's still questioning Chloe's reaction in his mind, but this appears to satisfy him for the moment. He relaxes his stance, even going so far as to offer me a handshake in greeting but continues to possessively keep his arm around Chloe.

"Eric Helsin. Chloe's fiancé."

Fiancé?

"Finn," I somehow manage to get out. I'm processing what he's told me.

"Finn?"

"Just Finn." Knowing my full name could give him power over me if he knew what to do and how to do it. He's human, but if he's seeing a witch, maybe he knows about demons, too. I'm certainly not going to give this prick my first name.

I'm trying to make sense out of what is happening because I'm clueless. I don't understand this at all. I play nice for Chloe's sake and shake his hand. He has a firm handshake. He tightens his grip as a warning. *Really? You seriously want to do this?* I tighten my grip in response. Neither of us smiles. I get it. It's a pissing contest and he's sizing me up.

Bring it.

He eyes me coolly as he withdraws his hand. I stick mine in the pocket of my jacket, hoping it keeps me from punching him in the face. Andrea attempts to distract me by introducing the guy she's with, but I'm barely listening to what she says. All I know about him is his first name is Brian and he has a weak handshake. Not to mention, his palm is sweaty.

I casually wipe my hand on my jeans. Now, we're all standing around in uncomfortable silence.

"We're going to see *Hamilton* at the Opera House." The tone of Andrea's voice continues to warn me not to say anything. She gestures toward the others. "We better go, or we'll be late."

"Right," Chloe replies, as if coming out of a trance. Her gaze settles on me for a moment, then she looks away again.

"Nice to meet you, Finn." Eric puts the emphasis on the F, like he's telling me to fuck off.

Yeah, fuck me. That's for sure. Fuck you, too.

The four go past me without a further word. Eric reaches over to take Chloe's hand as they start down the steps. She glances back at me, but I can't read her expression.

I'm left alone in the hall.

I go into Carol's apartment and do what any self-respecting demon would do. Since I couldn't punch Eric in the face, I make a large hole in the wall with my fist instead.

My hand hurts. My mood is worse. I'm back at my place staring at gray walls while Chloe is doing who knows what? It's after 10:00. Maybe they've made it back to his place, or maybe they're back at hers. An image of them naked together in her cozy bedroom, their bodies entwined together on her soft white sheets, enters my mind unbidden. I push the thought away. I know I shouldn't care, but I do.

I close my eyes. Last night was beyond amazing. Chloe chose me as her first. Not him. Me. But now she's out with him? I don't understand what happened between this morning and now. When I left her this morning, everything seemed fine. Not to mention the text she sent me. I'm completely and totally lost.

I reach for my third Fat Tire and try to concentrate on whatever it is I'm watching on television. I haven't paid attention enough to know what it's about, other than it's a horror movie that gives demons a bad name.

Trust me, anyone who summons a demon deserves what they get. You have no idea what it's like to be minding your own business, out doing your own thing, and then in an instant, you find yourself standing in some teenager's basement somewhere because they've seen one too many episodes of *American Horror Story.* Can you blame a demon if they get more than a little upset?

I give up on the movie and turn on the *Discovery Channel.* A pack of hyenas are stalking a lone wildebeest. Is this what my life has become? Inaccurate portrayals of demons and wildlife documentaries?

Seriously?

Perhaps, I should call Corsun. He's always up for a night of debauchery and partying to excess. The hostess at the restaurant the other night did have a certain charm.

Don't even think about it, Finn.

The last time Corsun and I partied together was in the early 1980s. We stole a goat, totaled a Ferrari, and ended up on a cargo ship headed to Shanghai. After that, my memory gets a little hazy. As for the week and a half that followed, I have no recollection at all.

The ping from my iPhone disrupts my increasingly dark thoughts. I reach over, picking it up off the coffee table. It's a text from Chloe. I tell myself I don't care, but my heart does the weird little pitter patter letting me know otherwise.

Can we talk? Call me.

My finger lingers over her number. I could call her, hear her out, see what she has to say. Maybe she has a good explanation for why she's with me one minute and going out with him the next. I mean, we didn't exactly say we wouldn't see other people, did we? Of course, she didn't exactly explain she had a fiancé, either. Maybe she has a good reason.

Good reason? Stop making excuses for her, Finn.

The best thing I can do is chalk it up to getting laid, call it a good time, and let it go. I'll round up Tommy tomorrow, drop him off at the shelter, and that's that. In the back of my mind, I'm questioning why I care so much about this, but I don't have a good answer for that, either.

Ignoring Chloe's text, I reach over for the remote and change the channel again. It's a show about a group of British people having a bake off. I have no clue what is going on, but it's not about demons or wildebeests, so maybe this is what I need to get my mind off my troubles. I'll only watch an episode or two in hopes it makes me sleepy.

Why have I not heard of *The Great British Bake Off* before? I have apparently missed seasons one and two, but I've now made it through most of season three. I'm relieved John didn't get eliminated after he cut his finger, but I'm not sure about Dani going over to help him. What was she thinking? At least no one got eliminated in this episode.

Something is seriously wrong with you, Finn.

I check my iPhone. It's after 4:00. I contemplate skipping sleep. I could watch a few—okay, several—more episodes since it's a marathon. Instead, I force myself to turn off the television and head for bed. Besides, I've discovered I can stream the rest of the episodes so I can watch them at my leisure, although I did set my DVR to record them.

Probably best not to tell Corsun about that, either.

CHAPTER 7

October 13:

The non-Chloe events from Monday and Tuesday all run together. There's not even one of those weird witch murders to help me differentiate between the days. Instead, it's a bunch of normal reaps, late-night television, and visiting Tommy. I make a half-hearted attempt to catch him, but he knows he's not going anywhere, and I do, too. The part of me wanting to see Chloe again conflicts with the part of me that does not.

I make a point to arrive late at night when I'm certain she's in bed, so I don't have to worry about running into her in the hallway. Except, if I admit it to myself, I do want to see her again. I find myself standing outside in the hallway, staring at her apartment door like I'm some kind of creepy stalker. Last night, I stood there for an hour.

I'm a mess.

Despite my hours of late-night television binge-watching the last few nights, this morning, I find myself awake before the alarm goes off. I have not slept well. I'm not even sure I've slept.

When I do try to sleep, I end up replaying the scene in the hallway over and over in my head. I can't get past how Chloe acted like we barely knew each other. I know technically we've only had one real date. Two, if you count the spur-of-the-moment dinner, but I thought we had a connection. I don't get it. This is why I don't do relationships.

I pull up my text messages to study her message again.

Can we talk? Call me.

I still have no clue what to say. I stare at the screen, then start to type.

No, I'd rather not.

Delete.

Hope you had fun on your date the other night.

Delete.

Glad I could help with that little virginity problem.

Delete.

What the fuck, Chloe?

Delete.

I give up. I check the Grim Reaper app to make sure there are no changes to today's schedule. There are. I now have three reaps instead of two. Two regular days and now this. I'd say it's getting old, but today, it's not a problem. I like the fact it will keep my mind occupied through most of the day. As long as I am working, I don't have time to think —about Chloe, I mean.

Tossing the phone onto the bed, I get up and wander into the walk-in closet. The sun is trying to make an appearance this morning, but October weather is so unpredictable. I decide to go for a run with the hope it will help me clear my head. I pull on a pair of black sweatpants and a gray Boston College Eagles sweatshirt, then find a clean pair of socks and my running shoes. I stick my iPhone into my pocket, and I guess I'm ready to go.

The air outside is cool and crisp. Perfect for a run. With Linkin Park's *Numb* playing through my ear buds, I head toward Atlantic Avenue before making my way over toward the Harborwalk. It's a little later in the day than I usually run. The fishing boats I normally see on my route have already headed out toward open water. There's a small crowd braving the morning temperatures to wait in line for one of those harbor cruises tourists like to take. I run past them, continuing to follow the waterline until I reach Independence Wharf. I stop to catch my breath before turning to head back.

I've kept Chloe out of my mind through my run, but once I'm back at my place, thoughts of her creep back in. Taking the phone out of my pocket, I stare at her text again. Why does she want to talk?

She used you, Finn. Maybe it was to make her fiancé jealous. Maybe she wanted to do something reckless. She didn't seem the type, but what do I know?

Apparently, not much.

The endorphins from my run had me feeling better, but my mood quickly sours again. I scowl at the phone, then turn it face down on the dresser. Stripping out of my sweatpants and sweatshirt, I head into the shower.

An hour later, I'm ready for my first reap of the day. I have just enough time to stop for coffee and a doughnut before my 10:35. It's a thirty-nine-year-old human female named Janice and her six-year-old dog, Spike. Cause of death? Carbon monoxide poisoning.

There wasn't a notation of a dual reap, but the dog is not my department. I have time, so I agree with Janice's request to hang around and see if another Grim Reaper or Angel of Death shows up.

An hour passes. We're still sitting in her living room.

"Stupid landlord." Janice glances up from where she sits on the couch. "I told him I smelled gas the other day. The furnace is probably as old as the house." She was Stage One when I first arrived, but she's quickly becoming a solid Stage Two. Even her dog notices she's agitated. Spike is a small brown and gray terrier. I have no clue what stage he is in. He has brought a small green ball over with him. Smart dog. I've been throwing it over and over again for him to fetch because he keeps bringing it back to me.

"How much longer?" Janice asks impatiently.

"It shouldn't be long now." *I have no idea.*

I glance at my watch. We could leave without the dog, but I don't know if she would go for that or not. I'm still okay on time, but I may have to skip lunch.

Spike tires of the ball. He lays down on the floor near the couch, wanting a belly rub. I oblige, then wander around the living room. Janice has an assortment of oil paintings hanging on the wall with her signature in the bottom right corner.

"These are yours?" I'm impressed.

She nods.

"I have a gallery opening next week." She frowns. "Well, I had a gallery opening next week. I don't know what they'll do now."

"They're quite good." I study the one in front of me. It's a red sailboat with bright white sails set against an evening sunset. I consider coming back later to get a couple of her paintings. The price will go up once people discover she's no longer around. "Any family nearby, Janice?" I ask casually. I remember that her file mentioned two sisters.

"One of my sisters lives a few miles from me." She gives me a puzzled look. "Why do you ask?"

"No reason."

She presses her lips together. "She's supposed to come by this afternoon."

It's almost like she's read my mind. So much for that plan.

Before I can say anything else, Spike goes on high alert. Janice and I both turn our heads toward the front door as we hear a noise outside. I watch as a tall Grim Reaper ambles through the door. Scratch that. He's not only tall, he's big. I'm guessing he's well over six feet. From his appearance, I suspect he pumps iron every day. He's got a thick beard, sideburns, and long brown hair that hasn't been washed in—well, forever. It's pulled back in a ponytail. An old denim jacket, dirty T-shirt with a yin-yang symbol, and a pair of torn faded jeans complete his attire. He's also wearing hiking boots.

"Sorry, I'm late. Busy morning." He stops to catch his breath. "Name's Hank."

"Finn."

"You're not Aiden Finn, are you?" He studies me. His eyes narrow.

"That's me," I reply, wary. I'm sure I've never seen him before. I'm hoping I haven't slept with his sister or done something else to offend him. He is huge.

He grins. "Holy shit. Aiden fucking Finn." He slaps me on the shoulder—hard. "I always hoped I'd meet you one day. This is great!"

Okay, not what I was expecting.

"This is Janice and Spike." I motion to our Charges, hoping to get him back on track.

"Right! Right." He nods. "I truly am sorry I'm late." His expression is contrite. "Had a hit and run. Had to talk her down from a tree." I'm guessing he's referring to a cat, but I'm not sure.

"No problem," I reply.

Janice glances at me. I shrug.

Hank's attention turns to Spike. "Who's a good boy? He's a good boy!" His voice goes several octaves higher. He bends down as the dog brings him the ball. "Oh, yes, he is!" He continues talking to the dog in a singsong voice while he takes the ball from his mouth. He throws it while pulling a red leash out of the pocket of his jacket. When Spike returns the ball, he attaches the leash to the dog's collar, then sticks the ball into the pocket of his jacket. "We're ready."

I turn back to Janice. "Time to go."

She gets up from the couch. The four of us pass through the door to the outside.

"Did you really toss your supervisor overboard in the middle of the ocean?" Hank peers down at me as we wait on Spike to finish whizzing on a bush at the end of the sidewalk.

Janice stares at me in alarm. I ignore her.

"I did," I respond.

We start walking again.

"Awesome!" Hank laughs. He picks up Spike, kissing him on the nose as the dog licks his face. He tucks him under his arm as we head west toward the Promenade Building. "Fucking awesome."

~

I'm normally not a big fan of fast-food places, but today I'm near Fenway Park and I can hear a Tasty Burger and fries calling my name. Yes, I admit it, I'm turning to comfort food now.

After receiving my order, I grab one of the picnic tables outside and settle in to people-watch. I sometimes wonder what humans would think if they knew angels, demons, and other creatures were living amongst them. We'd probably find ourselves back like it was in the 1500s during the Burning Times again. *Let's not go there.*

I pull out my phone. Once again, I'm back to staring at Chloe's text.

Can we talk? Call me.

What's left to talk about? She's in a committed relationship. He's her fiancé, for fuck's sake. Why am I so hung up on this?

Move on, Finn. Move on.

I set the phone down, swiping through my Grim Reaper app. My next Charge is human and my last one for the day is a witch. In the back of my mind, I wonder if this is another murdered witch. Guess I'll know soon enough.

I finish my fries and drink. My Charge isn't too far away. I decide to walk.

A Grim Reaper walks into a bar. I'm sure there's a joke in there somewhere. My next reap of the day is a twenty-eight-year-old human male named Earl. He's sitting at a table in the corner while police investigate the scene. It doesn't take much to figure out what transpired. Earl pulled a handgun on the bartender and the bartender opened fire on him with a shotgun. Shotgun always trumps a .38 if you get the shot off first.

Unlike most of my Charges, Earl hasn't grasped what happened to him yet. His soul carries the same gunshot wound his body does. Normally, by now a Charge is at least at the beginning of Stage One, but I don't think he's entered any of the Stages of Grief yet. Instead, he's just sitting there in shock, staring at his body.

The police are focusing on the crime scene itself, so they don't notice when two coffee cups disappear into thin air from behind the bar, or that I'm pouring coffee into them. I would like to pour us a couple shots of whiskey instead, but my Charge is already out of it and I'm on the clock. I take the coffee over to the table, setting one down in front of him. I take a seat, still holding onto the other. If he tries to lift the cup, his hand will go straight through it. I'm hoping he does, and it jolts him into realizing what has happened to him. I'm kind of having my doubts, though.

"You can see me?" His eyes grow big as he stares at me.

"Yes, I can." I take a drink of my coffee and try not to make a face. It's bad. Really bad. I think I may have killed off a few of my tastebuds. "How are you doing, Earl?"

He gapes at the hole in his chest. "How do you think I'm doing?"

Okay, not the best opening line, I guess. "Would you like me to fix that for you, Earl?" I motion toward his chest.

He nods.

I reach over, touching him on the arm. A soft glow of blue light shines from underneath my palm. The wound in his chest begins to disappear. Don't ask me how I do it because I don't understand it myself. I somehow know that when I need to, I can.

"Better?"

"Much." With the massive gunshot hole in his chest gone, I can now see he's wearing a dirty, green, long-sleeved shirt with the number '420' on it in red. Classy.

"Do you know what's happened to you, Earl?"

The 7 Habits of Highly Effective Reapers; Grim Reaper Training 101: *Dealing with Denial: Gathering the Information.*

"I was trying to get the cash. I got shot." He stares at his body, puzzled. "It doesn't hurt, though." He rubs his chest.

"And do you know why that is?" I ask gently.

"The drugs?"

I've got nothing. I try again. "No, Earl. Think." I motion from him over to his body and back again.

"I'm having a super weird dream?"

No, but I'm having a real facepalm moment here, Earl. "Try again."

Third time's the charm. "I'm dead?" The color drains from his face.

"That's right." Ding, ding, ding.

"No way!" He's fixated on his body now.

"Afraid so." I push the coffee cup far away from me. "Would you like to go for a walk, Earl?"

"I think so."

We get up from the table and head toward the door. The police are coming in and out. Instead of trying to get him to walk straight through the door, I wait until someone comes in and we shuffle around them to get out. The park where I sat with Carol isn't too far from here. My plan is to take him there and let him acclimate to the whole "I'm dead" thing before taking him to the ferry. As we cross the street, it becomes apparent Earl has other plans. He bolts. I've got a rabbit and now I have to catch him.

Fuck!

He takes off running down Avery Street. He's dodging most people, but occasionally he goes right through one. That's got to hurt. At least it slows him down. It's not like he can get away from me. I can track him if I have to, but I don't want the extra paperwork I'll have if he misses the ferry. Time is of the essence and all that.

We head toward the park. I gain some ground on him. When we reach a clearing, I close the distance and tackle him. He gets a lucky punch in directly below my eye as I work to pin him to the ground.

"Enough, Earl!" I growl as I finally manage to subdue him. He continues to struggle for a moment, but ultimately gives in.

"Okay. Okay," he mutters as I hold him down.

He's on his stomach and I'm straddled over his back. I wait to make sure he's not going to try anything else before releasing my grip on him. "I'm going to let you up now, Earl, but if you try that again, you won't like what happens next."

In truth, nothing will happen, but I don't want to have to chase him again. I could call in the authorities and let the demon magistratus handle him, but I'm not on the best of terms with them, so I'd prefer to handle this myself.

I get Earl to his feet, holding him by the arm—just in case. I'm out of breath and he is, too. I take my free hand and touch the spot below my eye. It smarts. I'll have a bruise there for a couple of hours at least.

"Am I going to Hell?" he asks.

Let's see. You died trying to rob someone. You were on drugs when you did it. You ran from Death. I would say that's a firm yes from me.

"I don't know." I suppose it's possible he's stored up karma points somewhere, but I doubt it. I glance at my watch. We're still good for time, but the sooner I can get him to the ferry, the better. I let go of his arm, giving him a shove. "Come on, let's go."

I get Earl to the ferry. I'm ready to go home, but I still have one more Charge to reap. Since it's so rare for me to have over two Charges in one day, especially since I'm a GR7, I wonder again what's up with the app. I consider mentioning it to Jack in case it's an actual glitch, but I suspect he doesn't want to hear from me after last week.

Just keep your head down and do your job, Finn.

The address I'm off to next is a good ten miles from the Promenade Building. I contemplate going back to the Echelon to get my bike but decide on a rideshare instead.

Because I'm trying hard to keep my mind occupied and off the Chloe situation, this reap is the one I've been wondering about all day. Tina Maddox. She's a forty-two-year-old female witch. Married. I read over her file on my iPhone while traveling in the backseat of a white Toyota. The driver is chatty. He makes it his mission to keep disrupting my concentration. He's constantly glancing at me through the rearview mirror and it's getting on my nerves.

"Here on business or pleasure?" he asks.

"I live here." I glance up at him, then back at my phone screen.

He tries a different approach. "How about those Red Sox? Think they're going to make it to the World Series this year?"

"Maybe." *Please stop talking.*

"My brother-in-law has tickets to Game Five of the

playoffs." He's watching me in the rearview mirror again. "Right behind the dugout."

I don't reply this time. I glance at my watch. It had crossed my mind earlier to arrive before the TOD to see exactly what happens, but the way traffic is, I may not make it on time at all. The address isn't in my usual area. It's in an older neighborhood, further out of town. Maybe it's a normal death.

"Traffic accident," the driver mutters. I'm not sure if he's saying it to me or himself.

I glance up as he maneuvers around a nasty two-car collision. An Angel of Death stands on the sidewalk, waiting for her Charge's TOD. She's dressed similarly to how Wallace and Nelson were the day of the multiple car accident. Shiny dress shoes. Tan pants. White shirt. She's even got on a tie. Maybe there is a dress code. I turn my head to look back, but she doesn't see me.

Once we're on the other side of the accident, traffic lightens up. Another glance at my watch confirms I won't make it to my reap before the death occurs, but I can check to see if there's a symbol. I ask the driver to let me out before we reach the house.

"Thanks for choosing Uber." He gives me a smile as I step out of the car.

I shut the door without commenting, then wait until he drives off. After double-checking to make sure no one is paying attention to me, I switch into Grim Reaper mode. It's 6:42. I'm five minutes late, but there's no sign of my Charge, so they haven't left the premises. I walk up the porch stairs and go straight through the door to let myself into the house. The television is on, but other than that, the house is quiet. There's no sign of a struggle.

"Tina?" I call out.

A noise comes from the hallway. I walk toward the sound. I don't see my Charge, but her body is lying a few feet inside her bedroom. It's another murdered witch.

Once again, the heart is missing, and she's also got a symbol drawn in blood on her forehead. I break a rule and take a picture of the symbol with my phone. It's different from the other one I saw. On some level, it's familiar to me as if I saw it once long, long ago, but I can't place it.

"Who are you?" A voice asks from behind me.

I whip around to see Tina standing there. I'm not sure where she came from.

Sticking the phone back into my pocket, I give her a curt nod. "I'm Finn." I study her. She's barefoot. She has on a pair of purple pajama bottoms with a matching purple sweetheart top. Her hair is wet.

She peers down at her body. "This is bad, Finn." She's already in Stage Five. Acceptance.

"I know." I break yet another rule. Management doesn't like us discussing how our Charges die. "Did you see who did this?"

She shakes her head. "They grabbed me from behind. I got out of the shower, went to the bedroom, and got dressed. When I came back out of the bedroom—" She stops talking. She stares at me, puzzled. "They must have stood behind the bedroom door while I was in there. I didn't see them at first."

"Man? Woman?"

"A man, I think, but I'm not sure. It's a little hazy right now. Why didn't I fight back?" She glances down at her body.

She's doing well to remember it at all. Often, they don't. It's better that way, but if I'm going to use this as a form of distraction, then I need the information to figure out what is going on. I think I've pressed her enough on this, however. "Okay, well, we should go," I tell her.

"Are my kids okay?"

"Are they here?" The app only had one reap.

She blinks. "I don't think so." I follow her down the hall to a child's bedroom. The bed is made. There's no sign of a struggle—or a body. The next room is the same. "Why can't I remember?" She stands in the bedroom doorway.

"You're in shock," I explain. "It makes events fuzzy sometimes."

She doesn't reply. Instead, she quickly heads down the hall. At first, I think I'm about to have another runner, but she stops in the kitchen. She points to an orange sheet of paper stuck behind a magnet on the refrigerator. It has a picture of a giant skate on it. It reads, *Wednesday Night Is Skate Night, 6 till 9*.

"My husband dropped them off. I should call and tell him—" Her voice trails off.

I'm not sure what to say. "We should go."

"Like this?" She holds out her arms. "I can't. I'm in my pajamas."

"You won't be the first." I start to tell her she's lucky she's wearing clothes. If she wasn't, it would make it awkward for us both.

"Let me at least get dressed."

"That's not the way it works." The deceased don't have to spend the rest of eternity in whatever clothes they're wearing when they die, but a wardrobe change rarely occurs until they're on the other side of the river. We make exceptions for people who aren't wearing clothes—well, most of the time. I've known a few demons who think it's amusing to escort their Charges to the ferry with nothing on. And I once had a ninety-two-year-old nudist who insisted on it. I still haven't gotten that image out of my head.

Tina folds her arms. She gazes at me. "There has to be something you can do."

"You can't change your clothes." I fold my arms, too. *You're not the only one who can play this game, Tina.*

"Please."

"No."

We remain in a standoff, staring at each other in the kitchen. I want to tell her I can do this all night. In truth, I need to get her on the ferry in the next few hours, so I'm going to have to get her moving, somehow.

The 7 Habits of Highly Effective Reapers: Grim Reaper Training 101: *Dealing with Difficult Charges; Sometimes Saying Nothing is the Perfect Answer.*

"You win," she says finally. She throws her arms up in defeat. "Can I at least put on my bathrobe?"

I consider this. "Where is it?"

"On a hook on the back of the door in the bathroom." She motions toward the back of the house.

I narrow my eyes. "You'll stay right here?" I'm not chasing another reap down today.

She holds her hand up. "Scout's honor."

"Stay right here." I emphasize the "right here" part this time. I tread back down the hall, grabbing the bathrobe from the hook in the bathroom. I stop to study Tina's body again. She brought up a good point earlier. These witches all have powers. Why are none of them fighting back? It's strange.

Back in the kitchen, Tina stands where I left her.

I motion for her to turn around. "Put your arms out." I help her get the robe on. "Better?"

"Yes, thank you." She peers down at her feet. "I don't suppose you could get my slippers?"

I raise an eyebrow.

"Okay, fine." She ties the robe shut. "I guess I'm ready to go now."

About time.

Tina makes her ferry departure on schedule. My job is done for the day. It's a little before 9:00. I want to go back to my place, but I need to stop and take care of Tommy first. Once I get back to the Echelon, I don't want to make another trip back out.

I start up the stairs. When I get almost to the top, I discover Chloe sitting on the landing with her back against the wall and her arms wrapped around her knees. Her head is down, but she raises it as I approach. Her eyes are red and puffy, stray tears still streak her cheeks.

I freeze.

Neither of us speaks.

"Hey," she says after a moment. She wipes her face with the sleeve of her sweater.

"Hey." I remain standing on the fifth stair from the top. I don't know whether to continue and walk past her or turn around and leave. I stay where I'm at, staring up at her.

"I've been waiting for you," she offers. "Since 7:00."

She's been out here for two hours? I'm not sure what to say. I climb the rest of the way up the stairs to where she's sitting.

"I want to explain about the other night." She glances up at me.

Tell her it's too late. She had her chance. Tell her, Finn. Tell her.

"I'm listening."

I know. I know.

She makes it to her feet and stands facing me. She takes a deep breath as if to steady her nerves. "First off, Eric's not my fiancé. He shouldn't have told you that."

"Okay." That's not what it looked like, but I let her continue.

"I mean, he was, but we broke it off a few months ago," she corrects herself. "Andrea is dating his best friend, Brian. The four of us already had tickets to go to the play months before I ever met you. Before we..." Her voice drops off. She knots her fingers, staring down at her hands. "And I wasn't going to go, but then he showed up at the museum. We got into an argument because I told him again I didn't want to go. He kept bothering me about it, so I finally said I would go if he would leave because I didn't want him to make a scene while I was at work." She pushes a strand of hair behind her ear. "I guess I thought since it was the four of us going, it wasn't a big deal. I insisted on paying for my own ticket, so I didn't even consider it an actual date." She waves her hand. "But then, you showed up when we were leaving the apartment. I didn't know how to explain things to you or him, so I didn't say anything. I handled it terribly, and I am so sorry."

I try to process what she's told me. Before I can respond, an older man with gray hair and a cane comes up the stairs. We move to one side so he can pass us. He walks by Chloe's door, then stops and looks back. He gives me a onceover.

"Everything okay, Chloe?" He grips his cane tight below the handle while he waits to see if she's going to need his help. I have to give him credit. He's got some balls. He probably weighs about a hundred pounds—wet. I could knock him to the ground with one finger.

"We're fine, Mr. Jensen." She gives him a warm smile.

"Well, all you have to do is give me a holler if you need me." He gives me his best *I've got my eyes on you* expression before continuing toward his apartment.

We stand in awkward silence as he fumbles with his key. His hand shakes as he attempts to align the key with the lock to the door of apartment 204. It's so exaggerated, I suspect it's intentional. It lets him stay out in the hall a little longer, so he can monitor us.

Chloe must think the same thing. She puts her hand to her mouth to hide her smile. As he continues, she turns her head away, hiding the amusement on her face. I find I'm trying not to smile, too. The tension between us eases as we watch him. Or rather, try not to watch him.

My patience only lasts for so long, however, before it wears thin. I'm about to yank the key from his hand to open the door myself, when, after what seems like an eternity of fumbling, he gets it unlocked. He holds the cane up as a final warning to me before disappearing inside.

"He means well, but I don't think he could hurt a fly with that thing," Chloe says as he closes the door. Her attention turns back to me. She's waiting for my response to what she said before he interrupted us.

I'm not sure which part needs addressing first, but there's one thing that's bothered me since Sunday night. "I don't understand. You were engaged, but you two never—" I don't quite know how to ask without embarrassing her. She's so sensual and willing. How could she not have done it before? And if she was engaged, the bigger question is—what's wrong with him?

She knots her fingers together. "His family is very religious. We were waiting until we got married. His idea, not mine. But I was okay with it because in the back of my mind, I don't think I ever wanted to be with him in that way. The first time I saw you, though, I just—knew."

Her comment catches me off guard. I'm flattered, of course, but now I wonder if she simply used me as a means to an end. With my past history of one-night stands, the irony of the situation is not lost on me. Trust me.

"I don't like to share, Chloe. When I saw you with him —" My voice trails off. If I tell her what I actually thought, what I wanted to do to him, she would run for the hills.

She takes a breath. "I know. And you both have a right to be upset with me, too. I handled it badly all around. If it helps, when we got back, I told him I met someone and we're serious. I think he figured out it was you." Her eyes meet mine. "Is it, though? Are we serious, I mean? Andrea says since we haven't known each other that long, she doesn't think that's possible. She thinks I'm imagining things or trying to make this—" She moves her hand back and forth, "—into more than it is."

I hesitate. It's a good question. I consider how I've felt since Sunday night. These are all new feelings for me. "No, you're not imagining things."

There's definitely something between us, but I'm not sure I can explain how I feel. I want to explore what that something is, but it will keep for later. At this moment, all I want to do is hold her in my arms.

So, I do.

I put my hand on the side of her face, running my thumb across her cheek. She presses her face into the palm of my hand. My plan is a simple kiss, but as soon as our lips meet, I want more. Reaching around her waist, I pull her close against me, kissing her hard. I want to claim her as mine again. I move her backward until she's resting against the wall, with me pressed up against her. Her hands come up to rest on my shoulders as she kisses me back. Pushing the material from her cardigan sweater away, I move my free hand down to her breast. My palm runs over the thin material of her shirt and bra. Her nipple grows hard beneath my touch. She moans. Vaguely, I'm aware we're standing in the hall, but I don't want to stop.

"Jesus, Chloe. What the hell are you doing?" Andrea's voice coming from the direction of the stairs startles us both.

Shit. Yeah, that puts a damper on things.

I push away from Chloe. We're both breathless and panting. Chloe's eyes meet mine. She grins at me. I grin back. We both laugh.

Andrea rolls her eyes at both of us and shakes her head. She glares at me as she walks between us to the apartment door. "Don't forget you have to be at work early tomorrow," she reminds her. She goes into the apartment, slamming the door behind her.

"She really does not like me," I comment.

Chloe giggles. "No, she does not." She sighs. "I should get to bed. To sleep, I mean," she corrects herself. "Can I see you tomorrow?"

"You can see all of me tomorrow, if you want." I raise an eyebrow, giving her my best demon smile.

"I'd like that." She gnaws on her bottom lip. "But there's this one little thing." She hesitates. "It's my birthday. I guess it's silly, but I always eat at the same restaurant. It's kind of a tradition, I guess. I've already made the reservation. We don't have to, but if you want to go with me—"

"Sounds nice." It saves me the trouble of having to figure out what to do for our first real date. She's got the telltale blush in her cheeks going on again, though. There's more. What is she not saying? "Is there something else?"

She knots her fingers together. "Andrea's off from work tomorrow."

She wants her to come with us to dinner? Not as much fun. "Okay, if you want the three of us to eat out together, that's fine." It's not fine at all. Inwardly, I groan. I'll have Andrea glaring at me across the table all night, but it is Chloe's birthday. What am I going to say?

Her blush spreads. "No, it's not that." She lowers her voice. "It means Andrea will be home when we get back—"

Got it.

I put my finger under her chin, lifting her face so I can see her eyes. "Would you like to spend tomorrow night at my place?"

"I'd love to." She rewards me with a shy smile.

"What time is the reservation?"

"7:00."

"I'll pick you up from work. Bring an overnight bag."

She throws her arms around my neck. "Goodnight, Finn," She kisses me softly on the lips.

"Goodnight."

"See you tomorrow," she adds bashfully.

I remain standing in the same spot for a full minute after she goes inside. The strange feeling is back, but I don't dwell on it as much this time. I smile. After three thousand years, I think I have a girlfriend.

CHAPTER 8

October 14 - Day:

It's a beautiful Thursday morning when I awake. The sun is shining. The skies are blue. Looking out the window, I can tell the temperature is mild. They call this time of year Fool's Fall because as soon as you get used to this type of weather, you'll wake up the next day and find the ground covered in snow. In the back of my mind, I wonder if I'm the fool because all I can think about is seeing Chloe tonight, and dare I say it? I'm happy.

You're a demon. Demons don't do happy, Finn.

I ignore the voice telling me I'm kidding myself and try to concentrate on my day. Checking my schedule reveals no changes for me to worry about. I have two reaps this afternoon, one at 1:15 and another at 3:22, but I don't have time to linger in bed because I have a 9:30 training session this morning at the dojo I frequent out in Newton. My sensei is a five-thousand-year-old demon named Iemon, who trained under a Buddhist monk over a thousand years ago in Okinawa. I suspect this is what made him a good assassin when he worked for the Yakuza back during the

1600s. Although I'm about two thousand years younger than Iemon, he still kicks my ass on a regular basis.

Until today.

"Something's different with you this morning," he says after I knock him to the mat for a second time. He studies me as I dodge his vertical punch, then blocks my palm strike with his arm. "You're more intense. More driven. Is it a woman? I think it's a woman. Better watch it, Finn, she'll make you weak," he goads me.

Stupidly, I take the bait, moving toward him. His roundhouse drops me to the ground in an instant.

Shit.

"What did I tell you about leading with your emotions?" He grins down at me before offering his hand to help me up. "Good job, today," he adds once I'm back on my feet.

"Thanks. I think." I scowl at him as I rub my shoulder.

We both bow.

Once we're off the mats, he hands me a bottle of water and picks up a towel, wiping the sweat off his face. "So, who is she?" He grabs a bottle for himself and unscrews the lid.

I take a drink, eying him uneasily. How does he always know this stuff? "She's a witch," I decide to share.

"Mmm." His head bobs up and down in agreement, like he knows something I don't. He takes a long drink, then puts the lid back on. "That explains it."

"Explains what?"

"Your aura is all shiny and black." He makes a circle with his hand. "I think you have fallen hard for this woman, my friend." He reaches out, touching me on the chest. "Don't forget about the demon inside, though. You must nurture him as well."

This is what Iemon does. He makes cryptic comments, then leaves you to figure out what all of it means. As I head into the locker room to change back into street clothes, I reflect on what he said. I'm sure it's another one of his lessons where the meaning is profound—if I can figure out what it is, that is.

I consider it some more. I've got nothing.

The rest of my morning goes smoothly, but I continue to have no idea what words of wisdom Iemon was trying to impart on me. After I finish my first reap, I put it out of my mind. I need to concentrate on bigger things, like my date with Chloe tonight and helping her celebrate her birthday.

I confess I've never understood why humans celebrate getting older, but I've always found birthday parties morbidly fascinating. Humans, and even witches, joining together to acknowledge someone becoming one year closer to death. I don't know what makes them so happy about it. Seems like it would make more sense if it were a day of mourning, but that's not the way they do it.

Demons don't celebrate birthdays. For one thing, it's fair to say it's impossible to get thousands of candles on a birthday cake without the risk of a major structural fire. But more to the point, most of us don't know exactly when we were born.

When getting a driver's license became a thing, I had to come up with a date. I chose April 25th because I thought it was a date I could easily remember. Every so often, however, I have to change the year of birth because it takes several hundred years before we show any signs we've aged. Most of the workers at the DMV are demons, so they take care of this type of thing when we need it. But I'm guessing you probably suspected they were demons before I told you. Admit it.

Before my second reap of the day, I have a few stops to make. The first is to Carol's apartment to take care of Tommy, so I don't have to interrupt our date later on. As I'm leaving the apartment, Andrea comes up the stairs. She's wearing black leggings and boots with an oversized purple long-sleeved shirt. It's the first time I've seen her in casual clothes. I remember Chloe telling me she's off work today. She's toting a bunch of bags from a party place.

"Hi," I say, locking the door to Carol's place.

"Hello." She purses her lips.

At least she's talking to me. She turns away as she fiddles with the lock on her apartment door. After a moment, she stops. She bows her head, mutters to herself, then, with a frustrated sigh, turns to face me again. "Are you busy tomorrow night?"

I'm not sure how to respond. I hope I'm seeing Chloe again, but we have to get through tonight first. "Not that I know of," I reply uneasily.

"Chloe told me she's staying with you tonight." She makes an unpleasant face like she's sucking on a lemon. "I need you to keep her away from here until around eight o'clock tomorrow night. I'm throwing a surprise birthday party for her."

"Okay. I can do that." I relax a little.

"Good." She hesitates before saying more. "Chloe's got a big heart, but it also means she's sometimes a little too trusting."

"Meaning?" I cross my arms. I know where she's going with this, but I'm going to make her say it.

"Meaning, it would be unfortunate if she got hurt." She gives me a pointed look, shifting the bags around in her arms. "Eight."

"Got it."

With a final disapproving look, she pushes the door to the apartment open and disappears inside.

That is one scary witch.

I leave the apartment complex and head back to my place for a shower and change of clothes. After that, I make a quick trip to the bank. Since I get reassigned to a different area every so many years, I have safety deposit boxes all over the world. Most contain money, but a few have collectibles, and some, like the one at this particular bank, are where I keep a lot of the jewelry I've acquired over the centuries. And by acquired, I mean a combination of pillaging, buying, and occasionally, yes, even stealing. As I've said before, it's what demons do.

Well, sometimes, anyway.

The reason I'm at this bank is because of the sapphire and diamond bracelet I keep here. It's from the Victorian era. The last time I had it appraised, it was worth around thirty-eight thousand dollars. Since it's Chloe's favorite time period, it seems like the perfect gift.

I open the black velvet box I keep it stored in. I can't help but take a moment to admire it. The bracelet is eighteen-karat gold and has twelve blue sapphires on it, each one surrounded by ten small diamonds. I almost forgot I had it until she mentioned her love for the Victorian era last week.

I check the rest of the contents of my safe deposit box but see nothing else I need. I put the box with the bracelet inside my jacket and I'm good to go. It's perfect for her. I hope she likes it.

I've only got enough time for a quick lunch, then it's on

to my second reap. No problems there, either. I get my Charge to the ferry early. It almost worries me because this day is going a little too well.

I've probably jinxed myself again. Meanwhile, it's almost time to pick up Chloe, but first, I've got two more stops to make.

CHAPTER 9

October 14 - Night:

I sit, waiting in my car parked in the employee lot next to the museum. It's 5:55. I've been parked here since 5:30, even though Chloe doesn't get off work until 6:00.

In the backseat, a single balloon bobs back and forth like a prize fighter itching for a fight. A bob to the left. To the right. Back to the left. I keep catching glimpses of it in the rearview mirror. It's dark blue and has Happy Birthday written on it in big yellow letters. It also has what looks like specks of red and green confetti dropping around the letters. I agonized over the balloon selection for a good twenty minutes. Why do they make so many choices to choose from?

I've attached the string of the balloon to the black velvet box with the bracelet inside, but I'm nervous about giving it to her. I mean, she'll like it since it's from the Victorian era, but is it too much, too soon? Probably not wise to mention how much it's worth.

Actually, I'm nervous about this entire date. I don't want to come across too strongly, but I'm still remembering the other night when Chloe asked if she was imagining whatever this is between us, and I told her she wasn't. I meant it, too. But I don't understand all these weird feelings I keep having. It's all so new to me. I confess, I find it rather disconcerting. Maybe this is what Iemon meant when he said to nurture my inner demon, or whatever it was he was talking about. I'm still not sure.

I glance up as the door opens, but it's only a security guard letting an older woman out. They chat for a moment, then he watches as she walks toward her car. The security guard waits until she is safely inside her vehicle before stepping back into the building. He closes the door behind him. I watch him do this a few more times as people leave, but still no Chloe.

I stare in the rearview mirror again. The balloon continues bobbing around. Maybe it's anxious about this date, too. Should I have gotten her flowers?

A glimpse at my watch shows the time is 6:03. I glance up again toward the door. The security guard steps out and suddenly, she appears. My heart does the weird little pitter patter thing that only happens when I'm around her or thinking about her.

As always, she's a vision. She's got on a long, gray coat and underneath, a sky-blue dress. She's paired it with those same black heels she had on the other night at the benefit. They make her legs look a mile long.

Her hair is different this evening, though. She's pulled it up in a messy bun with a few stray strands hanging down on either side of her face. It's a more sophisticated style for her, but I like it. I like it a lot.

She laughs at something the security guard says, then waves at him before heading over toward the car toting a black overnight bag. I get out to take the bag from her and open the car door on the passenger side. Her eyes light up as she sees me.

"Hello, Finn." She hands me her bag, then leans in to give me a kiss. She smells like lavender and vanilla.

"Hello, and happy birthday."

"Thank you." She smiles that special smile at me, and I feel ten feet tall. I hold the door open as she gets in, then stow her bag away in the trunk.

Getting back into the car, I reach for the balloon and the box. I probably didn't think this whole thing through because now the balloon is bobbing around up in the front seat with us, but I want her to wear the bracelet on our date. The sapphires will perfectly match her dress.

"This is for you." I give her the box. The balloon hits me in the face.

You had to go with the balloon, didn't you? Smooth move, Finn. Idiot.

I push the balloon down with my hand. It wants to put up a fight. I yank it over toward the steering wheel by the string. *Behave.*

She stares at me in surprise. "You shouldn't have. I wasn't expecting—" She runs her fingers over the velvet.

"Go ahead. Open it." I hold my breath.

She undoes the red balloon string from around the box. Glancing at me again, she pushes the lid open. She's silent for a moment before she speaks. "Oh, my God, it's beautiful, Finn, but I can't." She shakes her head. "It's too much."

I knew she wouldn't want to accept it. "I want you to have it. Happy birthday, baby."

She fingers the bracelet. I can tell she's wrestling with her desire to keep it. She gives in. "It's gorgeous. Thank you."

I shove the balloon into the backseat.

"Let's see how it looks on you." I reach over and remove it from the box. It's probably been around a hundred years or more since I last held it in my hand. I've kept it more as an investment than as a piece of jewelry. She holds up her wrist as I drape the bracelet across it. It takes me a couple of tries to figure out how the clasp works, but I finally figure it out.

She studies it on her wrist, then flings her arms around my neck and gives me another kiss. The balloon bobs in approval.

After a kiss like that, I'd like to skip the whole dinner thing and get her straight back to my place, but it is her birthday. I give her a smile, start the car, and we head out of the parking lot.

The drive to the restaurant takes us northward, out of the city. Chloe knows the way by heart, so I don't bother with the GPS. I've wondered why she doesn't drive. She tells me she has a license, but she no longer has a car. She used to drive her grandmother's Nissan, but the transmission went out.

"I can either save for a car or save money so I can go back to college," she says. "Andrea lets me drive her car when she doesn't need it, but I usually take the bus."

Maybe I should buy her a car as a birthday present. *She'll never accept it, Finn. Although, she might if she knew the bracelet costs almost as much as a new car. Stop it!*

I make conversation by asking her about the restaurant we're going to.

"My parents always ate there on their anniversary. When I was eight or nine, they brought me with them one time. I remember thinking it was the fanciest place I had ever seen. I told myself when I grew up, I was going to eat there, too." She laughs. "It's nowhere near as fancy as the restaurants in the city, but I always feel like I'm celebrating my birthday with them when I eat there." She sounds a little melancholy as she ends her story.

"What happened to your parents?" I ask.

"Car accident when I was ten." She stares out the window. "It killed them both instantly. They couldn't locate any of my mother's family, so I went to live with my dad's mother. My grandmother." She shifts in her seat. From the way she's fidgeting, I suspect she's uncomfortable talking about her childhood. "My grandmother was...difficult." She traces her fingers along the edge of the door. "How about you? Did you live with Carol after your parents died?"

Who?

"Your aunt." She sees the puzzled look on my face. "Did you ever live with her?"

Shit. Yes, Carol. The reason we're here together, now. My brain catches up.

"No." I recover quickly. No one has ever asked me about my childhood before. It's something I've tried hard not to think about over the years. There are no warm and fuzzy memories when you're raised by a pack of demons. "I didn't meet Carol until later in life." I sidestep my answer so as not to lie to her. "I was in and out of group homes until I was sixteen." And by group homes, I mean I lived in an orphanage for demons located in the Underworld.

"Foster system. That must have been hard," Chloe says sympathetically. "Turn right up here." She points to the upcoming road. "The restaurant is on the left. Since it's after six o'clock, you can park on the street." She waves toward an open parking space up ahead.

I breathe a sigh of relief we've moved on from the subject of our childhoods. The discussion was bringing up unpleasant memories. Ones I'd prefer not to dwell on.

We walk up the sidewalk next to the street, then up another sidewalk to a wooden ramp that stretches out over shallow water. From the outside, the building resembles a ship. We've made good time on our trip to this place. It's about five minutes before our reservation.

Although it's a Thursday night, the place is full. The inside of the restaurant is all dark, shiny wood. The interior keeps with the nautical theme and looks like the hull of a wooden ship. A carved masthead of a mermaid stares down at us from the wall next to the host station. Chloe approaches it to let him know we're here.

"Yes, we've already seated the other member of your party," the host advises Chloe.

"The reservation was only for two."

He checks again. "Someone must have written it down wrong." He hands two menus to a woman dressed in black. She gives us a weak smile. "Right this way."

We follow her toward a table near the back. A large window to our right draws my attention. Since the restaurant is on a dock situated over the water, guests can watch the activity on the incoming shrimp boats while they eat.

I'm distracted watching a fisherman spray down his boat when Chloe abruptly stops in front of me. I bump into her. At first, I don't understand why she stopped, but then I see where the hostess has led us. She's brought us to a nice, quiet table away from the flow of traffic. The only problem is that Eric, Chloe's ex, is sitting at it.

What the fuck?

The woman doesn't realize anything is amiss. She sets our menus down on the table. "Your server will be right with you." She gives us a bored smile this time before wandering off.

Eric gets up from his seat, ready to greet Chloe, but hesitates when he sees me standing behind her.

Chloe continues to stay right where she is, as if frozen to the spot.

She stares at him. "What are you doing here?"

He holds up a glass of what looks like bourbon. "It's your birthday, sweetheart," he says, as if that explains it. "This is where you always eat." He gestures toward the table where two empty glasses sit. His attention turns toward me. "You're the guy in the hall. The cat sitter." He swallows more of his drink, peering at me. "What was it? Finn, just Finn?" He swirls the liquid in his glass. "Have a seat." He waves to the two empty chairs across from him.

"You're drunk," Chloe says before I can respond. She grabs my arm. "Let's go."

"Chloe, if you want to eat here, I'll make him leave." It would make me quite happy to do it, too. Thrilled, in fact.

She shakes her head. "Please, don't do anything. I don't want to make a scene. Let's go." She walks past me before I can respond and heads back in the direction we came.

I seriously want to hurt this guy. I don't know what his deal is, but I'm tired of it. "Sorry, pal." I give an exaggerated shrug, then force myself to walk away before I do something I might regret.

By the time I catch up to Chloe, she has already told the host we've changed our minds and we're not going to eat here. Once we're outside, she takes off toward where we've left the car. I can't tell if she's upset and mad or upset and about to cry. I watch her go, not sure what to do other than go back inside and kill the guy. The idea does have a certain appeal to it.

"Chloe, wait!" Eric shouts as he follows us out of the

restaurant. He walks down the ramp and comes to where I'm standing on the sidewalk.

What is his problem? There's a weird dynamic going on between these two and I don't like it one bit. She doesn't seem afraid of him, but he's overly controlling. This is the second time he's shown up somewhere uninvited.

He's gone too far this time, though. I think I'm going to have to remind him they're not together anymore. That she's with me.

I stay on the sidewalk, blocking him from going any further. "Leave her alone. She doesn't want anything to do with you."

He gets up in my face. From the way he's sizing me up, I expect him to take a swing any second.

Do it. I dare you.

Chloe hurries back to us. She puts her hand on my arm, tugging at my sleeve. "Let me take care of this, okay?" She motions toward the car, indicating she wants me to go wait for her. "I'll be there in a minute."

I don't like this.

She points. "Please."

I scowl. "Okay." It's not okay at all. "I'll be right over there if you need me. For anything. Anything at all." I frown at Eric. *Asshole.*

I wait by the car. It feels like Chloe's put me in a time-out. I want to beat the shit out of Eric, but for her sake, I play nice. If I wanted to give them privacy, I would get in the car. Since I don't want to leave her alone with him—and more importantly, I want to hear what they say—I lean up against the car like I'm waiting for her instead. What neither of them know is even at this distance, I can hear every word as clearly as if I'm standing right next to them. My hearing is that good.

I cross my arms, watching them.

"What are you doing here, Eric?" she asks.

"I was hoping you would show up." He motions behind him. "I know this is where you like to eat on your birthday."

"You stole our reservation."

"No, I simply added myself to it. They said party of two, so I said party of three." He waves his hand in my direction. "I didn't know you would be here with him. I thought you would come with Andrea."

"I told you the other night I was seeing someone."

He reaches out to touch her face, but she steps back. He takes a breath. "I'm sorry. I know I shouldn't have come, but it's your birthday and I wanted to see you. Please, don't be mad." His tone changes. "So, you're, what, a couple now?" He lowers his voice. "Does he know about you?"

She hesitates. "I haven't told him yet." She shrugs. "I don't think he'll care. He's not like you."

This gets my attention, especially when they both peer in my direction. I reach into my pocket and take out my phone. I pretend to stare at the screen. *Nothing to see here. See?* I glance up at them like I'm surprised they're staring at me. They both turn away.

"I could tell him for you. Save you the trouble." He makes it sound like a threat.

"Go ahead."

That's right, call his bluff. I don't care what her big secret is. I suspect it's that she's a witch, but I'm not sure why he would make such a big deal out of it. Why would that matter to him?

I consider this for a moment. What if he recently found out she's a witch and that's why they broke up? That could make him hate witches. That could make him hate witches so much, in fact, that he's started killing them. I mentally move him up to the top of my list of suspects.

Okay, he's my only suspect. And he's probably not smart enough to carry out a bunch of murders like that. But still...

I get bored with my phone and stick it back into my pocket before turning my attention back to their conversation.

"You think he cares for you, Chloe?" He motions in my direction with both hands this time. "Look at him. You think he could care for someone like you? He's only going to use you."

Now, he's pissing me off. I fight the urge to go rip his head off. I don't care what he says about me, but I don't like the tone he's taking with her at all. I can't believe she was engaged to him. What could she possibly see in him?

"Maybe I want him to use me. Did you ever think of that?" She's angry now. "Or maybe, Eric, maybe I'm going to use him."

I keep my head down, so they don't see me grinning. *She can use me any way she wants. Stop it, Finn.*

"You don't mean that. What would your grandmother say?"

"I don't care what she would say. I don't know why you're even bringing her up."

He stares at her. "You're going to throw everything we have together away, so you can do what? Spread your legs for him?" He glares over in my direction.

I can't help myself. I fix my eyes on him and offer my best threatening demon smile I reserve for special assholes like him. Let him wonder about that. I seriously do want to kill him, though. I even know where I could hide his body so no one would ever find it.

She pokes him in the chest with her finger. "What I do or don't do isn't your concern anymore. Goodbye, Eric." She turns on her heel to walk away. Before she can, he reaches out and grabs her by the arm. This is the second time I've seen him do it to her. She flinches as he twists it, pulling her back to him.

She asked me to let her handle it but fuck that. I walk toward them, my fists clenched at my sides.

"You don't know him, Chloe. Not the way you know me." He continues to grasp her by the arm.

"I know him well enough," she argues back. "If I want to be with him, I'll be with him."

"I won't let you." He scowls at me as I approach. "You're not going to debase yourself with someone like him."

"Too late," she hisses. "I already have, and I enjoyed every minute of it, too. He can debase me however and whenever he wants."

I raise an eyebrow. I'm not sure she knows what she just said. She praised me, insulted me, and offered to let me do anything I want to her all in one breath. I'll have to think more about that later.

"Let her go." I close the distance between us, stopping a few feet from where they stand.

He glances from her to me. Letting go of her arm, he pushes her away from him in disgust. "I think your grandmother was right," he spits out. "She told me your mother was a whore. Maybe I should have listened to her when she warned me you were just like her."

Chloe slaps him hard across the face. "Say what you want about me, but don't you dare talk about my mother."

He makes a move like he's about to grab her again, so I step in between them. "Try it," I growl at him. I clench my fists harder. If he makes a move, he'll regret it.

"Finn, don't. That's what he wants you to do." She puts her hand on my shoulder. "Let's go."

I flex my fists. I seriously want to punch this guy.

"Please, Finn," she begs.

I exhale. "Stay away from her." I poke him hard in the chest with my finger, making sure I get the point across. "Or you won't like what happens next."

I put my arm around Chloe's shoulder and steer her toward the car. Thankfully, Eric takes the hint and remains standing in the middle of the sidewalk.

He's not going to let me have the last word, though.

"For their portions will be in the lake that burns with fire and sulfur, which is the second death," he shouts from behind us. "You're just like your mother, Chloe. You're just like your mother!"

She's shaking by the time we reach the car. I put my arms around her, pulling her close, but my concentration remains fixed on him. He's pacing back and forth on the sidewalk, mumbling incoherently to himself. It's disconcerting. Almost like he's having a mental breakdown.

Finally, he stops and stares at us. I pull Chloe closer. He looks like he's about to come this way, but he heads across the street instead. He approaches a white car parked on the other side of the road and talks to someone inside the car. After a moment, he goes around to the passenger side and gets in.

It's only then that I can see the driver. It's Andrea's date from the other night. The guy with the sweaty hands. He holds up his cellphone and points it straight at us. Now, I understand what Chloe was trying to tell me. He's been recording us the entire time. *Interesting.* I suspect Eric was hoping I would take a swing at him. I guess sending me to jail is one way to get rid of the competition. I'm glad Chloe stopped me.

"There's still time for you to head for the hills, you know," Chloe says a short while later. We've found a steakhouse about ten miles farther up the highway, courtesy of the GPS. It's not a bad place. There are western scenes painted on the walls, and they have a selection of mounted cow and bull heads on display. Overhead, to my right, there's one that's a brown longhorn steer. He's wearing a cowboy hat.

"Why would you say that?" I ask.

"Crazy roommate. Crazy ex-fiancé. I thought you might want to make a run for it after this last encounter. I couldn't blame you if you did."

"I'm not going anywhere." I reach across the table to hold her hand.

She shakes her head. "I still can't believe he did that."

"What's the story with you two?" I both want to know, and don't.

"We first started dating in high school. It was one of those religious private schools. My grandmother thought it would be good for me." She shakes her head. "She worked as a secretary part-time in the office, so my tuition was free. Most of the students who went there, though, came from money. Old money, to be exact." She crinkles her nose.

She stops talking as the server brings our drinks over to the table. He sets them down, then whips out a notebook to take our order. We both choose steak, salad, and home fries.

After he picks up our menus and leaves, Chloe continues. "I didn't date much because my grandmother never liked any of the guys I had an interest in. Well, until Eric came along, I guess. When he asked me out, she was more excited about it than I was. His family has donated a ton of money to the school over the years, so a lot of prestige comes with the Helsin name." She rolls her eyes. "She was so happy we were together, but I always felt like I was walking on eggshells around him. Like I couldn't be myself. We broke up when he went away to college but started dating again when he came home for the summer a couple of years ago." She stops talking as another server arrives with our salads.

"Would you like parmesan cheese on your Caesar salads?" The server brandishes a cheese grater in her hand. She looks disappointed when we both shake our heads. Setting a basket of rolls on the table, she disappears.

"He proposed last Christmas." Chloe picks up again where she left off. "He did it in front of his family and my grandmother. I didn't feel like I had any choice but to say yes. My grandmother was already sick. Our engagement made her so happy." Her eyes cloud with sadness. "She was always so mad at my father because he married my mother. She never approved of her, so I guess in some stupid way, I wanted to please her. After she passed, I broke off the engagement."

"And now he doesn't want to let you go?"

"He believes he needs to save me."

"Save you?" After hearing him quote scripture out on the sidewalk, I suspect this all leads back to the fact she's a witch.

I wait to see if she's going to tell me, but she shakes her head. "Another long story, for another time." She sticks her fork into a piece of lettuce. "What about you? Any crazy exes I should know about?"

"Not recent ones." I make it sound like a joke. In truth, I don't consider Ilene my ex since we weren't ever officially a couple. She couldn't pay her rent and I made the mistake of letting her stay over a few times back in the late 1960s. The next thing I knew, she had moved in.

Chloe notices I'm staring at my food. "She must have hurt you really bad." She studies me.

"What?" I shake my head. "No, nothing like that. It was a mistake on my part. It happened a long time ago. We were only together for a few months." I tell her the truth, glad I don't have to lie about that part of my life. I considered Ilene a pleasant diversion at the time. At least, I did until the night I came home early and found her in bed with a human she had picked up at a bar. I wasn't kidding when I told Chloe I don't like to share.

Even though it was my apartment, I packed up my things and left, but not before I tossed him out. And by tossed, I mean, I physically threw him out the window. I don't want to tell Chloe all the sordid details about that night, though. Thankfully, our entrees arrive before she can ask any more questions. As we enjoy our meal, all thoughts of exes, hers and mine, are forgotten.

Chloe and I arrive back at my place a little after 10:00. When I pull into the garage at the Echelon, it catches her off guard. The little V is back between her brows. It's her tell that something is bothering her. It occurs to me, we've never discussed where I live. She's quiet as I pull the car into my parking space. As we get out, she notices my bike.

"Nice. What kind is it?" She admires it as I walk around to the trunk of the car to get her bag. She's got the ribbon of the balloon weaved through her fingers. I think the balloon likes her. It doesn't fight her at all.

"It's a 1956 Harley Davidson KH." I refrain from mentioning that the black paint is still the original—or that I got her brand spanking new back in the day. "Do you like to ride?"

"I've never been on one before," she confesses.

"Maybe we can go for a ride tomorrow when you get off work." What I would like to do is head out in the morning and spend the day with her, riding up the coastline. She has to work, though. Plus, Death doesn't take a holiday. I have to work, too.

"I'd like that." She smiles.

But I have to have you back to your apartment by eight or Andrea will have my balls...

Quickly shoving the thought of Andrea neutering me out of my mind, I reach for Chloe's free hand. We walk toward the elevator. After our run-in with Eric, I want to make the rest of the night perfect for her.

No pressure, Finn.

The ride to the penthouse is the longest elevator ride I've ever taken in my life. The familiar shade of pink creeps into Chloe's cheeks. I suspect she's thinking about how she wants the rest of the night to go. I am, too.

The elevator doors open.

She lets out a little gasp as we step out into the foyer. "You live here?" Her eyes grow wide.

"I do."

"It's the penthouse."

"It is."

"And it's yours."

I'm not sure where she's going with this. "Yes, it's mine." We're still standing in the middle of the foyer. I go over and open one of the double doors for her. "Do you want to see the rest of it?"

The atmosphere between us grows colder in the blink of an eye. She says nothing as she walks past me, dragging the balloon in behind her. It's almost like she's suddenly upset or angry with me, but there's no hint as to why.

"Do you live here alone?" Undoing the ribbon from around her hand, she passes the balloon to me. She slides her coat off, handing it to me as well. I watch, concerned, as she wanders away from me and heads into the living room. Her fingers run over the back of the couch as she walks by it. She cocks her head, studying the gray and white painting on the wall to the left of the fireplace. Then, with her jaw set firm, she turns back to stare at me. Her fingers play with the bracelet on her wrist. She is definitely acting strange.

"Yes, it's just me," I reply as I walk into the kitchen. I set her overnight bag on the island and place her coat over the back of one of the stools. I tie the ribbon of the balloon around the back of another. "Do you want a glass of champagne?" I come back to the living room to see what she's doing.

I find her standing next to the couch with her arms folded. "Not at the moment."

"Something wrong?"

She shakes her head. "No, everything's fine." Her voice takes on an unusually high pitch.

It doesn't seem fine. "Would you like the grand tour?" I ask, trying to lighten the mood.

She shrugs. "Sure."

Living room, study, library, guest rooms. She remains quiet as she takes it all in. I still can't tell what she's thinking. I intentionally skip the master bedroom, showing her the exercise room instead because it feels awkward to take her into my bedroom. *Here's where I thought I would sleep with you tonight. Now, I'm not so sure—*

She figures out we missed a door, though, and opens it on her own. Her lips form a thin line. She turns on the light, walks past me, then stops in the center of the room. I haven't drawn the curtains over the windows yet. Her attention shifts from the room to the view outside. The bay is dark, but the navigation lights twinkle on the water from a boat or two.

She's too quiet. It's worrisome.

"What's wrong?" I can't take the odd silence anymore.

"Andrea is right." Her voice is flat.

Her back is to me, so I can't see her expression.

"What do you mean?" I try to keep the edge out of my voice.

"That you're out of my league." She turns around to look at me. "How many women have you brought here, Finn?" She waves her hand around the room.

Where is this coming from?

"I haven't." I answer truthfully. "After Ilene, I've never brought a woman home. Until now."

Her lips form a thin line again. "Why me?"

"What do you mean?"

"With all of this." She motions around the room again. "You could have any woman you want." She fidgets with the bracelet like she wants to tear it off her wrist. "Why me?"

I'm not sure I can explain it, but I take a breath and try. "Because since the first moment I saw you, you're all I think about. I've never felt this way about anyone before."

She's still wary, but her expression softens. "But I've got no experience. I'm sure there are plenty of other women who are beautiful, who know more about how to—" Her eyes drift over to the bed.

I close the distance between us. "Chloe, you're beautiful." I wish she could see herself the way I see her. My hand reaches out to tuck a wayward strand of hair behind her ear. "I thought we were great together the other night. I don't want anyone else. I want you."

"I'm sorry. This is kind of overwhelming." She's back to waving her arms around the room again. "When I told Andrea about your car, she was convinced you borrowed or rented it." She hesitates. "Well, she thought you might have stolen it." She has the grace to appear embarrassed.

"Oh, she did, did she?" I can't decide if her friend is simply overprotective or if she truly hates me.

"Plus, I know you're older than me. You obviously have a lot of experience." Her gaze drifts over to the bed once more. "As you saw with Eric, my track record with men isn't too good. Andrea thinks I'm too trusting. She says I'm setting myself up to get hurt."

"And what do you think?"

She doesn't reply. She stares down at her fingers as if maybe she's trying to gather her thoughts. I prepare for her to tell me she wants me to take her home and never wants to see me again, but then she looks up, straight into my eyes, and does that thing where she bites her bottom lip. "I think I'd like that champagne now."

I let out the breath I wasn't aware I was holding. "You would, huh? You're sure?" I give her one more opportunity to back out.

"Yes, please." She playfully bats her eyelashes at me.

I hold up a finger. "I'll be right back."

I somehow refrain from running out of the room and down the hall. For some stupid reason, my heart is beating like mad in my chest. Maybe I'm afraid if I don't move fast enough, she'll change her mind.

I get to the kitchen, grab two crystal champagne flutes out of a cabinet, the champagne from the refrigerator, and a box of chocolate-covered strawberries from the counter. I probably should have gotten her a cake, or at least one of those fancy cupcakes, but hindsight is twenty-twenty and all that.

Returning to the room as quickly as I can, I find her sitting on the edge of the bed. She's taken off her shoes. The moment she was having appears to have passed. I set the champagne flutes and the box of strawberries down on the bedside table. Then, with a twist of the cork, I open the champagne bottle with a bit of flourish.

When I planned the evening out in my mind, I was presenting her with all of this in the living room in front of the fireplace, but I stay in the moment. I pour the champagne and hand her a glass. The box of strawberries has a red bow around it, and it takes me a while to figure out how to undo it. Instead of coming across as suave, I'm all thumbs. I don't know why, but this woman seriously does things to me.

Chloe puts a hand over her mouth, trying not to laugh.

Smooth, Finn. Real smooth.

Inwardly, I sigh with relief once I get the knot of ribbon undone. I open the box, giving her a small bow as I present the contents inside. "Strawberry?"

"Don't mind if I do." She peers up at me demurely, choosing a strawberry covered in white chocolate.

I set the box on the bedside table and pick up my champagne. "Happy birthday, baby." I raise the glass to her in a toast.

"Thank you." As usual, she does the unexpected. She

dips the strawberry into her champagne, then brings it to her lips to lick it off. It feels like she's made a direct hit when she bites into the berry. I suppress a groan. Taking a long drink, I empty the contents of the glass in one swallow.

She takes a couple more sips of hers, then sets it down next to the box. Standing up, she takes the glass from me, puts it next to hers, then places her arms around my neck. She leans up on her tiptoes to kiss me, and I get a taste of sweet strawberries, chocolate, and champagne. Still kissing me, her hands reach for my belt and undo it. Mine strays to the zipper on the back of her dress, but she steps out of reach once it's down. She pulls on the material of my shirt. I raise my arms as she lifts it up over my head, then tosses it somewhere over to my left. Instead of proceeding to my pants, she stops. She bites her lip.

What's this?

She slides around me, heading toward the door to the bathroom. When she reaches the door, she gestures back toward the bed. "Make yourself comfortable. I'll only be a minute. She slips into the bathroom and shuts the door.

I'm guessing she's heeding the call of nature, but I'm not sure. I sit on the edge of the bed, taking off my shoes and socks. I remove my pants but leave on the black boxer briefs. She's still in there, so I slink over to my underwear drawer and pull a foil pack out of the box. On second thought, make that two foil packs. If she's going to stay over more often, maybe I should move the box to the nightstand.

Getting way ahead of yourself, Finn.

I set the foil packs next to the champagne glasses. I make it back to the edge of the bed right as the bathroom door opens. Running my hand through my hair, I try to play it cool.

She emerges from the bathroom, wearing a lacy black pushup bra, which reveals more than a generous amount of cleavage, and a black lace thong. She's let her hair down. It cascades in loose curls around her shoulders.

My mouth drops open. I stare at her like an idiot.

Holy shit.

She puts her arm up against the frame of the door in a sexy pose, but the red in her cheeks gives away her nervousness. Dropping the pose, she bites on one of her fingernails instead. "Do you like it?"

My brain ceases to function. I can't get my mouth to shut. I can't even figure out how to form words.

She is a goddess. Beautiful. Sexy. Chloe.

Sauntering over to me, she continues to bite the edge of her fingernail. "Finn?"

"Yes." I'm not sure if I'm responding to her question or to the sound of my name.

Her walk ends in front of me. She places her fingers under my chin, tilting my head up so I'm looking straight into her eyes. "Breathe, Finn." She smiles.

I can't help myself. I reach for her, bringing her down onto my lap. "You look amazing. I love it."

She squeals as she puts her arms around my neck. "You should have seen your face," she giggles. "I sort of blew it, though. I meant to wear the shoes, but I forgot to bring them into the bathroom with me. I also bought a black garter belt to go with it, but I tried to wear it this morning. I couldn't figure out how to make the stockings stay up the way they are supposed to and—"

It barely registers what she's saying. I kiss her on the

neck, and she stops talking. I pull her with me as we tumble backward onto the bed. We land where I can roll us over, and she ends up beneath me. We grin at each other, savoring the moment. I kiss her again, with fervor this time. First, her lips, then I leave a trail of kisses down her neck. Reaching down, I cup her breast. My hand moves over the silky material. To my delight, I discover the clasp of the bra is on the front. Corsun refers to bras like this as front loaders. *Where the hell did that thought come from?* I quickly push the random thought away.

Chloe tries not to giggle as it takes me a second to unhook it. She gives a small sigh when I finally get it undone.

I push the material back. "You are so beautiful," I whisper as she raises up for me to remove the bra. Leaning down, I worship her breasts, first with kisses and my tongue, then with my lips as I start to suck. She cries out as she arches up for more. Her fingers make their way to my hair, pulling at it while I give attention to one breast, then the other.

"Oh, Finn."

I move lower, kissing and nipping at her skin. My tongue licks and laps and explores, dipping into her navel. She bows again as I brush my hand across her skin. Slipping my fingers under the strings on each side of her panties, I pull them down.

"I want you so much." She rubs her hips against me.

"Baby, I want you, too." Sliding the thong down her legs and over her feet, I discard it onto the floor. I scramble out of my boxers, adding them to the pile. I reach for the foil pack on the bedside table and tear it open.

"Are you going to show me how to do it differently?" Her question comes out of nowhere.

"What?" I stop.

"Last time, you said if I had told you before, we could have done it differently."

I guess I did say that, didn't I? That wasn't exactly what I meant, but she wouldn't know that.

"Something different, huh?"

She gives me a playful smile. "Yes, please."

"You didn't like how we did it last time?" I raise an eyebrow.

"Oh, I liked it very much. It's all I've been able to think about. But I wanted to know how else—" She glances up at me, embarrassed. Her cheeks blush scarlet red.

It's all she's been able to think about? *You better make this good for her, Finn.*

"Well, I guess since it's your birthday, we can accommodate requests." I lean down to kiss her as she beams up at me. "Sit up," I instruct her.

She's not sure what we're doing, but she's game. She brings herself to a sitting position. "Like this?" She places one hand on each of her thighs.

"Perfect." I get up on my knees, bringing her closer and closer until she's straddling me.

"Now what?" She tries to figure out what comes next.

"We fuck." I give her my best demon smile. She gasps at my language, but the fire in her eyes tells me she's turned on.

Grabbing her hips, I lift her up, slowly bringing her down on me. Her lips form a perfect O. I continue flexing my hips, slowly filling her inch by inch until I'm buried deep inside her.

I pause, giving her a moment to adjust to how it feels. She's so tight. At this rate, I won't last long. I grit my teeth, trying to distract myself. She moves her hips a little as she adjusts to the sensation, then drops her head back, leaning away from me. "This feels incredible," she purrs.

"You like that?"

"Mmm hmm." She tosses her hair back behind her shoulders. Leaning forward, she places her hands on my shoulders. Her lips touch mine, and her tongue slides in and out of my mouth in a slow rhythmic tease. It's unexpected and extremely hot.

I move my hips, keeping it slow and steady at first. Her eyes lock with mine. A fast learner, she instinctively moves, copying my rhythm. As we collide against each other again and again and again. I wrap my arms around her lower waist, increasing the intensity.

I change the angle slightly until I feel her nails dig into the muscles of my neck. When she cries out my name, it's my undoing. I groan, unable to hold on any longer. We find our release together as I explode inside of her. Breathless, we collapse into each other.

Moving her to my chest, I wrap my arms around her and give her a kiss. My heart thuds hard inside my chest. It takes a moment before I can speak coherently. "Chloe, you are amazing. That was—" Once again, I can't form the words in my mind to describe it. When we're together, it's like nothing I've experienced before.

"For me, too. But as you know, my experience is somewhat limited." She gazes at me, running her fingers through my hair. "But I do believe it's the best birthday present anyone's ever given me." She grins.

"Oh, really?" I smile back at her.

"Mmm hmm. Best. Ever." Her eyes sparkle.

"Happy birthday, baby." I kiss her again.

CHAPTER 10

October 15 - Day:

I wake before the alarm goes off. For once this week, I've slept well. Stretching my arms overhead, I'm surprised to find my body is completely relaxed. That doesn't happen very often, especially once I hit the three-thousand-year mark. My head turns to the pillow where Chloe slept, but she's not there. Her absence catches me off guard, but then I hear the sound of water running in the bathroom. She's in the shower. My first thought is to join her, but no doubt it would make her late for work. It could make me late, too.

This reminds me, I didn't check my app last night.

Bit distracted, weren't you, old boy?

Another one of those stupid grins appears on my face and I can't seem to get rid of it. Picking up my iPad from the bedside table, I scan over my schedule for today. It's two normal reaps. No changes. The first one isn't until 9:47 and the other one is at 3:23. This means I can drop Chloe off at work, pick her up when she gets off, and most importantly, get her to the party on time to avoid Andrea's wrath. The sun is out, so we can even take that ride on my bike. I love it when everything comes together.

Chloe comes out of the bathroom, her hair still damp. She's wearing a pair of dark jeans along with a tan bra, but no shirt.

Speaking of coming together—Behave. Work, remember?

"I couldn't find your hair dryer and I apparently forgot to pack a shirt." She gives me a bashful look. "I was wondering if I could borrow one of yours?"

Before I can answer, she comes over to the bed and sits down next to me. "I'll work in the back of the museum all day so I can dress more casually."

She reaches out to push a lock of hair off my forehead. It catches me off guard. Belatedly, I realize I still have the Grim Reaper app pulled up on my iPad. The information for my second reap is on full display. I distract her by pulling her into an embrace. As I give her a kiss, I reach over, quickly shutting the app.

That was close.

She leans back, biting her bottom lip. A sly smile spreads across her face.

Okay, what's this?

Reaching behind her back, she undoes her bra. She holds it up in her hand before dropping it onto the bed.

Something tells me neither one of us is going to make it to work on time.

The day drags to a standstill after I take Chloe to work. She is a good forty-five minutes late. That is all I will say about that, except she looked quite fetching in my black Boston Eagle hoodie when I dropped her off at the employee entrance. It's way too big on her, but she looks adorable in it.

Who are you? What have you done with Finn?

As expected, I'm late to my first reap of the day. I nudge my Charge into acceptance fairly quickly, though, and there are no complications getting him to the ferry. I'm walking back toward the elevator when Jack calls my name.

"Finn, wait up!"

Shit. Now what?

I turn, waiting for him to catch up.

"Jack," I reply cautiously. I was hoping to stay off his radar for a while.

We walk to the elevator together. He pushes the button. "How's it going?"

"Good." I give a small shrug. *Why are you asking?*

"Good." He studies me. "You seem different."

"Do I?"

"You do."

Okay.

"Listen, I wanted to check with you. That witch thing you mentioned at the hearing." He hesitates. "Is all that okay now?" He watches me expectantly.

Witch thing? I consider showing him the photo. I could ask him if he thinks it's okay, but it's not what he wants to hear. "Yeah, it's good," I say instead.

"Good."

I can't help myself. "Why do you ask?"

Now, it's his turn to shrug. "No reason. I got a little kickback from the angels the other day. You know they don't like anyone making waves. I told them you were simply curious, and you told me you would let the whole matter drop. You did, right? Let it drop?"

"I did," I reply because, again, this is what he expects me to say.

"Good."

The elevator doors open. Two angels with their Charges shuffle out past us. We get on the elevator. Jack pushes the lobby button for me, the twenty-first-floor button for him. The doors to the elevator shut. We both stare straight ahead.

"If you've got enough bandwidth, we should do lunch next week," he says out of nowhere.

"Sure," I reply because he is, after all, my boss.

"Good. I'll text you."

"Sounds good."

The elevator doors mercifully open.

Jack raises his eyebrows at me as I get off the elevator. "Finn."

"Jack."

He acknowledges a human who is getting into the elevator, then gives a final nod back at me before the doors close.

I have no clue what just happened.

My second reap for the day, a fifty-eight-year-old human named Greg, goes smoothly as well. I drop him off at the ferry, grateful not to run into Jack again. I'm still not sure what all of that was about earlier. We used to occasionally hang out before I got sent to Hell, but the only interaction we have now is when it's work related. I decide not to dwell on it, though, because I'm about to head home to get my bike.

Keeping in mind I am to deliver Chloe to the party later

on, I change into a black sweater and my nicest pair of jeans. Instead of wearing my favorite biker boots, I settle for a newer pair, but they aren't nearly as comfortable. I finish my attire by adding my leather jacket to the mix. I study myself in the closet mirror. I've been told I give off a bad boy vibe, but all I see is a scrappy-looking demon. Maybe I should have gotten a haircut.

I arrive at the museum about ten minutes before 5:00, the time Chloe gets off on Fridays. At 5:00 on the dot, Chloe walks out of the employee entrance. She gives a wave, and after talking to the security guard for a moment, heads over.

I get a sweet smile and a kiss from her, but she's tense. I hope it's not about riding on my bike.

"What's wrong?" I ask.

She lets out a breath. "I have to go out of town tomorrow for a conference. The curator and her assistant were planning to go, but the assistant had a family emergency. They want me to go in her place."

"And you don't want to go?" I don't want her to go, either, but I don't have the right to stop her.

She shrugs. "It's a great opportunity, but Beth is rather intense and then there's—" Her voice drops off. She waves her hand in my direction. "I feel like we're in a good place and I don't want to leave you."

She's going to miss me. My heart does the weird little pitter patter thing.

"How long will you be gone?"

"Until Thursday."

I try to act nonchalant. "That's not too bad." *I miss her already.* "We can text, do Facetime. Maybe try a little sexting." I wiggle my eyebrows and give her my best demon grin.

She narrows her eyes at me as if she's outraged, then playfully punches me in the arm and laughs. "You're bad."

"I try." I offer her a helmet. "Come on, let's get out of here."

She puts on the helmet. Getting onto the back of the bike, she puts her arms around my waist. "Where are we going?"

"Plymouth."

She squeals as I peel out of the parking lot.

Traffic is heavy, but it clears as we leave the city. I follow the road along the coastline. It's a perfect fall night. This is the kind of trip memories are made of. Me, my bike, my girl, and the open road.

CHAPTER 11

October 15 – Night:

I've done my homework and chosen a seafood place overlooking Plymouth Harbor. The ocean breeze makes it chilly, but Chloe likes the idea of dining outdoors, so we grab a table out on the deck. We go all in and order two clambakes. It occurs to me only after we've feasted on clam chowder, lobster, fries, and coleslaw that I hope Andrea's birthday party wasn't a dinner. She never mentioned food, so I believe we're safe.

Keeping a close eye on the time, I casually suggest it's getting a little too cool to keep riding north. We head back toward the city. I pull up into the parking space outside Chloe's apartment building a little before 8:00.

"That was so much fun. I wish we didn't have to come back so soon," Chloe says as I secure my helmet to the bike. "You know you don't have to do this, right?"

"What do you mean?" I turn away from my bike to look at her.

She rolls her eyes as she hands me her helmet. "The

party. I know you're supposed to have me back here by eight o'clock."

"I don't know what you're talking about." I feign ignorance. I certainly don't want Andrea to think I've spoiled the surprise.

She folds her arms. "I overheard Andrea on the phone the other night. She told someone the party begins at eight and everyone should be at the apartment no later than seven-thirty." She pushes back a strand of hair that's escaped from her ponytail. "I don't want you to feel you have to stay."

She's correct. I don't want to attend a party, but it is for her birthday, even if it is a day late. I study her. Maybe she doesn't want me to stay. "Do you not want me to meet your friends?"

"It's not that. They're not exactly my friends," she says uncomfortably. "It's more like people I know through Andrea and a few people from work I'm sure she's invited. I think she feels bad because I don't have any family left, so she does stuff like this. I'd rather have spent another night with you." She gives me a suggestive look.

I raise an eyebrow. "Would you, now?" I put my arms around her waist, drawing her close.

She places her hands on my shoulder. "Mmm hmm. Especially since I have to go on that trip tomorrow." She leans up, kissing me. "Even if it is a great opportunity," she adds wistfully.

"Yeah. I wish you didn't have to go, but it's only until Thursday."

She stares into my eyes. "Will you miss me?"

More than you could possibly imagine.

~

We stand at the door to the apartment. Chloe pulls her keys out of the pocket of her jacket. “Last chance.” She gestures toward the stairs. “I won’t think less of you if you make a run for it.”

I consider it for about half a second but continue to stand by her side as she puts the key into the lock. Slowly turning the doorknob, she reaches back for my hand, then pushes open the door. I’m not sure if it’s more for moral support or if the hand holding is to keep me from trying to take off.

The living room is completely dark, but I can still see fifteen or twenty people standing inside, waiting for Chloe to enter the room.

“Surprise!” They all shout at once as the lights come on, then break into an off-key rendition of *Happy Birthday* as we walk inside. A bunch of flashes from phone cameras go off at once.

Shit! I was not expecting that.

I blink repeatedly to clear my vision. Hopefully, no one will think too much about it when they see my eyes glowing an odd greenish yellow color in all their photos instead of the usual red eye from the flash. Demons have the same reflective tapetal layer beneath our retinas certain animals do. It allows us to see better in dimly lit situations. We can also see in almost complete darkness, but our eyes turn entirely black. They will also turn that way if we’re extremely angry or startled. Lucky for me, that didn’t happen. It would have made things awkward, to say the least.

As my vision returns, I take in the room. Lots of witches here and about five humans.

We both stand awkwardly through the slew of birthday greetings for Chloe. Finally, Andrea rushes forward to hug her. I release Chloe's hand as she throws her arms around her neck.

"Happy birthday, honey!" Andrea gives her a hug. She steps back and turns toward the people standing behind her. "Everyone, this is Finn." Andrea waves her hand in front of my face. "He's Chloe's boyfriend."

The room goes silent at the news. Several people murmur to each other, asking what happened to Eric. Andrea must have given them all one of those scary looks she likes to give because suddenly they stop, and the conversations go back to normal.

"Sorry," Chloe whispers. "Andrea shouldn't have done that without us talking about it first."

"It's okay." I'm not sure if I was ready to officially put a label on what we are out into the world. I mean, witch and demon as girlfriend and boyfriend? That combination qualifies for the *it's complicated* box if we need to check one off. But the weird little flutter in my chest suggests I like the idea of everyone knowing she's mine. Actually, I like it a lot. I don't have time to dwell on this revelation, however, because the guests start pushing their way up to have their own moment with Chloe and meet me.

"How did you meet?"

"How long have you been dating?"

"Are you from around here, Finn?"

It's all a bit much, and after a few minutes, it feels like the room is closing in.

Thankfully, Andrea takes control of the situation. She backs everyone away from us with the promise of cake, snacks, and drinks in the kitchen.

"Let's give Chloe a chance to catch her breath," she says, motioning for them to give us, or at least Chloe, some space.

"Well, this is—" I start as I help Chloe out of her jacket.

"Overwhelming," she finishes.

I'm not exactly sure what word I was going to use, but I'll go with her choice.

"I don't know what Andrea was thinking," she mumbles under her breath. I suspect she's referring to the boyfriend comment or maybe it's the number of people crowded into the apartment. I'm not sure. "To be fair, I did offer to let you make a run for it." She jokes, holding out her hand. "Give me your jacket. I'm going to go freshen up a bit."

I slide off my jacket and hand it to her. She runs her fingers through my hair to straighten it a bit, then kisses me on the cheek. She heads into the crowd, working her way through the room while I remain standing next to the door. Now, I'm in the awkward position of not knowing what to do with myself. No one is sitting on the couch, so I head that way.

From there, I can see what's going on around me. The room looks different. The coffee table, the Queen Anne chairs, and the small table normally sitting between them are gone. Some folding chairs have replaced them, and the kitchen chairs are now in the living room. People have already claimed most of them and I suspect it's only a matter of time before someone joins me on the couch.

At the entranceway to the kitchen, someone has strung fairy lights overhead and there's a huge HAPPY BIRTHDAY, CHLOE banner underneath. It's crooked, but probably no one besides me will notice.

What are you doing here, Finn?

I remind myself I'm here for Chloe, but this is so not my thing.

Fifteen minutes later, Chloe has yet to reappear. I

occupy my time watching the guests. I recognize a few of them from the museum the other night. They're all human. The rest are witches and I suspect they're the mutual friends Chloe told me about. It would appear everyone is enjoying her party. Maybe because it's not their birthday?

"There you are!" Chloe works her way over to me through the crowd of people. She has two pieces of cake on paper plates in one hand and two red Solo cups filled with drinks held between her fingers in the other. She has changed into a fuzzy green sweater. Her hair is now down and loose around her shoulders. She looks as beautiful as ever. She hands me a plate and a drink, then sits down next to me.

I can't help but smirk. She's brought me devil's food cake. I guess that's appropriate. The slice she's given me has a giant C on it. I think back, but I don't recall ever having birthday cake before. I've certainly never celebrated anyone's birthday.

"Penny for your thoughts." Chloe bumps her leg against mine.

"I was thinking—good cake," I lie.

We eat mostly in silence. A few people come up to talk to Chloe, and I get a lot of uncomfortable side glances thrown my way. I'm sure they're wondering who I am or comparing me to her ex. By their expressions, I'm guessing most are hashtag Team Eric. Chloe must feel my tension level rising because she reaches over to grab my hand. She gives it a big squeeze.

I finally settle back down, but then Andrea reappears.

"Chloe, it's your party. You need to mingle some." She shoots her a pointed look before giving a disapproving glance over at me.

Something unspoken passes between them. Chloe turns to me. "Will you be okay?"

"Sure." I mean, what else am I going to say?

Letting go of my hand, she gets up off the couch and follows Andrea toward the kitchen.

Now, I'm all alone again, and yep, it's back to feeling awkward.

I return to people watching. They're all curious about me, so I brush it off at first when I get the feeling someone is also watching me. But then, it happens again, and I spot the older gray-haired woman standing near the entranceway to the kitchen. She's got the telltale purple aura of a witch. If I didn't know better, I'd say she's giving me the evil eye. When she realizes I'm paying attention to her, she turns away.

What is her problem?

I shift my attention to a group of five who have made a circle with their chairs and are sitting off to the side in front of the bookcase. More witches.

"Has anyone heard any news?" A male witch quietly asks the others. He's got a Gandalf thing going on with his long gray beard.

A female witch dressed in bright purple, which is a perfect match for her aura, shakes her head. "She's been missing a month now. The police are absolutely useless."

"That's at least three. You know one was from Raven Oak, and I heard they have one missing from Silver Cloud, too," a dark-skinned witch with a thick British accent says. From the way they talk, I'm guessing these are coven names, although, they also sound like good names for a campground.

"Maybe one of us should try a locating spell. What if

someone is holding them all somewhere?" Gandalf speaks again.

"We need to do a protection spell," a younger male witch suggests. The witch in purple bobs her head in agreement.

This validates my concerns about the murders. It's almost a relief to know I'm not the only one noticing something strange is going on.

Before I can work through all that's been said about the missing witches, goosebumps dart up the back of my neck. I glance up to find the old woman staring my way again. Her eyes remain on me as she walks over to the group of five and whispers something. It's in English, but her accent is so thick, I can't clearly hear what she tells them. I do catch the last word, however. "...Der Teufel." She purses her lips and makes a spitting noise.

All eyes turn my way. My German is more than a little rusty. I haven't been in Germany since 1799, but unless I'm mistaken, the old woman just called me the devil. This could mean one of two things. Either she's a staunch supporter of Team Eric, or more likely, she has picked up on the fact I'm a demon.

Fuck.

Nervous laughter comes from the group, then they all turn back around. I believe they think she's joking. Thankfully, a human comes up to talk to the old woman. While she's distracted, I decide it's a good time to go in search of Chloe.

I find her in the kitchen cornered by one human, one witch, and Andrea.

Okay, let's not go over there.

I head out to the balcony to get some fresh air instead.

Brian, Andrea's date from the other night, is leaning against the railing smoking a cigarette.

Fucking great.

I didn't notice him earlier or I would have had my guard up. I start to go back inside.

"I told Eric he should keep an eye on you."

His remark stops me. I turn back around. "What did you say?"

He flicks the ashes of his cigarette over the railing. "The night we ran into you in the hallway. Eric thought we'd all go out together and it would be like it was before they broke up," he snorts. "Not me. From the way you were watching Chloe, I knew something was up. I told him he better keep an eye on you. I guess I was right." He pulls a pack of menthols out of the pocket of his shirt. "Cigarette?"

"No, thanks." I haven't smoked since the 1940s. Although after tonight, I may want to rethink that.

"Andrea wants me to quit. I'm not having much luck." He sticks the pack back into his pocket. We stand there in silence while he takes another drag on the cigarette. "You know, if I were you, I'd watch my back."

"Is that a threat?" I come a little closer to him.

He puts his hands up. "No. I'm simply saying, I've known Eric since we were kids. He doesn't like to lose—at anything." He motions behind me. "I figure as long as you and I are dating roommates, our paths are going to keep crossing." He flicks ashes from the cigarette. "I thought I should give you a friendly little warning."

"Thanks, but I can take care of myself."

"No doubt." He snubs the cigarette out on the balcony railing, then tosses it over the side. "But like I said, Eric doesn't like to lose, and you don't know who you're dealing with."

It still sounds like a threat.

I'm about to respond, but Chloe appears at the balcony door.

"Everything all right?" She studies us uneasily.

"It's fine." Brian gives her a smile. "I was just having a friendly little chat with Finn." He embraces her in a hug, giving her a kiss on the cheek. "Happy birthday."

"Thanks, Brian."

He gives me one last glance before going back inside.

"What was that all about?" Chloe asks once he's gone.

I shake my head. "Nothing."

She doesn't buy it for a minute, but she doesn't push me to say anything else. Instead, she puts her arms around my neck. "I get the feeling all of this is not your kind of thing, but thanks for staying." She gives me a long kiss and a hug. Suddenly, my night becomes a whole lot better.

CHAPTER 12

October 17:

Andrea dropped Chloe off at the airport yesterday morning, so I haven't seen her since Friday night. That's one day, ten hours, twenty minutes, and forty-two seconds since we were last together. Not that I'm counting.

Overnight, the temperature plummets, and with her gone, so does my mood. I get out of bed, then stand staring out the window. I don't even have to check the weather to know the chance of rain is almost certain. The water in the bay is a murky gray. The waves are choppy, and the wind is picking up.

I want to blame my change in disposition on the weather, but that's not exactly true. I'm not sure if the real problem is that Chloe is out of town, or if it's because I'm missing her more than I thought I would. Either way, it's a strange feeling for me and I don't like it one bit. The only good thing is, she misses me, too.

I say this because we were sending texts all day yesterday, then we video chatted last night when we discovered neither one of us could sleep. She's got a busy day today, however, so all I've gotten this morning is a couple of texts that she was on her way to breakfast with all the attendees at the conference.

Regardless of my mood, I have Charges to look after today, so I shift my focus to the three reaps on my schedule. When I went to bed last night, today's schedule had one witch and a human. Now, it shows two witches and a human. If both witches are murder victims, it could mean the killer is escalating. At least, that's what they always say about the unsubs on reruns of *Criminal Minds*, a show I sometimes may or may not watch.

The problem is it would seem I'm the only one concerned about it. Well, except for those witches at the party on Friday night. They don't know their friends are dead, though, only that they're missing. As for Management, I suspect they believe it's another one of those crazy serial killers like Jack the Ripper or that Zodiac Killer guy, but this feels different to me.

The bad thing is I have heard nothing about a rise in local disappearances on the news, so it would appear the police haven't connected all the dots together yet, either.

I'm still trying to wrap my mind around this as I get into the shower. By my count, there are at least six witches who are dead. While I'm not the only one escorting them to the other side, they seem to turn up on my schedule a lot for some reason. It's strange.

Plus, every time it happens, their deaths occur the same way. They're stabbed and their hearts are removed. Then, there are those weird symbols. I'm mid-shampoo in the shower when it dawns on me—if I could get a hold of the books Chloe mentioned, I might have a way to decipher what they mean and use the information to figure out what exactly is going on. It could give me the proof I need to take all of this to Jack or an angel in Upper Management and show them there's something strange going on.

Not a good idea, Finn. You know what Jack said. He told you to drop it, not dig deeper.

I think about this before I rinse my hair. Lost in thought, I let the hot water cascade over me. Chloe told me the books had gone back to the library. If the witches today have the symbol like the others, maybe I can go to the library tomorrow, see what the books have to say, then figure out what to do. There. Now, I have a plan. My inner demon tells me it's a bad one, but at least it's a plan.

The good news is the first witch on my schedule today is not a murder victim. The bad news is on Thursday night, Latisha, a thirty-three-year-old witch, dental hygienist, and soccer mom from the Emerald Pines community, ate not one, not two, but three servings of chicken casserole because she hates to waste leftovers. Latisha informs me she thought the entire family had the flu the next day. It wasn't until late Friday night at the emergency room when she discovered she was wrong, and it was salmonella poisoning instead.

The other three members of her family have been treated and released. Latisha is not as lucky. A compromised immune system and past health issues swung her over into the column of being one of only 0.6% of people who die from salmonella poisoning each year. She's been in the ICU with kidney and liver failure while the rest of her family made a full recovery.

Latisha feels bad for leaving her family, but she feels vindicated when the doctors confirm to her husband it was bad meat and not her cooking that did her in. She boards the ferry at 11:57 as a solid Stage Five, and I have just enough time to take an hour for lunch.

My second reap of the day is a thirty-seven-year-old human. Karen is the victim of a hit-and-run. She tells me she was in the crosswalk, simply trying to get from one side of the street to the other. A drunk driver hit her with his car and kept on going. She knows it's a hit-and-run driver because she heard the police officer who responded discussing it with the paramedic trying to revive her.

Karen is angry about a lot of things, and I get to hear all about it. Currently, she is upset with me because I don't have an umbrella and we are both standing in the rain. I don't have an umbrella because I'm always setting them down and forgetting them. Plus, the idea of a demon carrying around an umbrella is, in my opinion, a little silly.

That, and yeah, I lose them. A lot.

I would say she is somewhere between the denial of Stage One and the anger of Stage Two. Make that extreme anger of Stage Two. The kicker is, she hasn't even officially met her time of death yet. She made one round trip so far and has three more to go.

"I will haunt him until the end of his days." She clutches her beaded necklace while pointing a perfectly manicured red fingernail at me. "I will hunt him down and I will make his life a living hell." A second later, she disappears.

I wonder for a brief moment if she found him, but she is, as Roz likes to say, a Yo-Yo.

I stand behind the paramedics as they discuss whether she's stable enough to transport. Once they determine she is, they load her up into the ambulance. Before they can close the doors, however, one of them says her blood pressure is dropping. She goes into cardiac arrest.

Karen reappears and we're now both in the ambulance. She is incorporeal. She'll return to her body soon.

She cringes as one of them takes a needle and injects something into her arm. "I hate needles." She plays with her necklace again. "What did they give me?"

Like I'm supposed to know.

"Amiodarone," I casually reply. It makes me appear like I'm all wise and stuff, but what she doesn't know is that from where I sit, I can see it written on the box the paramedic took the needle from.

Karen disappears again.

I glance at my watch. Five minutes to go. The ambulance driver is having a hard time maneuvering around all the traffic. The drunk driver apparently caused a chain of accidents, and the street is all but impassable.

"Why are we still in the ambulance?" Karen is back. Her form is more solid than before, but I can still see through her.

"Traffic."

Her lips form a straight, thin line. "Well, which hospital am I going to?"

"Probably Lowell. I think it's the closest."

"Well, that won't do at all. I want to go to Mass General."

"Karen, it doesn't matter because—"

And she's gone.

And...she's back.

"Are we going to Mass General?"

"No, they're still headed to Lowell, but we're not making good time. We're stuck in traffic."

"I want to go to Mass General." She puts her hands on her hips.

"It doesn't work that way."

"Mass. General."

The 7 Habits of Highly Effective Reapers: Grim Reaper Training 101: *Keeping Your Voice Calm When the Charge is Upset.*

"Karen." I keep my voice neutral.

"Mass. General."

"Listen, I understand you're upset, but I don't have the authority—"

"Mass. General."

The paramedics use the defibrillator again, but she doesn't notice. She's still more concerned about which hospital the ambulance is taking her to. Karen is now corporeal.

The 7 Habits of Highly Effective Reapers: Grim Reaper Training 101: *Things to Do if You Disagree or Cannot Fulfill a Charge's Request.*

"Karen, I understand this is distressful for you, but you have to realize—"

She doubles and triples down. "Mass General. Mass General. Mass General. I want to go to Mass General."

I can't see either of her feet, but I'm fairly certain she stomped one of them. She is seriously pissing me off.

I take a breath, waving my hand toward her body. "Think about it. Does it really matter, Karen?"

"Mass—" She stops. The heart monitor shows a flat line. One paramedic shakes his head at the other. Her mouth forms a little O, goes back to a straight line, then back to the O again. She reminds me of a goldfish gasping for air.

"Well, then," she sputters. She watches as they shut

down the equipment. "This wouldn't have happened if they had taken me to Mass General."

Time of Death 3:23.

~

My original plan for today was to make it to the death of each witch early. That way, I might see who the killer is and perhaps figure out what it is they are trying to do. While I was there in plenty of time for Latisha's death, I'm quite certain I will not make it there on time for the next witch's death. I'm not even sure I'm going to make it to the reap itself.

Unfortunately, my adventure with Karen does not end with our arrival at the Promenade Building because she has asked to speak to—wait for it—a manager.

This means I'm now sitting in the waiting area of customer service, paging through a battered copy of *Life* magazine with a young Elizabeth Taylor on the cover while Karen is inside an office with the manager on duty. I suspect she is giving him a piece of her mind.

Technically, we don't have customer service in the afterlife, but occasionally a Charge wants to file a grievance against one of us. When this happens, they instruct us to take them to the holding area next to the elevator. This is where the supervisor on call for transportation issues has their office. Since most of the Charges who want to complain identify with customer service, some of us may refer to it as such when someone wants to talk to a higher authority.

In my defense, I did everything by the book with Karen, although I may have forgotten to mention that she wasn't on her way to Hell when we took the elevator down to the Underworld.

Okay, I didn't forget, but she had it coming.

I sit for ten more minutes before the door to the office opens. Karen and Mr. Fitz walk out together. I'm surprised to see him. I wouldn't have thought, at his rank, he would be on duty here in the Underworld. I'm not one who believes in signs, but I have to admit it's interesting to run into him like this.

"Stella, can you escort this passenger down to the ferry?" Mr. Fitz asks the bored blue-haired demon sitting behind the reception desk.

No, there aren't normally blue-haired demons running about. She's dyed it, but it's an impressive shade of blue all the same. She's also got a nose ring, an eyebrow ring, and a black widow spider tattoo on her neck. Karen is terrified of her, and I am secretly glad. The demon gives me a sly smile as they go past me, which luckily, Mr. Fitz does not see.

"Got a moment, Finn?" He signals for me to come into his office after they've left.

Shit.

I follow him inside, and as he shuts the door, he motions for me to take a seat. This is not good.

He sits down behind the desk. I've been in this room a few times over the last several decades. It was here long before they built the Promenade Building. A boarding house once sat on the property until the early 1990s, and if I'm not mistaken, this space may have once been a bomb shelter, although I'm not sure why Management would need one in the Underworld. The time period lines up, though. The first time I recall stepping in here was back in the 1970s.

"How are you doing today?" Mr. Fitz leans back in his chair, studying me.

"Okay, I guess." I'm not sure what answer he expects. I try to act casual.

"She was a handful, wasn't she?" He gives me a tense smile.

"Yes, sir. She was."

"After all that," he says, waving his hand around, "I probably would have let her believe she was going to Hell when she came down here, too." He keeps smiling.

"Sorry about that, sir."

"Not a concern. She was rather unpleasant." He runs his hand under his chin. "The reason I wanted to talk to you, though, is because I remembered what you said in your hearing. I wanted to find out if you had experienced any more of the glitches you mentioned. I think you said it was only occurring with the witches."

"Sir?" I act like I don't know what he is talking about. Now, I'm thinking this is less of a sign and I'm wondering why he is bringing it up.

"At your hearing, it came up that you had questioned an AoD about one of his Charges. A murdered witch, as I recall."

I open my mouth, then shut it again. This is my chance to share what keeps happening with someone who is higher up, but in the back of my mind, I remember Corsun telling me about the angels manipulating the Times of Death. Is Mr. Fitz actually interested, or is he in on it?

"I had one the other day." I try to sound casual. I debate about showing him the photo I took and wonder whether I should mention the other witch scheduled for later today. I decide not to say anything until I figure out where he's going with this.

"I checked into it some more after you mentioned it," he tells me, and I get the feeling he's studying me for my reaction. "There's no record of any changes to your schedule other than when they needed you for the multi-car accident." He puts his hands together, propping them under his chin. "You know, those kinds of changes aren't unusual when they occur, Finn. Creatures have free will. If they alter their destiny, our network system simply makes the change and accounts for it."

"But that rarely affects the time of death," I argue.

"No, it doesn't affect their time of death, but how they die can change. When that happens, it may get pulled and reassigned to another Grim Reaper or to an Angel of Death, for that matter."

"This isn't like that." I throw caution to the wind. "Here, I'll show you." I pull out my phone and bring up my app. "When it happens, they're always added to my schedule during the night, and it's always a murdered witch. Like this one at 4:27 this afternoon." I hand the phone to him.

He stares down at the screen, then swipes it with his thumb. "Except this one is a human."

"No, that's not right." I take the phone back from him. The file I'm staring at has the information for a forty-two-year-old human named Charles. This morning, it was a fifty-four-year-old male witch named Charlie something. I stare at my phone. "It was a witch. This has changed again since this morning."

He watches me with concern. "When was the last time you requested time off? I know demons don't do that very often. They believe it shows a sign of weakness, but we encourage our angels to—"

"It was a witch. I know it was a witch." I mumble to

myself. I swipe back to the others. "See, these are all witches."

"But not the two for today."

"I had one this morning."

"And that witch was murdered?"

"No, it was food poisoning, but—" I go back to the Charge's file. "I don't understand."

He looks at me sympathetically. "Maybe you misread it?"

"No, I didn't," I snap.

He raises an eyebrow. I'm sure he thinks any minute now, he's going to have to press the button underneath his desk that Management occasionally uses to call for help when a soul refuses to get on the ferry. Of course, it's not usually done for the one responsible for getting them there. The way he's looking at me, I fully expect someone to come in, tranquilize me, and carry me away.

Get it together, Finn.

I want to argue. I know what I saw, but this is something I can't win. I even consider showing him the photo I took of the seal, but taking the photo broke a privacy rule, so I dismiss the idea. Plus, if he discusses any of this with Jack, I'll find myself eternally assigned to the graveyard shift. After this last hearing, I'm in enough trouble.

I take a breath. "I apologize. I haven't been sleeping well." I stick the phone back into my pocket. "I think I was mistaken."

The gentle smile returns. "Of course," Mr. Fitz replies. He slides his business card over to me. I guess he doesn't remember he already gave me one. "If you do run across another one of these witch murders, or maybe find some actual proof that someone is doing something to intentionally change your schedule, please give me a call." He stands, signaling our meeting is over.

"Sorry about that." I stand as well. I give him my *crazy overworked demon* smile.

He puts his hand out to shake mine. I continue to hold my smile through it, but I am fairly certain my fingers now have frostbite.

"Thank you, Finn. I appreciate all your hard work."

"You, too."

Idiot.

CHAPTER 13

October 18:

After my encounter with Mr. Fitz yesterday, it's a relief to find my schedule for today has not been altered and both of my Charges are human. On the other hand, it's now been two days, eight hours, fifteen minutes, and forty seconds since I last saw Chloe. I miss her.

I tell myself having a little space and time to myself is a good thing. And perhaps, this is true since I still can't figure out what happened with my third Charge yesterday. I am ninety-nine percent certain the file on the app said witch and not human when I checked my schedule yesterday morning. I've never had a sudden change like that, so I'm second-guessing myself. Or, maybe I'm obsessing about these witch murders too much.

My thoughts turn back to Chloe as I go into the bathroom to shower. When I come back out to get dressed, I find a text from her on my phone.

Thinking of you. <3

I put my finger over the little heart. She's thinking of

me. Me. I still don't know how I got so lucky. I try to come up with something witty and clever to text back to her.

Thinking of you, too.

I take a breath and hit send.

How is that witty or clever, Finn? They are going to take away your demon and your man card.

Okay, maybe I can come up with something witty and clever after I've had my caffeine and doughnut fix.

I set the phone aside and start to dress. It feels like the temperature has dropped some more. We have another day of clouds and rain on the way. I go with a black long-sleeved T-shirt, jeans, and black Brooks running shoes. I check my phone again as I step into the elevator. No new messages from Chloe. It's a little after 9:00. I suspect she's in her first meeting, workshop, or whatever they're calling it.

I have two reaps this afternoon, but my morning is wide open. With nothing to occupy my time, my thoughts keep coming back to the witch murders. Mr. Fitz wants proof. What I should do is leave it alone, but maybe finding out about those symbols can help. I stop at Dunks to grab my usual coffee and an old fashioned doughnut, then head over to the library.

There are quite a few people inside the library for a Monday morning, but it's strangely quiet. You could literally hear a pen drop in here, and I do because one falls out of the pocket of my coat when I pull out the piece of paper I wrote the book titles on. A couple of people glance in my direction as I bend down to pick it up.

I haven't visited this particular library in years. And by

years, I mean, since around the time it opened back in 1895. Oddly, little has changed. They've kept the long wooden tables, which were here when it originally opened. Even the smell is the way I remember. Taking a moment, I look upward to admire the stained glass windows and tall, coffered ceiling.

Back from my trip down memory lane, I go over to the counter where a young brunette with streaks of green in her hair sits in front of a computer.

"I'm trying to track down these three books." Despite my attempt to whisper, my voice comes out louder than expected. I cringe. I slip her the piece of paper with the titles on it.

She peers up at me over the top of her tortoiseshell glasses but doesn't comment. Setting the paper down next to the computer, she taps around on the keyboard.

"All three are out on loan at the moment," she says finally.

"On loan?"

"The library occasionally loans out manuscripts to certain people and institutions. You know, for research or for item documentations." She hands the list back to me. "These three are on loan until the end of the month."

"Can you tell me who has them now?" I rest my arms on the counter and give her my best smile.

"We're not supposed to—"

I cock my head to the side, using every ounce of my demon charm. "Please."

She blinks. "I don't know—" She glances around nervously. I continue to stare at her. She purses her lips before finally giving a little sigh. She writes down the name and address, then flips the paper over. She scribbles down something else before handing the paper back to me.

F Michael

1545 Hanover Street

"Thank you." I take the paper from her.

"My number is on the back."

I give her a wink and head toward the door.

Back outside, the expected rain has arrived. Rather than walk, I opt for a rideshare. Ten minutes later, I'm at my destination. I shake my head as I get out of the car.

Unbelievable.

The address she sent me to belongs to St. Peter's Cathedral. Just my luck. It's a church.

Shit.

I stand in the middle of the sidewalk on the other side of the street, staring up at the Gothic arches and the cross atop the roof. Obviously, F Michael stands for Father Michael. I question why the good father is borrowing manuscripts about demonology, mythology, and archaic languages from a library. In as many days, I also question again exactly why I'm doing this. I don't have a good answer for that, either. It's like an itch I keep needing to scratch.

You might think since I've got the whole demon thing going on, I can't enter a church. This is incorrect. My understanding is that I won't burst into flames, but I can expect a lot of nausea, and if I stay inside too long, my skin will feel like it's crawling to the point where I could go mad. Oh, and there's also the little fact that should the priest discover what I am, he may want to perform an exorcism on me. So, it adds an extra element of fun to this little adventure. I frown as I consider whether I seriously want to do this.

My first thought is to forget the whole thing. Or maybe I could run inside in Grim Reaper mode and see if I can locate the books, but I wouldn't know where to look. Plus, I don't want to explain to Management why I'm visiting a church, so that's not happening. After the incident the other day, I'm sure they wonder what is going on with me, and I honestly don't understand it myself.

I take a deep breath.

You can do this, Finn.

My inner pep talk to myself doesn't work.

With as much determination as I can muster, I march across the street before I change my mind. Climbing up the three steps, I reach for the doorknob. My hand stops in mid-air. The large circular handles and framework of the massive wooden doors of the church look suspiciously like wrought iron. The builders of these old Gothic churches loved to demon-proof everything.

Luckily, I caught it in time, or I'd have one nasty burn. I remember my driving gloves in the pocket of my raincoat. Pulling them on, I put a single gloved finger on the handle. When I'm sure nothing bad is going to happen, I put my entire hand on it. It feels like I am taking something hot out of the oven, but with the glove on, my skin's not burning.

The first wave of nausea hits me before I even get my foot completely over the threshold. I immediately feel incredibly warm. Stepping inside, I worry for a moment I'm wrong about churches. Maybe I am about to catch on fire. If a demon walks into a church and bursts into flames, does that mean they committed suicide? An odd giggle escapes from my lips. I slap a hand over my mouth to stifle it.

What the hell?

I push everything out of my mind, then take a few more steps inward until I'm about three feet inside the door. I move forward another three feet, and another. I regret eating breakfast. This is such a bad idea. From the recesses of my mind comes the old saying about "sweating like a whore in church on a Sunday morning." This is how I feel. I am so hot. It's like I'm burning from the inside out.

I don't think I can do this.

"Are you here for confession? We normally only hear confessions until 11:00, but if you need me to—" A voice starts, but quickly fades away. I gaze to my left. A short gray-haired man with a prominent bald spot on his head stares at me in concern. He's standing in front of what I'm guessing is a confessional. The black pants and shirt, along with the white collar and purple stole he wears, gives away he's a priest.

I fixate on the purple stole. It's the same color priests wear when they perform exorcisms. My stomach rolls.

"You don't look so well." He peers at me over his round-rimmed glasses. "Are you feeling okay?"

"I think I've made a mistake." I somehow get the words out. Coming in here is positively one of the dumbest ideas I have ever had in my life.

"Coming down from a high, are we?" He sounds a bit condescending, but his expression is sympathetic. "Do you want me to call your family or an ambulance?"

I shake my head. "No, I'm okay."

I. Am. So. Not. Okay.

"Alright then." He gives me a gentle smile. "Come on, we'll get you some tea. You'll feel better." He walks past me. I turn to see where he's going. There's a downward staircase to the left of the door I came in.

"Narcotics Anonymous meets down here every Tuesday evening and Saturday morning. I'll get you a pamphlet before you leave," he tells me as I follow him down the stairs.

I must really look bad.

We end up in what I assume is a reception hall. In the

center of the room are several round tables with metal chairs for seating, and to the right is a kitchen with an open pass-through. Beneath the window sits a coffeemaker, a coffee urn, condiments, stirrers, and rows of stacked white Styrofoam coffee cups. The church is apparently not into saving the planet.

"Actually, I'm here to see Father Michael." I will the bile in my throat not to come up as I follow him into the darkened kitchen. I blink rapidly when he turns on the fluorescent lights overhead. I still feel ill, but at least down here I don't feel like I'm about to puke my guts out like the little girl in *The Exorcist*. I'm cold and clammy now, so maybe I don't have to worry about spontaneous combustion after all. Still, I wish he would get rid of the purple stole. The sight of it is hard to take, and for some weird reason, I have the urge to hiss at it. Unfortunately, he seems to have forgotten he's wearing it.

"I'm Father Michael, but everyone calls me Father Mike." He gets a metal tea kettle with a dent in the side off the stove and takes it over to the sink. Glancing over at me, he asks, "What can I help you with?"

"The library told me they loaned you a few books." I watch as he returns the kettle to the stove and turns on the burner. He takes two brown coffee mugs off a rack on the counter, then starts opening and closing cabinet doors. He goes down the line, opening one door after the other.

"I wish they would quit moving the teabags," he mutters. Opening the last door in the row, he brings out a yellow box with a red label and a second smaller one with peppermints on the front of it.

He takes another look at me. "Peppermint tea, I think." He puts the bigger box back before taking two teabags out of the smaller one and placing one in each mug. "Which books?"

I take the list out of my coat pocket and hand it to him. He unfolds the paper. His eyebrows go up. He stares at me over the top of his glasses again. "You're obviously not a cop." He eyes me suspiciously. "Reporter?"

Sure, let's go with that. "Yes, I'm working on a story—"

"I'm uncertain about whether the police would want me talking to reporters about an open investigation." He cuts me off. He turns his attention to the teakettle as it whistles. "I don't think they want anyone to know I do consulting work for them." He pours the hot water into the two coffee mugs and hands me one.

It's the books I want to see, but I'm curious now. "Do you consult for them often?" I ask as I take the cup from him. He stares at my gloves. I forgot to take them off.

"Off the record?"

I follow him out of the kitchen to where the coffee supplies are. "Yes, off the record." I watch while he takes the teabag out of his mug. He tosses it into the garbage.

"They call on me from time to time. It might surprise you to learn how often the devil, demonic creatures, and other things like that come up in criminal cases." He picks up a canister of sugar, adding a generous amount to his mug. "Or since you're writing a story on it, maybe not." He considers this while he stirs his tea.

I ignore the fact he's called me a creature and a thing in one breath. I'd like to see his face if I told him he was talking to one of those creatures. My eyes land back on the purple stole and I quickly table the idea.

Turning my attention to the teabag in my mug, I attempt to remove it first without taking my gloves off but realize that's not happening. Setting the coffee mug down, I remove them and stuff them into the pocket of my coat. "There are some symbols I've heard about. I'm trying to do research on them."

I've never had peppermint tea before. After adding my teabag to his in the trash, I pour only the smallest amount of sugar into the tea. I take a sniff. As far as tea goes, it doesn't smell too bad.

"You must have a source inside the police department. They haven't released that information to the public yet." He sets his mug down on one of the tables. "Have a seat. I'll be back in a second."

I wait until he's gone, then pull out a chair. Tea with a priest. This passes over some of the strange things I've done in my life and goes straight to the bizarre.

In front of me, there's a giant bulletin board on the wall. It's decorated with cutouts of pumpkins and autumn leaves for the month of October. I study the flyers pinned to it. There's a potluck dinner next Saturday, the church wants donations for a winter coat drive, and they're having a Trunk or Treat the week before Halloween. I raise an eyebrow at the skeleton in the upper right corner, and yes, an image of a Grim Reaper in the bottom left, complete with black robe and scythe.

You can't make this stuff up.

As I'm eying the images on the flyer, Father Mike returns with a large leatherbound book. It has seen better days. The leather is peeling off the cover and the binding is completely worn out. He sets it down in front of me, then takes a seat on the opposite side of the table. I'm relieved to see he has removed the purple stole. He can't help himself, though. Without saying a word, he also sets down a NA brochure.

Subtle, Father, subtle.

He picks up his mug and takes a sip. "I believe what you're looking for is in there." He gestures toward the book. "Page three hundred and fifty-three."

The text is an ancient language, which predates Latin. I've seen it before, but I don't remember enough of the language to read much of it.

"The book is *The Study of Demonology: Guide to the Nine Keys and the Book of Nightmares, Volume One*," he says as I stare at the cover. He sets the mug back on the table and puts his hands around it as I turn the pages. "Researching demonology is a hobby of mine, I guess you could say. Well, anything to do with the occult and the supernatural. It fascinates me."

I wonder what the church thinks about this. I'm not sure how to respond. I remain silent as I carefully flip through the pages. The book is heavy on illustrations. They portray almost every kind of demon you can imagine and several that don't exist. Most of the drawings are wildly inaccurate. If this is the first volume, I wonder what's in Volume Two. I can't read most of the text, but from the images, it's safe to say this volume has some unusual ideas about demons.

I keep turning the pages until I reach page three hundred and fifty-three. It has illustrations for nine symbols, but from the few words I can make out, they are called seals. I've seen two of them, and Nelson drew me a picture of the one he saw.

"It took me a while to translate, but from what I can understand, each seal is a key. This was on one of them." He points to an image of a triangle inside a square with smaller circles around it. It matches the one Tina had. "And this one was on the forehead of the body they found in the woods maybe four weeks ago or so." He moves his finger on top of another image. "This is the one that was on the first body they found a few days after Labor Day." It's a circle with three lines and a star inside. "And I believe this is the one they found about four days later. That's when the police called me for a consult."

The police have found four bodies? They must have found two I didn't hear about.

"What do the keys do?" I scan the text, recognizing an occasional word or two.

"Are you familiar with the poem, Dante's Inferno?"

"The nine Circles of Hell?" I try to hold back my amusement. "Yes, I'm somewhat familiar." I want to tell him the descriptions of the rings are wildly inaccurate, just like the images of demons in this book, but I refrain. Case in point, they are physical levels rather than metaphorical, and they aren't circles; they're rectangles. There are nine of them, though, and I guess I should know. I did almost all my time in Hell on Tier Seven. I even have the scars on my back to prove it. In truth, the levels are more like cell blocks in a prison, but I guess in every story lies a bit of truth.

"You think each symbol is a key to one circle?" I push the thoughts of my incarceration out of my mind.

"I think someone believes they are. Especially since they desecrated the bodies."

Meaning they took their hearts. He continues telling me what the text says while I carefully turn through the pages of the book. He doesn't realize the victims are witches, but the gist of what he tells me is that each murder creates a key, which allows the bearer to enter one level of Hell. Opening the ninth level on one of the four equinoxes can, for a lack of an easier way to explain it, could let someone overthrow Lower Management and rule Hell. In other words, somebody is planning a coup.

"So, each death unlocks one level. That's interesting." I don't realize at first that I've said what I was thinking aloud. I'm unconsciously scratching the top of my hand with my fingernails. It feels like a bug is walking across it. I have to get out of here soon.

"Yes, but using all the keys won't do any good unless the killer has one of these." Father Mike points to another illustration. It's an image of something that looks like a cross between a dagger and a short sword, but the blade resembles a long ice pick. "It's made of silver. The Order of Reformed Cistercians of Our Lady of La Trappe forged it back in the 1600s. Supposedly, it's the only thing that can kill Satan."

Chloe didn't describe the blade stolen from the museum, but I'm willing to bet my Harley the missing blade is the one in the drawing.

"What else would someone need to do this?" I run my fingers under the collar of my shirt, trying hard not to scratch my neck. I pick up the coffee mug and drink a few sips of tea, hoping to distract myself. It doesn't help. Now, it feels like something is crawling up my leg. I tap my foot.

"I'm still researching that part of things. I suspect you would need something like an incantation. What you would call a spell. Of course, if whoever is doing this truly believes they can open the gates of Hell, they might make one up. Lots of sick minds out there." He taps the side of his head. He leans back in his chair, studying me. "Do I need to be concerned about whatever it is you've taken? You're looking worse."

I set down the coffee mug. "No, I'm fine." I rub at my wrist. "I've probably taken up enough of your time, though." Picking up my gloves, I quickly pull them on, so I don't claw at myself. "You've been most helpful."

We both stand.

"Glad to do it. Remember, it's all off the record, so don't quote me." He winks, reaching down to pick up the brochure. "Tuesdays and Saturdays. Everyone is welcome." He hands it to me.

I nod. Saluting him with the brochure, I look for an exit. I need to go. Now.

"Come on, I'll show you out."

I follow him back up the stairs. The door to freedom is in sight.

"Thank you."

"My pleasure." He puts his hand out to shake mine.

Shit. What's this?

I stare at it. I'm wearing gloves, but he's a Holy man. This could go either way. I'm not sure what will happen if he touches me. Gingerly, I stick my hand out. I close my eyes. His hand is overly warm, just like the door handle. I open my eyes again. *Phew.* I'm okay.

"What is your name?" He places his other hand on top of mine.

Seriously? Any respectable demon knows not to give their name to a priest.

"What?" I stare at him.

"Your name?" He fixes his gaze on me. "I'll pray for you."

I blink. "Corsun."

He nods. "Good to meet you, Corsun."

"You, too."

He lets go of my hand, and I turn to push on the door. It doesn't open. I try again. Nothing.

I'm trapped.

Fuck. Fuck. Fuck.

Eyes wide, I whirl around to face him.

"Sorry about that." He gives me an odd look. Shuffling past me, he gives the door a hard shove with his shoulder. "It sticks in wet weather sometimes." He holds the door open. "Have a nice day."

I walk by him as calmly, but quickly, as I can. I feel him watching me as I run down the church steps.

Almost there, Finn.

I drop to my knees on the wet sidewalk, throwing up in the church flower bed. Long and hard. The little girl from The Exorcist has nothing on me. Peppermint tea, breakfast, coffee, maybe even the undigested remains from last night's dinner along with the lining from my stomach—it all comes up. Then, the dry heaves start. My eyes water. When it's finally over, I sit back on my heels and wipe my mouth with the back of my glove.

"Tuesday evenings and Saturday mornings." Father Mike's voice rings out from the open door of the church. "All are welcome."

I ignore him.

CHAPTER 14

October 20:

My schedule is normal yet again. Just like it has been since Sunday. I have one early morning reap and one in the late afternoon. Both humans. I got a little distracted texting with Chloe this morning, so I'm running late. I skip shaving, take a quick shower, dress for rainy weather, and I'm out the door. I don't have time for my coffee and doughnut, so I head straight to the intersection of Blue Hills Avenue and Morton Street.

My first Charge is a twenty-four-year-old man named Jeremy, who in about three minutes will become the fatality of a two-vehicle accident.

Jeremy is the only one scheduled to die, so I stand on the side of the road in the rain by myself, waiting until another car hits his. Not the fault of my guy, though. Jeremy is turning left when the other driver runs the red light. Jeremy stays with me for a few minutes as we watch the paramedics try to revive him.

"This sucks." He flickers on and off like a light bulb.

Then, he's gone.

One of the paramedics tells the other he's got a pulse. They confirm which hospital they are transporting him to, then load him into the ambulance. There's not much room for me, but I squeeze in beside them. They also have a third paramedic riding along, a trainee or something. It's about to get crowded in here in a few minutes when Jeremy joins me again. We're about five minutes out from the hospital when he goes into cardiac arrest. He watches as they try to revive him again.

"This really sucks."

"I know."

He's not completely convinced he's dead, so we end up following his body into the emergency room while they attempt to revive him for a third time.

Time of Death 10:02.

My second reap for the day is at 4:50. Gordon is a sixty-three-year-old CEO who passes from a brain aneurysm with no symptoms at all. He tells me he felt fine one minute and now he's with me. He bypasses Stages One and Two and goes straight into Stage Three. Well, I assume it's Stage Three. He offers me a bribe if I'll send him back. I guess that counts as bargaining, doesn't it?

"It's tempting, Gordon, but no." Even if I was interested, I wouldn't know where to begin.

I'm still thinking about this after I drop him off at the ferry. Did Corsun know what he was talking about when he told me some of the angels were manipulating the times and days of death? Sometimes, he knows things, and other times he just likes to say things to sound important and hear himself talk.

It occurs to me as I'm riding the elevator back up to the lobby that all the murdered witches I've dealt with were last-minute additions to my schedule. The so-called glitch I've been noticing. And there's still that strange one from Sunday, the one I thought was a witch who changed to a human on my app.

What if something more sinister is going on and it's not simply a crazy human serial killer out there? Is it possible I've overlooked the obvious and it's an inside job? Maybe it's one of the partners from Corsun's law firm or someone from Management moving the death dates around and murdering witches. What if they really are trying to take over Hell? The autumn equinox is at the end of the week, so if it's true, the killer is running out of time. If I knew how many witches they've murdered, maybe I could get a better sense of what is going on and either prove or disprove my crazy theory.

The problem is that I know how I can find out, but I have no clue how to go about it. I'm going to have to rely on a higher source for information. And by higher source, I mean Corsun. I know exactly where to find him.

One thing I can say about Corsun, he's a creature of habit. On Wednesday nights, he's at his favorite watering hole on Dalton Street. It's his go-to place for eating chili and drinking beer.

As usual, he's sitting in his regular spot, the last bar stool on the left. It's situated next to the side exit door, and he's got his back to it. This sitting arrangement makes me uneasy. I prefer a table toward the back where I can keep an eye on things. I suspect he likes it because he can make a quick getaway if a jealous husband or boyfriend shows up looking for him. He'll take a stand if he has to, but Corsun considers himself more of a lover than a fighter.

The bar is busy for a Wednesday night. I slide onto the stool next to his, catching him by surprise. A bottle of Tabasco sauce and an empty bowl with a spoon in it sits in front of him. He's finished his meal and is chatting up the bartender in between drinks of his beer. She's bleach blonde, tan, and well-endowed. Definitely his type.

"Same." I motion to the mug Corsun holds when she looks my way.

"Finn, my man, what are you doing here?" he asks as she goes to fetch my drink. I suspect he came here straight from work. He's wearing a navy suit and a white shirt, but he's undone a couple of buttons and taken off his tie. It's lying on the bar a couple inches from the empty bowl. There's a chili stain on it.

"Just in the neighborhood." I try to sound casual.

"Mmm hmm." He narrows his eyes. He's not buying it for one second.

I wait until the bartender returns with my beer before I speak. "I need some information."

"I thought so." He sets the mug down. "What's up?"

Where to begin? "You remember at the hearing, when the angel from Upper Management wanted to know why I was asking about the murdered witch Nelson handled a couple of weeks ago?"

"Yeah, so?"

"I think the murder is related to some kind of ritual." I glance around to make sure no one is listening. It's mostly humans, but I spot two demons sitting at a table back in the far right corner. It doesn't appear they're paying any attention to us at all. I listen in on their conversation for a few seconds to confirm they aren't. They're having a debate over whether Johnny or Daniel is the better sensei in *Cobra Kai*.

Oh, please. It's Johnny, of course. Discussion closed. I roll my eyes.

I turn my attention back to Corsun. "I believe someone is planning to overthrow Lower Management and take over Hell."

He is mid-drink as I say this. He stares at me dumbfounded, then bursts out laughing. Part of his drink spews out of his mouth in a spray. Luckily, not in my direction. He continues to laugh as he grabs a napkin off the bar.

Okay, not the reaction I was expecting.

He wipes his mouth, his smile fading. "Shit, you're serious about this, aren't you?" He sets his drink down again. "What the hell are you talking about?"

I tell him about the symbols on the witch's foreheads and my visit to the church. He shakes his head at me. "You've lost your mind."

That's highly possible.

I dig the phone out of my pocket to show him the photo of the symbol on the last witch's forehead. "Here, I've got a photo of one of the seals. There are supposedly nine of them in total."

He pushes my arm away. "You're taking photos of dead people now?" For a moment, he looks like he's about to toss his chili back up.

I glance around to make sure no one heard him. "No!" I reply sharply. "Well, only her forehead." I shrug.

"You are one sick puppy." He gives me a smile and what I think is a nod of approval.

"It's not like that."

He takes the phone from me, studying the photo. "It's

probably one of those Satanic devil worshipers. I dated one of those once. They are so into demons. She liked to paint symbols, too. All over my—"

I snatch my phone back from him, hoping to divert him from giving me a play-by-play. After hearing the stories about a few of his sexual exploits over the years, I have a lot of images stuck in my brain I've never been able to get rid of. I don't need another. "I don't think it's like that. Devil worshipers, I mean."

"All I was going to say was she liked to paint all these pentacles on my chest. She was like a wildcat in bed. Liked to claw and scratch—"

"Let's try to focus here." I work to get him back on track. I tell him about the blade that was stolen from the museum. "I believe it's all connected."

He finishes his beer, then waves at the bartender for another.

I still haven't touched mine. I take a sip. It's not Fat Tire, but it's not bad.

"Well, if it's true. I'm sure the Big Guy has a lot of security in place. You've been there, you should know."

He just had to bring that up. "Thanks for the reminder."

The bartender sets another beer in front of him. She picks up Corsun's empty mug and dishes before giving me a wink and heading off toward the kitchen. Corsun scowls at me as I suppress my smile.

"What kind of information do you need?" he asks, taking a swig of his second beer. Or maybe it's his third. I'm not sure how long he was here before I arrived.

"I want to know how many witches they've murdered. There's got to be a way to find out." I tell him about the ones I know of, and how my schedule has been messed up on the day the deaths on my watch have occurred. By my count, the number of deaths is already up to six.

"Mate, you need to let this go." Corsun shakes his head. "Seriously. You're already on thin ice after the incident with the angel. If they find out—" He takes three or four more swallows of beer, then wipes his upper lip with the back of his hand. "Why are you still pursuing this?"

"I don't know," I reply. It's an honest answer. "For some reason, I feel like I need to see this through. Figure out what is going on. Isn't it strange to you that all these latest murdered witches keep ending up on my schedule? That's three of them now, and I think there might have even been a fourth one before it got changed." I still can't figure that one out. "It can't be a coincidence. I'd like to know who is targeting me and why."

Corsun is silent for a moment. He stares down into his beer. Finally, he takes a deep breath. "Look, the only way you're going to find that kind of information out is to check the data on one of Management's computers. They classify all that stuff. Even my office doesn't have access to it."

"Do you know a way I can do that?" I run my finger over the handle of the mug in front of me until it hits a chip in the glass.

"You're sure you want to get involved in whatever this is you think you've discovered?" He makes a motion with his hand. "I mean, if they are planning to off Lucifer, they may be someone you don't want to mess with."

Do I? I'm not sure. "I think I have to follow it out," I tell him with more conviction than I feel.

"Your funeral." He finishes off his drink.

I raise an eyebrow.

"Well, you know what I mean," he says. "Besides,

having a hostile takeover of Management might not be such a bad thing. Have you thought about that?"

"They're murdering witches," I remind him, but I can't help myself. "Plus, better the devil you know than—"

He sighs, shaking his head. Pulling out his billfold from the pocket of his jacket, he takes out his key card. He slides it across the bar to me. "Security changes out about a quarter to eleven. They won't have anyone manning the desk for about forty-five minutes because they are a bunch of slackers. The graveyard shift takes its sweet time coming back to man the desk. Use this to get in the front door. They lock it after eight o'clock, but this will open it. Don't use the elevators."

"How do I get upstairs?"

"Take the fire escape on the left once you're inside. Use it to get up to Jack's floor. If anyone asks me about the log entry, I'll tell them I forgot a file I needed." He lowers his voice. "Jack can never remember his password. He keeps it taped inside the desk drawer."

I pick up the key card, sliding it into my pocket. "How do I get back out without being seen?"

"Well, if it were me, I'd do that little invisibility trick you do." He twirls his finger in a circle.

My little invisibility trick? What am I, a trained seal? *Seriously?*

"They'll know I was in the building."

"Oh, yeah. I always forget about that." He taps his finger against his lips. "Okay, your other option is to go down to the basement when you're ready to leave. Open the fire door on the opposite side of the room and go out that way."

"Sounds easy enough."

"The alarm will go off when you do. You better be ready

to run. You'll have demon and angel magistratus there in minutes, if not seconds."

"Not so easy, then." I want to ask why he knows all this but decide it's better not to know.

"You'll figure it out." Pulling out his billfold, he sets a ten-dollar bill on the bar. He chugs down the rest of his drink, then holds it up like he's about to make a toast. He checks to see where the bartender is. "I've got somewhere I've got to be in about twenty minutes." He raises his eyebrows and grins. It means he's two, three, or four-timing the bartender. "Good luck."

"Yeah, thanks." I scowl.

He gets down off the bar stool, then motions to the bartender for the check. "He's paying," he tells her when she walks over. Corsun slaps me hard on the back, leaving me to settle his tab.

Why am I not surprised?

I'm not new to breaking into places, but I'm not exactly comfortable breaking into the building I frequent every day. Plus, since it's a neutral zone between Upper and Lower Management, I don't know who would have jurisdiction if I get caught.

In case you're wondering, the ferry doesn't shut down at night. It's only this port of entry that closes. The night shift uses the back entrance at one of the 24-hour superstores over on Commonwealth Avenue.

I wait until 11:47 to enter the Promenade Building using the key card Corsun gave me. He was right. The lobby is completely empty. In all the years I have been coming here, I've never noticed a door to the fire escape near the front entrance. It's the same gray color as the wall and blends perfectly into it. I don't know how I've missed it. I open it and quickly shut the door behind me.

Jack's office is on the twenty-second floor. I start up the stairs, then make the mistake of looking up. There are a lot of stairs. I'm in shape. No big deal, right? I can do this. I start climbing. Lobby to the first floor. First floor to the second. I pass the third, the fourth, and the fifth.

This isn't so bad.

Sixth, seventh, eighth, and ninth. I stop to take my jacket off on the landing of the tenth. I'm still doing okay as I make it to the fifteenth floor, but I'm feeling it a little by the time I get to the seventeenth.

Crap, that's a lot of stairs.

Only five more floors to go. I can do this. I've lost count, but there's twelve steps to each flight, so I think this is number 203 or 204.

I get to 232, or maybe it's 233? I stop for a moment to catch my breath. I am feeling every bit of my three thousand years. Bending over, I rest my hands on my legs for a minute.

I've got this. As I open the door to the floor where Jack's office is, it occurs to me I'll have to go back down the same stairs in a little while.

Yeah, let's not think about that right now.

I walk down the hall to Jack's office. The top of his desk is a mess. He's got folders piled everywhere and my file is sitting on top of the stack in the middle. It's about four inches thick and full of papers. I didn't come here to read my file, but I'm not about to let a chance like this pass, either. I scan through it, but there's not much I don't already know about. My latest disciplinary action is on top, along with my most recent transportation statistics. I'm insulted to read Management considers my performance rate average, but whatever.

The folder also contains printouts of my reaps from the last few weeks. I recognize the names, but they all have a series of letters and numbers next to them. I suspect it's a type of coding Management uses for tracking purposes, but none of it makes sense to me. I put my file back in its place and concentrate on why I'm here.

The password is exactly where Corsun said it would be. It takes me only a couple of seconds to log in. I would think Management would have the latest technology, but the computer looks old. No, not old. It's ancient. There is also something sticky all over the keyboard I'm trying hard not to think about.

The problem is, I don't know what I'm searching for. I stare at the screen. Jack's computer has a Grim Reaper icon on it that looks the same as my phone app. I click on it. It takes me to a screen with a list of names. I recognize several of them as other Grim Reapers in the area. I scan until I find my name. Since it's after midnight, it already has the schedule for my reaps on it for later today. No names. It only has the times for the reaps and some codes. GH473, GP8T6. A quick check shows the times match the ones I have on my app. Only I have the names of my Charges along with their information instead of the codes.

I click on an arrow to switch to Friday's date. That page is blank except for the word *Pending*. Dead end.

I go back to today's date, then back to the one from yesterday, then the day before, and back, back, back. Same variation of the codes every day except on the days when I have three reaps. On those days, there is a third code.

GS66S. I saw this somewhere else. It was on the printout of my performance over the last few weeks.

Grabbing my file, I open it and check the report. There it is. The same code. I flip through the pages. The report is the passenger manifest for the ferry. Besides the TOD, it has their exact clock-in time through the turnstile, then a breakdown of my transportation times. By checking it against the files on my app, I notice both Carol's name and the witch named Tina have the GS66S code. It doesn't mean witch because there are other witches who don't have the same code, but these two were both murdered the same way.

That's what the code means. Not that they were murdered, but that the Charge is an addition to an already established schedule. Since all the additions have been murdered witches, however, it might as well mean the same thing. The question is, how do I find out how many murders there have been when I can only see my reaps on the screen?

I run a hand through my hair.

Think, Finn. Think.

I go back to the list of Grim Reaper names. There's a lot of them. Some I know and some I don't. If I go through them one by one, it will take all night. I'm about to give up when I spot the three little lines up at the top right side of the screen. When I click on them, there's a menu. It brings up a search option, which opens on another screen. Now, it wants another password. I try Jack's, but it defiantly beeps at me.

A quick glance at my watch tells me it's now 12:20. I've got maybe ten minutes left if I want to go out the front door and not set off an alarm in the basement. I'm running out of time. I don't know enough about Jack to make a guess what he would use for a password. Corsun said Jack couldn't remember his password, though. I stare at the screen.

Inspiration strikes.

P-A-S-S-W-O-R-D.

And, I'm in. *Seriously, Jack?*

I quickly type in the code and hit search. I get five hits. Two are from the middle of September that were handled by other Grim Reapers, then the most recent three Charges, which are all mine.

What the fuck? I thought I was imagining it, but it really is almost like someone has singled me out for whatever is going on.

I do some quick math in my head. Nelson had one Charge murdered this way, and the priest mentioned two others I hadn't heard about. Those were probably handled by the Angels of Death since he said the deaths happened in early September, and I don't see any corresponding dates on the list for that time period. That makes eight murdered witches all killed the same way. A sick feeling enters my stomach. Someone has one more witch to kill before they can unlock all nine seals. If I'm right, someone really is planning to overthrow Hell.

I confess, I was hoping I was imagining all of this. But I'm not. It's real.

Holy shit.

I snap a quick photo of the computer screen and the ferry manifest with my phone before logging out of the system, then quickly head for the stairs. It's much easier going down than it was going up, but it still takes time to do it, and I was on the computer longer than expected. By the time I make it to the lobby, over fifty minutes have passed. I don't even have to peek out the door to know security is back in the lobby. I can hear the loud music playing from here.

I continue down the steps until I come to another metal door. I open it just enough to make sure no one is waiting for me on the other side. All is quiet, except for the hum of the electrical equipment. There's a heavy smell of machinery oil, and brown water is dripping from a pipe overhead. Most of the fluorescent lights are burnt out, but one keeps flickering on and off like a strobe light.

Ever see one of those movies where a serial killer leaves a body for the police in some out-of-the-way location, then they hide in the shadows waiting for the detective to show up? The basement of the Promenade Building is a lot like that. Creepy doesn't begin to describe it, and that's coming from a demon.

I find the door Corsun told me about. The sign above it informs me it is indeed an exit, although the X isn't lit. The sign on the door notes it's for emergency exits only. More importantly, it states an alarm will activate if I open it. *How does Corsun always know this stuff?*

Now comes the fun part, evading the magistratus. In my favor, they are big and husky, meaning they don't move particularly fast. They are also not always the brightest of demons, so my chances of getting away from them are fairly good. Of course, if it's the angel magistratus, that's another story altogether. The few I've had to deal with are more like Wallace. Tall, arrogant, no-nonsense types who take their jobs very seriously. There's no fighting one of them off if they catch me.

Since the Underworld is directly below where I'm standing, I'm betting it's the demon magistratus who will make an appearance. The problem is the alarm going off could summon one or two of them, or if it's a slow night in Hell, fifty of them could appear. If the security tonight is angel, I honestly don't know how it would go down. I try not to think about it.

In retrospect, perhaps this was not the smartest of plans. It might work out better if I spend the night in Corsun's office and leave first thing in the morning. I actually like that plan a lot better. I head back to the stairwell door and—it's locked.

Out the fire exit, it is.

Hood up. Gloves on. I open the door. The alarm goes off immediately. It's ear-splitting and loud enough to wake the dead. Figuratively speaking, that is. Alarms won't wake the dead, although it wouldn't surprise me if this one did. It really is loud.

The sound is bad enough, but my timing is so incredibly perfect, I open the door right into a human security guard standing in front of it. It knocks the cigarette he's smoking out of his hand. We're both so surprised, neither one of us moves for a couple of seconds.

"Shit." The security guard stares at me.

It's dark and I'm wearing the hoodie so he can't see my face, but I can sure see the startled expression on his.

"Fuck," I mutter under my breath.

I recover first and take off running. He's human, but he's fast. I'm slightly faster, but not by much. He calls for the other security guard on his radio. This sucker is directly behind me, and he might have a chance at catching me.

Shit. Shit. Shit.

A tan Peugeot screeches to the curb up ahead. The door swings open.

"Get in!" It's Corsun.

I don't hesitate. I jump in the car. He hits the gas pedal, throwing me back in the seat.

"What are you doing here?" I ask when I can sit up straight again.

"Saving your ass." Corsun shifts from first to second. The transmission grinds in response.

I reach for the seatbelt as he cuts a car off in the turning lane. He makes a sharp left turn, then follows it with a quick right before going down a back alley. His driving is erratic even when we're not on the run from someone. Which, I guess, is why when I know we're going to have to make a quick getaway, I usually never let him drive. I snap the seatbelt into place, putting my hand on the dashboard as the right tires go up over the curb.

To my relief, he slows down to a normal speed by the time we reach Atlantic Avenue. Since I encountered the human security guard, it's unlikely the magistratus will respond at all. Even if they do, they won't go any farther than a few blocks on foot for a simple break and enter. They won't investigate either since I escaped their jurisdiction. I am, thankfully, in the clear. I let out a breath.

We come to a red light, and the Peugeot rolls to a stop. A patrol car pulls up next to us in the turning lane. Corsun glances over as the light changes to green. The officer bobs his head at us. Corsun smiles and waves. We go straight as the patrol car turns.

Corsun bursts out laughing. I laugh, too. I'm not sure why. It takes us a good two minutes before we can stop.

"You are one crazy demon." He shakes his head. "Did you get what you needed?"

"Yeah, I think so." I tell him what I found.

"What are you going to do with the information?"

I shrug. "I'm not sure yet. Jack doesn't want to know

about it, and I'm not certain I can trust the angels. Even Mr. Fitz."

"You could contact—" Corson glances downward.

Lower Management? I frown at him. He shrugs. That would force me to deal with my old supervisor. The one I tried to kill. "Only as a last resort," I mutter.

Corson pulls the car up to the entrance of the Echelon. "Well, let me know what you decide."

"I will." I reach into my pocket, pulling out his security card. "Before I forget. Thanks."

He waves his hand. "Keep it. I lifted it off an angel a few weeks ago."

He opens the glove compartment. It's full of cards, three or four phones, and several billfolds.

I narrow my eyes at him.

"What? It's not like the angels need any of it. Don't they take a vow of poverty or something?"

"You mean priests."

"What?"

"Priests take a vow of poverty. Not angels."

"Oh, well, whatever." He reaches over to grab a phone. He hands it to me. "Hey, I know what you can do. You'll have to find a charger for it, but you can text the information to your angel friend anonymously."

"He's not my friend. Plus, he'll know who it's from. My name is on the transportation report and was on the computer screen, too. Besides, he's the one who said to get him some proof." I start to hand it back to him.

"Well, take it, anyway. I've got more in the trunk."

I shake my head, but I stick the phone into the pocket of my jacket. I open the door. "Thanks for that back there," I say as I get out.

"Anytime." He nods. This means I now owe him a favor.

I shut the door.

Corsun gives a wave before pulling out of the driveway.

I continue to stand there, watching the tires go up over the curb again as the car makes a right. I wait until it disappears around the corner before heading inside.

CHAPTER 15

October 21 Day:

Chloe is back in town. While I was out breaking into a building last night, she was flying home. I stare out the window at the gray skies, wondering when I'll get to see her again. I had hoped I would get to pick her up from the airport, but her boss already made plans to have a car pick them both up and drop them off.

As I get out of bed, my phone pings. It's a text. It's from her.

Got in late last night. Leaving for work now. Andrea's schedule is back to days. :(Maybe we can go out on Saturday, or see you for dinner tonight?

I smile as I read her text. Dinner is great, but I don't want to wait until the weekend to spend time alone with her. I almost text back to let her know she can stay at my place tonight, but if she got in late last night and went into work this early, she's probably tired. I'll have to see what she thinks. The way Andrea's schedule keeps shifting around, it wouldn't surprise me if she's changing it intentionally to keep us apart. Maybe I should see if Chloe wants to move in with me.

Where did that come from? That's a big step, Finn. Remember how it turned out with Ilene?

I'm sure Chloe would agree we're moving things too fast, but I wonder what she would say if I asked. I ponder this as I open the Grim Reaper app. I frown. My schedule has shifted around again. This is the first time it's happened since Sunday. If it actually did change, that is. I'm still undecided about whether it happened or if I imagined the whole thing.

Regardless, I have three reaps today instead of two. If it is another murdered witch, maybe I should send the file to Mr. Fitz, along with the information I got last night.

My first two reaps are both human. A sixty-year-old male at 11:43, and a thirty-one-year-old female at 3:19. My thumb swipes to the next file. It's a 25-year-old witch. Female. Time of Death 7:06. I continue scanning, then check the photo.

And it's Chloe.

What. The. Fuck?

My breath catches. I'm sure I didn't read that right. I start over, rereading the file from the top. I sit down on the edge of the bed because my legs are threatening to give out from under me. In my chest, my heart beats out a staccato like a rampant herd of hopping bunny rabbits.

This is a joke. This is someone's idea of a sick joke. There's no way this is real. Who would do this? Is this Corsun's doing? He has a sick sense of humor, but even he wouldn't do something like this. I dismiss the possibility.

I continue reading. It's Chloe's address. The location of death is at her apartment. It even has her parent's information listed as family waiting for her on the other side. All of her information is correct. The file appears legit.

My entire body goes numb except for the sick feeling in the pit of my stomach. My Chloe is scheduled to die tonight, and by a bizarre twist of fate, I'm the one assigned to get her to the ferry. How is that even possible?

Shit. Shit. Shit.

I forget about the run. My first thought is to go to Chloe. I need to tell her what's going to happen.

No, Finn. She won't believe you.

I could tell her what I am. I could show her the app. I could warn her. Maybe I could try to stop it.

Except I can't. It's against the rules and not in a little "slap on the wrist and don't do it again" kind of way. This is messing with the Universe. It's disrupting fate and the Grand Plan. It's trying to outrun destiny, and it never works out. This is the one law no Grim Reaper or Angel of Death can break. Face it, there's no cheating death.

But it's Chloe.

I need to think.

I take my shower, hoping inspiration strikes while I'm standing under the hot water. It does. Last night, I never asked Corsun about the angels fixing the Time of Death dates. He's going to have to level up. I'll make him tell me if the story is real or if it's only a rumor he's heard.

I finish my shower, fasten a towel around my waist, and pad back into the bedroom for my phone. I haven't completely dried myself off, but I don't care. Sitting on the edge of the bed, I dial Corsun's number. The call goes straight to voicemail. I hang up and try his office number. It goes to voicemail as well. I call back his cellphone, and this time I leave a message.

"Corsun, it's Finn. Call me as soon as you get this message. It's important."

Shit.

I put my head in my hands. How is this happening? It's like a sick cosmic joke and I'm the punchline.

I get it together enough to pull some clothes on. I put off leaving for as long as possible, but finally I have no choice. It's time to head out for my first reap of the day. Meanwhile, Chloe has nine hours, thirty-two minutes, and ten seconds to live unless I can come up with a plan. I skip my daily doughnut and only order coffee. It barely stays down. I chuck the almost full cup into a garbage can a couple of blocks later.

My next few hours all run together. I get my first Charge to the ferry on time but can't remember a thing about him. I spend the next couple of hours wandering aimlessly around the city, thinking, hoping, trying to make sense of this. Looking up, I discover I'm in front of the museum. I have no clue how I got here, but I need to see her. I need to see Chloe.

Inside, I approach the ticket counter. The man sitting behind the window doesn't acknowledge my presence. It takes me a moment to realize I'm still in Grim Reaper mode because I never changed back. Shaking my head at my stupidity, I walk past him.

Get it together, Finn.

The museum is full of loud, screaming school children who apparently are all on a field trip. They're young, maybe third or fourth grade. A volunteer from the museum is giving them a lecture about the T-Rex sitting on the giant platform in the middle of the museum. I remember walking by it the night of the benefit. The night Chloe and I—

I stop myself. I won't think about that now. I need to find Chloe. I check to see if she is helping with the occult exhibit today, but I don't see her. It's only a couple of volunteers keeping an eye on a few of the museum visitors. I continue my search, finally locating her in the back room near the loading docks.

She's dressed almost the way she was on the first day we met. Pale green shirt and a pair of gray dress pants along with those hideous sensible shoes. Her hair is in a ponytail. She yawns, and the circles under her eyes tell me she didn't get much sleep last night.

One of the delivery men chats her up as she looks over an invoice. He mentions one of the new bars in town, then asks if she has plans for the weekend. She sidesteps the question and keeps it all business with him. When she's done checking in the boxes from the truck, she sets down his clipboard on one of the crates and goes back to work. She doesn't give him a second look.

That's my girl.

Realizing she shot him down; he picks up his clipboard and walks back toward the loading dock with his tail between his legs. He can't help himself, though. He stops and turns to watch her, but Chloe doesn't notice. With a sigh, he admits his defeat and finally leaves.

I can't help but smile. She had to have known he was asking her out.

My attention goes back to her as she picks up a small crowbar. She uses it to pry open the smallest of the crates, then sifts through the packing material. It looks like straw.

She chews on the tip of her pen, lost in concentration. I want to make myself known, but how would I explain what I'm doing here or how I appeared out of nowhere?

Taking a seat on one of the nearby crates, I watch as she removes a small statue made of clay. It's Egyptian, perhaps, a warrior with a spear in his hand. The spear is intact, but the head of the statue has broken off. Chloe holds both pieces in her hands, studying them. She carefully glances around. For a moment, I think she senses someone is watching her, but she's only checking to make sure she's alone. She holds out the smaller piece of the statue in her hand, whispering something under her breath. The head disappears from her hand and reappears attached to the bigger piece of the statue.

I smile. Clever. It's the first time I've ever seen her perform magic. I'm impressed, but I may never get the chance to tell her I saw her do it.

She puts the statue on top of a second crate and marks something down on the clipboard, then digs into the crate again. She brings out another statue similar to the first. This one is intact. She sets it down beside the other one.

I continue watching. Time slips by. When I glance at my watch, it's almost time for my next reap. If I don't leave now, I won't make it on time. I don't want to go, but I don't have a choice.

I am a Grim Reaper. This is my job. This is what I do.

It's 6:59. Chloe isn't home yet, and my numerous calls to Corsun have gone unanswered. I wait outside her apartment as the minutes tick away. In a little over seven minutes, she will die. It's her time and there is absolutely nothing I can do about it.

When I first became a Grim Reaper, the death process fascinated me. I would arrive way before a Charge was scheduled to die, specifically so I could watch it happen. I'd even make a guess to determine the outcome. This is one reason I can predict automobile accidents so well. It's like playing a game of chess and knowing you only have so many potential moves.

I've seen every kind of death imaginable. Murder, suicide, accident. I've never enjoyed watching someone die or the aftermath like some demons do, but there is something primal about it that made me want to see it up close and personal. It's never affected me. So what if one person killed another, or someone decided they no longer wanted to exist? Even watching someone do something stupid and pay for it with their life—none of it touched me, so none of it mattered.

At some point, it got to where I no longer wanted to watch. It made me feel like a voyeur invading a Charge's last private moments. Or maybe that's simply what I told myself. It was easier not to care.

Today, it matters. Today, I care. I've told myself all day this is part of the job. Humans and witches care about people, yet they still lose them all the time. It's a part of life. I try to convince myself it's better that I'm escorting Chloe to the ferry than some other Grim Reaper, or worse, an Angel of Death. I'll get to spend a little more time with her. Most of all, I won't have to lie to her anymore.

The problem is, I'm not sure I can let her death happen. I glance at my watch. Two more minutes pass. Time is running out. I want to warn her. I want to stop it. I want to break the unbreakable rule. I want to help her cheat death. But—

This is the Grand Plan of the Universe. It's her fate. Her destiny. Her time. Altering it would have catastrophic consequences for us both. It doesn't matter how much I want to, I cannot interfere.

Almost as if on cue, she arrives at the top of the stairs. She's breathless. Her hair is damp from the evening rain even though she's wearing a coat with a hood.

That's my Chloe.

"Hey!" Her eyes light up as she sees me. She's happy I'm here. "Did you come to see me, or are you here to see Tommy?"

"Both." I try to smile, but I can't. Before I can stop myself, I pull her into my arms, burying my face in her wet hair, so I can memorize her scent. I want to remember what it's like to hold her. We stand like this for a minute in silence. I can feel the seconds drifting away. I don't want to let her go.

She pulls back from me. "What's wrong?" Her eyes study me with concern. "Did something happen? What is it, Finn?"

I can't get the words out. I stare at her, and I can't make a sound.

"Nothing." *Yeah, that sounds real convincing. Keep it together, Finn.*

"Okay, now you're scaring me." Her eyes narrow as she stares at me. She takes her keys out of her purse. "Andrea's asleep, but let me change clothes. We can go get dinner and talk." She puts the key into the lock and turns the knob. "Go feed Tommy. I'll meet you in the hall in a few minutes." She kisses me on the cheek.

I put my hand out to stop her. My fingers touch the

material of her raincoat, but I force myself to pull them back. Her eyes show she's worried about me. The little V forms between her brows, but she gives me a shy smile and disappears into the apartment. She shuts the door behind her. I check my watch. One minute and counting. That's all the time she has left.

Everything around me feels like it's spinning. I slump against the wall next to her door and close my eyes. All I can see is the image of her face. I replay the moment I first saw her, our first kiss, the way she looked at me the first time we made love—

Something crashes in the apartment. My eyes snap open. There's a noise like a thud. Glass breaks. I check my watch again. Forty-five seconds. Forty-five seconds and it's over. Forty-five seconds and I lose her forever.

I. Can't. Let. This. Happen.

Fuck!

Am I doing this?

I'm doing this.

I'm really going to do this.

Taking a deep breath, I start to kick the door in, but my hand goes to the doorknob first. Chloe didn't lock it behind her. I rush inside. A broken lamp is on the floor. There's a strange yellow glow from it streaming across the entire living room floor. I move farther into the room. Another loud thud directs me toward the hallway near the kitchen.

Chloe's purse and keys are on the floor. Going toward the noise, I find a figure dressed in black with their gloved fingers around Chloe's neck. She's trying to fight back, but they've pinned her against the wall. In the back of my mind, I wonder why she isn't using her magic to defend herself. She's probably so scared, she can't.

"Leave her alone!" I charge toward the figure. They

push her aside before turning to face me. The intruder is a man. He takes a swing at me. I deflect the blow and land a surprise punch to his midsection. It catches him off guard, but he quickly recovers. His eyes stare back at me through his ski mask.

I study him for signs of weakness. He's more muscular than I am. He's got some height on me, too. The punch I made barely fazed him at all.

Before I can sidestep, he swings. His fist slams into my jaw. The force knocks me backward. I stumble, falling into the bookcase against the opposite wall. The shelves jolt forward, their contents falling to the floor.

"Finn, watch out!" Chloe shouts from somewhere in the hallway.

The man turns to follow the sound of her voice, but he pivots back when he hears the shards of porcelain crunch beneath my shoes as I regain my footing. All my focus is on taking him down, so I don't see the long narrow blade in his hand until a second too late. He shoves the blade in hard, directly below my ribcage. It slices through the material of my shirt and goes through my skin, piercing deep into my side. The blade must contain silver because there's an immediate severe muscle contraction followed by an icy cold stinging sensation. The pain is excruciating.

Holy fuck!

I stagger back. My eyes turn completely black. I snarl, advancing on him again. I let the demon inside take over and run on pure adrenaline. All my senses are heightened as my focus homes in on my target.

My left fist finds his cheekbone, but the material of the mask keeps me from fully connecting. With my other arm, I aim for the bend of his elbow. A hard chop and the blade flies from his hand. It trails along the wooden floor onto the linoleum in the kitchen.

"I'm going to kill you." I lunge at him. We slam into the opposite wall, dislodging a row of pictures. Several crash to the floor. The frames and glass shatter into pieces.

He breaks away from me. We both scramble for the blade. I skid across the floor on my knees, reaching it first. Blade in hand, I struggle to regain my footing, but he doesn't come at me. He hesitates, stares at the blade, then looks at me. For the briefest moment, there's a sense of familiarity, like I've seen him before, but I can't place him. It throws me off guard. He uses my hesitation to push past me, fleeing into the kitchen.

He bolts through the open balcony door. I turn to go after him, but before I get far, something knocks me hard on the back of the head. I lose my grip on the blade and it falls out of my hand.

Everything goes into slow motion. The floor rises to meet me. As an inky blackness closes in, a pair of ugly shoes appear in front of my eyes. I gaze up in confusion and see Chloe's face. Her lips move, but I can't make out what she's saying. A voice calls out my name from far off in the distance, but I'm unable to respond. It fades away and everything goes dark.

CHAPTER 16

October 21 Night:

My eyes open and I'm staring at an unfamiliar ceiling. It takes me a second to figure out where I am. I'm lying on the floor in Chloe's living room, but I have a pillow under my head.

Strange.

I take a deep breath. My side hurts like hell. Actually, my entire body hurts, and my head is pounding. Events come back to me in bits and pieces. Opening the door and rushing into Chloe's apartment. The fight with the masked intruder. The intruder who would have taken her life but stabbed me instead.

Oh yeah, and I got hit on the head. My hand reaches up to feel the knot forming there. It's about the size of a goose egg and painful to touch. My hair feels wet and sticky.

Is Chloe okay?

I lift my head high enough off the pillow to glance around. She's watching me from a chair across the room. She appears okay, but I can't read her expression. Worry? No, it's fear. She's scared.

"Hey." I give her a weak smile, croaking the word out. My throat feels parched. "You okay?"

She doesn't answer. Instead, she gets out of the chair. She walks closer, but for some reason remains several feet away.

She bites on the tip of her thumbnail. "Andrea, he's awake," she hollers toward the kitchen. Folding her arms over her chest, she silently stares down at me.

I attempt to sit up, but I'm dizzy. Belatedly, I notice my shirt is missing and I have a large bandage below my ribcage. I run my hand over it. Farther down, I'm relieved to find I'm wearing my jeans since Andrea is about to make an appearance, but my shoes are gone. At least I'm still wearing my socks.

"Chloe, what's wrong?" *Besides the fact someone tried to kill you, I mean.* I don't understand why she is acting so odd.

She says nothing as she continues to stare at me.

It's a struggle, but I pull myself up into a sitting position with my legs straight out in front of me. Why am I so weak? I can barely move. I survey my surroundings. I'm more or less in the middle of the room. Someone has moved the coffee table. It's now up against the couch. None of it makes sense until I notice the trail of salt on the floor. It goes all the way around me in a circle. There are also groups of symbols written in chalk on the other side of it.

A Demon Snare. Really?

What. The. Fuck?

I stare hard at Chloe. I'm not sure if I'm mad or my feelings are hurt. Does she not know what I've done for her? Everything I've sacrificed for her?

No, of course not. She has no clue.

I break eye contact to study the snare they've trapped me in. The circle of salt—it's doing no good at all. Someone watched one too many episodes of *Supernatural*. The symbols, on the other hand, well, there is a little dark magic there. It will temporarily hold me in place for a while, but not forever. If I have to, I can wait it out.

I suspect Andrea put Chloe up to this. As if on cue, she walks into the room from the kitchen and stands next to her. She's holding a baseball bat. I believe I know what hit me on the back of the head.

She looks at me as if I'm something vile. "You're a demon," she spits out. I'm not sure if she means it as commentary or an accusation. She puts her hand on Chloe's shoulder. "You should go. I'll handle this."

Chloe purses her lips but doesn't move.

"And you're a witch," I hiss back. I soften my voice as I turn to Chloe. "And you are, too." I need to make her understand. "I'm not here to hurt you, Chloe. I was trying to protect you."

She remains silent. Her stance shifts, but Andrea nudges her. "Show him."

Chloe reaches into her pocket, flushing guiltily. She pulls out a phone. It's mine. *Shit!*

I know where she's going with this. She must have seen me use my passcode. They've accessed my phone.

She stares down at me uneasily as she taps on the screen before turning it to where I can see what she's staring at. She's in the Grim Reaper app. It's displaying her file.

"You're not only a demon, are you?" she asks. "What are you, a serial killer? A demon assassin? What the hell is this? Why is my name on here?" Her voice rises and her hand shakes. She takes the phone and begins swiping with her finger. She stops and turns the phone back toward me again. It's Carol's file. "Did you kill her, Finn? Where is she?

What did you do to her?" She swipes some more. "Did you kill all these people?"

It feels like a slap in the face.

I stumble to get to my feet. All I want to do is take her in my arms and reassure her I'm not any of these things she's accusing me of, but I can't move forward any farther than to the edge of the stupid salt circle. I stare down at my socks. It feels like I'm standing in front of an invisible wall made up of some kind of an electrical current. I suspect it's what's draining my energy. That, and having a blade stuck into me earlier. Since it was silver, it will take a while for it to heal and I'm going to have a scar. I guess I'm lucky the killer didn't stab me in the heart. Silver is another one of the few things that can kill a demon, and it wouldn't have been pretty.

I shake the thought out of my head and focus on the present. The absurdity of my situation almost makes me laugh. I'm shirtless and shoeless, trapped inside a circle of salt because of some symbols on the floor. Andrea talked Chloe into this, I just know it.

"Chloe, I can explain." I run my hand through my hair. "If I can just talk to you alone." I won't get anywhere with her as long as Andrea is in the room.

"I'm not going anywhere, freak!" Andrea snarls at me. If looks could kill, I would burst into flames right about now. It's a good thing I know, even though she's a witch, that's not actually possible.

"Chloe, please. I can explain." I try again, waving my hand in front of me. "It's not like I can do anything to you as long as you have me trapped here." *Not that I ever would. I'd rather die first.*

The guilt returns to her face. Her eyes meet mine. "It's okay," she turns to Andrea. "I'll be fine."

Andrea whispers something to her, and Chloe whispers something back. I can't hear what they're saying at all. The snare has dampened that ability, too. They whisper some more.

Andrea finally nods. "Try anything, and I'll use this to end you." She holds up the bat. "I'm warning you." She does one of those gestures where she motions at her eyes with two fingers, then points them at me. It's almost comical, but she did knock me out with that thing. She glares at me as she walks out of the room with the bat over her shoulder. I feel confident her plan is to stand in the hallway, listening to every word we say.

Chloe retrieves the chair, dragging it across the floor so she can sit closer to me, but she remains on the other side of the circle. I sit cross-legged on the floor, getting as close to her as I can.

Neither of us says anything. She pushes a strand of hair behind her ear. "So, start explaining." She motions at my phone. "What is this?"

I have no clue where to begin. I decide to jump right in. "It's an app. It tells me when and where someone is going to die, so I can be there to escort them to the other side." I tell her the truth. "I'm a Grim Reaper."

"I thought you were a demon." Her lips form a thin line like she's already caught me in a lie.

"I'm both. I'm a demon and my designation, or what you would call my job, is a Grim Reaper."

"You take them to Hell?"

I shake my head. "No, my job is to get them to the ferry so they can cross the River Styx to the other side. Where they go after that gets sorted out over there."

The little V between her eyebrows is back as she takes it

all in. She's trying to grasp what I'm telling her. "So, you're a Grim Reaper and you're a demon."

"Yes."

"So, you're possessing that body?" She motions at me.

"What?" Where did that question come from? "No, I'm not that kind of demon." It would take hours to explain the hierarchy of demons in Hell to her, and we don't have that much time. "What you see, this is me." I place my hand on my chest over my heart.

"You look human, though."

I smile. "You do, too, even though you're a witch."

She appears to accept this. Maybe we're making progress.

"Your blood is black."

"Actually, on the inside, it's a lot like yours. When it hits the air, it becomes black, the same way your blood turns red."

See, Chloe, we're not that different.

Her expression is blank. I can't tell what she's thinking. She stares down at my phone again.

"Am I going to die?"

"I don't know. You should have died earlier tonight, but I interfered and stopped it." I run my hand over the bandage. "I broke the rules."

For you, Chloe.

I'm in major trouble, but I don't know what will happen when her soul doesn't get on the ferry. To say all Hell is going to break loose doesn't begin to cover it. I need to make a plan. I need to get her away from her apartment. Somewhere safe.

First, though, I've got to get out of this stupid snare. She still wants to play Twenty Questions, though.

"Did you already know this was my day to die when we first met?"

"No, I only got the notice this morning. That's why I was so upset when you saw me in the hall." I take a breath. "I'm sorry. I wanted to tell you, but I didn't know how."

"Then, when we met...why me? When we—" She can't say the words. She stares down at her hands, then raises her head. "Was any of it real?"

Oh, Chloe. I am completely helpless here. If I could take her in my arms and show her, she'd know she means the world to me. I want to tell her—what? *That I love her.* The thought remains unsettling, but it's true. I've loved her from the moment I first saw her, but I didn't recognize what it was.

"Yes, of course it was real. It still is." I stand up again and pace in the small area I can move around in. I need to get her out of here. Hell, I need to get me out of here. I'm like a dog trapped in a cage.

"Look, Chloe, I'm happy to answer all your questions, but we need to get you as far away from here as we can get. It's not safe." I don't want to scare her, but she needs to know the truth. "How long was I out?"

"I—I'm not sure," she stammers.

"Think, Chloe. It's important."

She shrugs. "Maybe two hours. Why?"

Her time of death should have occurred at 7:06. The countdown started then, so there's about a four-hour window before she has to board the ferry. When she doesn't, it will cause a departure delay, which will shut things down for at least an hour. We've got maybe three hours to get as far away from here as we can, and even then, I've never known anyone able to cheat or outrun Death for long.

"Okay, we've got maybe three hours before they come here to get you. We need to get out of here."

"They?" She's confused. "Who are they?"

"The magistratus. They're like the police," I reply. "I promise you, I will explain everything to you later. All of it. But we're going to run out of time." I stop pacing. "Chloe, please, you know me. You need to trust me. I saved you. I would never hurt you. Surely, you know this."

She doesn't reply. Instead, she continues to sit and stare at me.

Biting at one of her fingernails, she looks from me toward the hallway. "I don't know, Finn. This is a lot to take in at one time." She takes a deep breath. Putting a finger to her lips, she gets up from the chair and comes as near to the edge of the circle as she can. "I trust you. Tell me what to do," she whispers.

I point to one of the symbols and make a motion with my hand for her to erase it. Unless Andrea rigged the snare with a backup spell, that should do it.

She bends down. Using the sleeve of her sweater, she erases the symbol. There is a whoosh noise and a small pop. I instantly feel better. I gingerly put my foot over the salt line. When nothing bad happens, I take a step outside of it. Chloe buries herself in my arms. "I'm sorry," she whispers against my chest.

I stroke her hair. "It's okay."

I want to keep standing here with my arms wrapped around her, but the clock is running out. I lift her chin with my fingers. "You need to pack, and we need to go. Do it now."

She nods and hands me my phone, then heads toward her bedroom. I spot my shoes next to the couch but have no clue what has become of my shirt or my coat. I sit down on the couch to put my shoes on. It hurts to bend over. Any quick movement makes me dizzy, but I ignore both the dizziness and the pain.

Andrea and Chloe whisper back and forth in the hallway, then Andrea appears. She stares at the empty circle, then presses her lips together. A sullen look appears on her face. She disappears back down the hall. A door slams, followed by the sounds of a heated argument. In a couple of minutes, Andrea reappears, and she holds my shirt in her hand. She throws it at me. I catch it. The hole where the blade went through is gone. There's no sign of my blood on it, either. I stare at it, puzzled.

"Chloe fixed it for you. She tried to heal you, too." She motions at my abdomen. "It didn't work, so I stitched you up."

I reach down, touching the bandage. "Thank you." I force the words out. I'm betting Chloe didn't give her a choice. I pull the shirt over my head, inhaling sharply at the pain as the movement of my arms tugs on the area beneath the bandage.

"Where is the blade?" I ask after I'm dressed again.

"Chloe's got it. I told her if she's determined to go with you, she should keep it close to her in case you tried—"

I raise an eyebrow, mentally daring her to finish her sentence.

She gives me an icy stare instead, then puts her hands on her hips. "What's your plan exactly?"

"For now? Get Chloe somewhere safe where they won't find her."

"Like where?"

I honestly don't know. "I haven't gotten that far with the plan yet. The only thing I know is they are going to come for her soon. She can't stay here."

Andrea scowls. She shakes her head in disapproval as she passes by me. Grabbing her purse from a table near the door, she opens it and pulls out a set of keys on a ring. She takes one off the ring and holds it up. "Will this work? My grandfather has a cottage in North Waterboro. It's isolated. One road in, one road out."

I don't know if anything will work, but at least it sounds like a start. I nod.

She brings it to me, but holds it back as I reach for it. "If anything happens to her, I'm holding you personally responsible." She gives me the address, then hands me the key.

"I would expect no less," I tell her as we continue to stare at each other.

"What should I tell them when they show up?"

I'm in uncharted territory here and I don't know how to reply. I don't think she'll have the ability to see them when they show up, so it probably doesn't matter. I explain about the invisibility part and suggest she not do or say anything that might indicate where we are. When I'm finished, she seems unnerved by the possibility of having beings in her apartment she can't see. I almost forget, but in the back of my mind, I remember my nemesis across the hall. I fish the key to Carol's apartment out of my pocket.

"Tommy." I hand her the key. She starts to say something, but as Chloe comes out of the bedroom, she shoots me a look, leaving whatever she wanted to say unsaid.

"I guess I'm ready," Chloe announces. She's toting a small carry-on, her purse, and my coat.

"Leave your phone here," I instruct. "They can track us through anything with GPS or WiFi."

She takes the phone out of her pocket and hands it to Andrea.

I run my hand through my hair. "We'll need to do something else for transportation, too. They'll be able to trace the GPS in my car," I say, more to myself than to them. If it wasn't raining, we could take my bike.

Chloe raises an eyebrow at Andrea. She rolls her eyes. Reaching back into her purse, she retrieves another set of keys.

She throws them at me. "Promise me you'll keep her safe."

"I promise."

The two hug, and Chloe and I are on our way.

By the time we get to the Echelon, a plan forms in my mind. Not much of one, but it's all I've got at the moment. Chloe has said little on the ride over. She's not only scared, she's reeling from all the information she has learned during the last hour. About her date of death, about me, about everything.

We take the elevator up to the penthouse in silence. I half expect to find someone from Management or the magistratus waiting for us when the doors open, but all is quiet. I guess my imagination is getting ahead of itself.

"So, does this place belong to someone who is dead?" Chloe studies the place as if she's seeing it for the first time.

"No, it's mine," I reply, taking what is possibly my own last look around. I won't miss all the gray. "Make yourself at home. I've got to get a few things. It won't take long."

I leave her in the living room and head to my bedroom. In the closet, I grab my gym bag off the floor. Opening the wall safe, I remove all the cash from inside, lining it across the bottom of the bag. I take out my passport and stuff it into the pocket of my coat and tuck my gun into my waistband. It gives me a surreal feeling, almost like I'm playing out a scene from a movie.

So, this is your life now?

I shut the safe.

Regardless of what humans believe, they're not watched over every single moment of every single day. That would make it all rather creepy. There are entities who come as needed, but it is possible to go "off grid." I'll need to talk to Chloe about this so she doesn't attract attention to herself. I'll also need to tell her not to use any magic or they could track her energy. I mentally make a list.

I finish packing, putting the clothing on top of the money. Taking out my phone, I stare at it. I'm still not a hundred percent sure what I'm about to do is a good idea.

I consider Corsun a friend, but demons are an untrustworthy lot, and as I said before, most will turn on you in a heartbeat. If it comes down to him or me, he'll sell me out without a second thought. I'm about to take a huge risk. I dial his number.

"Hey, mate." He answers on the first ring. It sounds like he's at a bar. "I tried to call you back earlier. We were in meetings all day."

"Can you talk?"

"Sure," he replies. "Is this about the witch thing again?"

"Sort of. I've got a situation."

"You've always got a situation. Hang on a minute, okay?" There's the sound of muffled voices and loud music. The music fades away. A door creaks open and closed, then silence. "Okay, brother, tell me what's going on."

"That stuff you were telling me about changing the TODs, was it true?"

He remains silent.

"Is it true?" I try again.

"You know how I get when I've had too much to drink, Finn," he says slowly. "Why do you want to know?"

I take a deep breath, then launch into an abbreviated version of what's happened since Wednesday night.

He's silent again. "Shit." He takes a breath. "Is this the one you introduced me to at the benefit?"

"Yes." I'm not sure why it's important. "Why?"

"I'm simply trying to figure out why you've gone and thrown your entire life away for her, that's all."

"Can you help me or not?" I pinch the bridge of my nose with my fingers.

"I may know someone."

"Who?"

"It's better if you don't know." He lowers his voice. "It's going to cost you, though."

"How much?"

"Two hundred and fifty thousand, at least."

"Not a problem."

This catches him off guard. "What do you want as the new TOD?"

Witches have the same normal life span a human does. "Have them make it for when she's a hundred." I swallow. "I don't want to know the exact date."

"Okay, I'll make some calls."

Since we won't have our phones with us and he's not sure it's safe for me to use the burner phone he gave me, Corsun agrees to drive up to the cottage in the morning to either let us know it's okay to come back or provide us with new passports and fake IDs. If nothing else works, I'll use my real passport to make the magistratus follow me, and Corsun will get Chloe to the airport on a private airplane and as far away as possible. I'm trusting him with a lot.

"I hope she's worth it," he says after we've worked out all the details.

"She is." I hang up.

I get out my wallet and fish for one of the cards Mr. Fitz gave me. I'm even less sure if this is the right thing to do, but I do it, anyway. Typing his number into my phone, I send him the photos I took of Jack's computer screen and the manifest report to him in a text message.

I toss the phone on the bed and grab the gym bag. I guess we're ready to go.

The traffic is light on our way to Andrea's cottage. Chloe goes from staring out the window to looking over at me, down at her hands in her lap, and back to staring out the window. She has been doing this on and off since we left the Echelon. I would have thought by now she would have asked me some questions about what happened back at her apartment, but she's been strangely quiet about it. I suspect she's in shock.

Meanwhile, the only good part of the trip so far is that it's stopped raining, but now I'm driving in the fog. The headlights on Andrea's car barely cut through it, so I'm forced to keep my concentration on the road.

"It must pay well," she says, breaking her silence.

I don't respond. I have no clue what she's talking about.

"The Grim Reaper thing." Her focus shifts away from the window, watching me instead.

"It's not exactly a paying type of job."

"Your place. The car you took me home in the other night." She continues to stare at me. "That all belongs to you? Not to someone else?"

She's already asked me about my place twice. I guess she's unsure now because the first time we met, I told her I was Carol's nephew. And yeah, she's still processing the whole demon thing, too.

"It's all mine," I reply, wanting her to know the truth. It's important to me that she trusts me, and we're not there yet. "I've made investments over the years. They've paid off." I hope she doesn't ask me where the money came from. The things I've done in my past, I would rather not share with her, at least not when I'm trying to get us back on track.

"Have you been doing this for a long time?"

"No, this is the only time I've ever been on the run with someone whose soul I was supposed to take. It's a first for me." I look over at her with a hint of a smile, which I'm sure she can't see. She's not asking questions about the afterlife; she's asking questions about me. I'm hoping it's a good sign.

"And it's the first time I've ever been on the run with a Grim Reaper, who is also a demon." She lets out a huff as she pushes a strand of hair behind her ear. She folds her arms over her chest.

"Touché," I reply. "Three thousand years, give or take." I don't believe she's ready to hear about my extended stay in Hell, or why I was there. I know I'm not ready to stir all those memories back up. The fog grows thicker. I keep my attention on the road, but I feel her eyes back on me.

"You're making that up."

"What?"

"That you're three thousand years old."

"I'm not."

"Promise?"

"Promise."

"You swear?"

"I swear."

"You don't look it."

"That's good to know."

She shakes her head in disbelief, but at least the tension between us is easing. Even she seems to realize how far down the rabbit hole she's gone. She's either handling it well, or I'm right and she's in shock.

"And you're a witch." I shift the conversation away from me.

She nods. "It was a big part of the problem between me and Eric. I wanted to be honest with him, so I told him. I guess I thought he would accept me for who I am, but he didn't. He never wanted me to use my magic because he said it would corrupt me. My grandmother was the same way. She couldn't stand the fact my father married a witch. When she found out I took after my mother, she wanted nothing to do with me, but I guess she didn't feel like she had a choice. I know she always resented having to take me in, though." She glances in my direction. "I'm glad you found out. I wanted to tell you when we were at the museum, but I wasn't sure how you would react."

I don't mention I've known she was a witch since the first time I saw her. "I wanted to tell you, too," I say instead. I resist the urge to reach over and take her hand. If she pulls away, I don't think I could take it.

"The irony is, of course, that this is both my grandmother and Eric's worst fear, and it came true." She waves her hand back and forth. I catch a touch of humor in her voice.

"What do you mean?"

"Consorting with the devil." She makes air quotes with her hands and a smile plays on her lips. "Well, a demon, but still—"

I wonder again if she's okay because she's taking things a little too well, but then she changes the subject. "Do you know who it was that tried to—" Her voice drops off as she reaches up to touch the bruises on her neck. "Or why they wanted to kill me?"

I tell her about the murdered witches, Father Mike, and how I found out about the seals. Since this person had a silver blade and Chloe's a witch, I'm certain it's all connected.

"I told Andrea you weren't evil." She comes back to the demon topic. I watch as she nervously twists her hair around her fingers. "But you did the thing with your eyes, and we saw your blood—" She's studying me again. "Is that the only thing different between you and a human?"

"Well, you've seen all of me." I try not to, but I smirk. "Maybe you should tell me."

"That's not what I meant," she says in a huff. I don't have to look to know she's blushing.

I play nice. "Our anatomy is basically the same as yours, or any human, but demons can see in the dark and we have excellent hearing. We're not what you would call completely immortal, but we're hard to kill. Extreme blood loss can do it. Cast iron or silver straight to the heart will do it the quickest, though." My hand leaves the steering wheel. I run it over my shirt where the bandage is. "That, and decapitation." I mention a few of the other differences, such as our high metabolism and how little sleep we need, but before I can tell her anything else, I spot the sign for the road the cottage is on ahead on the right.

Slowing the car, I check the rearview mirror again to make sure no one is following us before turning onto the dirt road. Andrea has told me there are only a few other cottages on the road and most of them are rentals. I count the mailboxes as we pass by, then see the driveway on the left. It takes us farther back into the woods. Andrea was correct—one way in, one way out. As far as hideaways go, it's a good choice. The clock on the dashboard turns to 1:15 right as the car's headlights shine onto the cottage. Chloe has officially missed her departure time. We're now both MIA.

I park the car. We sit in silence for a moment. Part of me expects to find the car surrounded by demon magistratus as soon as we step out of it, but the rational part tells me it won't happen. Well, not right away, anyway. Hopefully, Corsun is in the process of getting Chloe's TOD changed and we've simply made a wasted trip out here to the middle of nowhere. Although, if he does pull it off, it's probably for the best. She does still have a killer after her that we'll eventually need to deal with, but at least for now, she's safe.

One step at a time, Finn.

We both get out of the car. I grab my gym bag and Chloe's carry-on. The rain has stopped and it's only a mist now. I scan the darkness, but I don't see or hear anything out of the ordinary. We make our way onto the porch, then head inside.

The cottage is small, but clean and efficient. Chloe tells me Andrea mentioned a lake behind the property where her grandfather likes to fish. I survey our surroundings. There's an open living room with a fireplace and a small kitchen. I'm unsure about the sleeping arrangements after the whole demon revelation, so I set my stuff next to the couch while Chloe wanders off to inspect the one and only bedroom.

I note there are wall units for heat, but it's going to take a while for the place to warm up. I saw a pile of wood on the porch, so I decide to build a fire in the fireplace to speed the process along.

Chloe returns from the bedroom and investigates the kitchen. "We've got beer," she informs me as she checks to see what's in the refrigerator. "I also see eggs, bacon that's still in date, and a questionable block of cheese." She opens a few of the cabinets. "And lots and lots of cans of soup."

"Well, at least we won't starve," I reply dryly. We should have stopped for supplies, but almost everyone has a security camera these days. I didn't want to tip off which direction we were heading in.

She walks over to where I stand in front of the fireplace. She's opened two bottles of beer. "Thank you for saving me. I should have already told you that." She hands me one bottle before taking a drink from the other. "What will they do if they catch us?"

I take a sip. "I'm not entirely sure. They would adjust your TOD, I mean, your Time of Death, and more than likely you wouldn't even remember you missed it." This is only partially true, but I don't want to scare her. Upper Management would most likely loop time, and without me there to save her on the next go around, she would die. From that point, everything would go on as it should.

"What would they do to you?"

Another tour in Hell, or complete annihilation. Take your pick. "I broke the rules. Punishment. Nothing I haven't been through before." I shrug.

"The scars on your back?" Her eyes widen.

Yeah, let's not go there right now. I take another drink of beer. "You need to eat. How about some of that soup?"

Neither of us is hungry, but we go through the motions of getting out the bowls and heating the soup, since it gives us something normal to do. Chloe locates a box of crackers in another cabinet. They're out of date, but not stale, so we end up with vegetable soup and saltine crackers.

We sit on a faded brown couch in front of the fireplace to eat. I make a mental note to check out the old rifle hung on hooks over the mantle. If it's loaded, it could come in handy. It won't kill a demon or an angel, but it can slow one down if we need to make a getaway. Above the rifle is a painting of a black and white cow with grass hanging out of its mouth. It's an interesting choice for a piece of art. Okay, it's strange. The cow looks menacing. I don't like its eyes. They're creepy. Chloe is staring at it, too.

She finishes her soup and sets the empty bowl on the coffee table. "Is that what it's like?" She motions to the flames flickering in the fireplace. "Hell, I mean."

"For some," I reply. I don't exactly know how to explain it to her. "Souls create their own version of Hell. Whatever you fear in life gets magnified when you're down there. Since some people have the fear of burning in Hell, they get to repeatedly relive it. For others, it's simply having their worst fear play out in all different ways. Stuck endlessly on a plane if you're afraid of flying, thrown into a pit with vipers if you have a fear of snakes—"

She appears to accept this explanation and moves on. "And you've been there?"

"Yes, twice."

"Is that how it was for you?"

"Not the first time." I set my bowl on the coffee table next to hers. "When I was growing up, I lived in the Underworld. Since I received the Grim Reaper designation at birth, I didn't have it as bad as some demons. It was more like living in a military barrack or maybe an overly strict orphanage."

"But it was like that the second time?"

I don't want to have this discussion with her—or anyone, for that matter—but she's brought it up again. "No, I didn't have any fears they could play on. For me, it was more like being held prisoner in a dungeon where they would repeatedly torture me." I choose my words carefully. "I heal quickly, so they would torture me to the point where I would lose consciousness, let me heal, then start it all over again the next day. Our skin can only take so much of that, though. Then, it doesn't repair itself correctly."

"Why were you there the second time?"

That's a harder question to answer. "I tried to kill the demon who was my supervisor."

Her eyes grow wide. "Why did you do that?"

"He made me break a promise to some of my Charges. It's what we call the souls we reap." Now, it's my turn to stare at the flames in the fireplace. "Have you ever heard the story about what happened on the Island of Pompeii?"

"The volcano?" She looks at me incredulously. "You're saying you were there? In 79 CE?" She stares at me like I've told her a joke and she's waiting for the punchline.

"It's a long story, but the ship we were on would only hold so many of us. The demon who was in charge—well, he lied. He told us other ships were coming to help transport the rest of the souls, but they weren't." I take a breath. "And I had promised some of my remaining Charges that someone would come back for them, but then I found out he planned to leave them there. When the volcano blew, it basically obliterated their energy, and they were gone."

"That's terrible."

I frown as I remember seeing the volcano erupt while watching from the ship. "When I found out the truth—that he had always planned to leave them—I tried to kill him. I also tried to take over the ship to go back, but it was too late. I got charged with attempted murder and mutiny. And that was that."

In truth, to this day, my only regret is that I didn't kill him, but it wasn't for a lack of trying. I decide that's probably not something I should share with her, at least not right now when I'm still not sure how she feels about me.

"Oh, Finn. I'm so sorry." Chloe reaches over and takes my hand. "I can't imagine. It must have been awful for you."

"It was a long time ago." I give her hand a squeeze. "It's late. You should try to get some sleep."

"Do you think we're safe here for tonight?"

"I do." Unless Andrea messes up and gives away our location, but I don't tell her that.

"I'm going to take a shower, then." She gets up off the couch and disappears into the bedroom.

While she showers, I decide to check outside again to reassure myself the magistratus aren't out in the dark silently surrounding the cabin. Once I'm back inside, I lock the door securely behind me. I clear our bowls off the coffee table and put them in the sink. I also check to see if the shotgun hanging over the mantle is usable. It is. Someone recently cleaned it. I'm happy to discover it's also loaded.

I'm about to settle down on the couch when Chloe opens the bedroom door with a yellow towel wrapped around her. She's barefoot and her hair is still damp from the shower. She watches me quietly for a moment, then walks over to stand in front of the fireplace. She holds her hand out to me. “Coming to bed?”

“Are you sure?”

“Yes,” she replies, and I see the heat in her eyes. She nods. “I’m sure.”

I get up from the couch, take her hand, and follow her into the bedroom.

CHAPTER 17

October 22:

I awaken to find Chloe sleeping peacefully beside me. It takes a second to remember where we are and why we're here. Yesterday seems like a bad dream. I pick my watch up off the nightstand. It shows it's a little after 8:00. Over twelve hours since Chloe's time of death, but so far, she's safe.

I dress without waking her. Slipping the gun off the bedside table, I tuck it into my waistband—just in case. I half expect to find the magistratus waiting in the living room, but it's quiet except for the humming of one of the heater units on the wall. Corsun will arrive in a couple of hours. Chloe and I will both know our fates then.

I hunt through the cabinets for coffee. The coffeemaker is one of those you fill with water and put on the stovetop. I haven't used one like it in years. I also fill the tea kettle and put it on another burner to heat.

Although I can cook, I usually choose not to. I decide I'll make Chloe breakfast and we can discuss our next move while we eat. If her time of death has changed, we can head back home. If we're going on the run, we'll need to decide where to go. I haven't had to do anything like this since the Burning Times back around 1450, when things got unstable for a while in the part of Europe I was living in. At least then, Management was around to help plan everything out. This time, I'm on my own.

I bring my focus back to the present. I grab the eggs and bacon out of the refrigerator. Digging around in the freezer yields an unopened box of frozen waffles hidden in the back. They'll do. I pour myself a cup of coffee and get to work.

Chloe comes out of the bedroom just as the waffles pop up in the toaster. I survey my work. The eggs are a little brown and the bacon extra crispy, but it's edible. I said I could cook. I didn't say I was good at it. She puts her arms around me, kissing me on the cheek.

"Good morning." She smiles. She's dressed in jeans and a long-sleeved blue shirt with my black T-shirt from yesterday on underneath.

"Good morning," I reply, hugging her back. "Are you hungry?"

She glances up at me. "Starving. I worked up quite the appetite last night."

"Did you now?" I try not to grin too big as I recall our late-night extracurricular activities.

She picks up a piece of bacon, sticking it into her mouth. "Most definitely."

"There's hot water over there for your tea." I motion with the spatula to the kettle next to the coffeemaker on the stove.

"You remembered." She beams at me. She picks up the mug I set on the counter for her. I found out she prefers tea over coffee when we had breakfast the morning after she spent the night at my place.

We take the plates, coffee, and tea over to the small table near the window. The sun is out this morning. In the daylight, you can see the lake. If we weren't hiding out, this might make for an enjoyable long weekend getaway. As it is, I remain on edge.

"This is good." Chloe takes a bite of her waffle after drowning it in syrup. I'm glad I found a bottle in one of the cabinets.

We're just finishing our breakfast when we hear the sound of tires crunching over gravel. A car is coming up the driveway. I get up and peer out the window of the front door. A black SUV I don't recognize pulls up. It stops next to Andrea's car.

"Is it Corsun?" Chloe joins me.

"I'm not sure. It's not his car." I look at her. "Remember what we discussed. Stay in the bedroom until I let you know it's safe to come out."

"Be careful." She gives me a kiss, then heads into the bedroom. If things go south, she's to go out the window and run toward the lake.

I wait until she closes the door before stepping out onto the porch. I'm expecting Corsun to get out of the car, but when the door to the SUV opens, there's a flash of reddish-brown hair instead. I don't recognize who it is at first until they go around to the passenger side and retrieve something from the backseat. It's the angel from Management. Muriel.

She's alone.

I quickly turn to go back into the cottage but stop as she waves at me.

What the hell?

Well, this is certainly strange. Reaching my hand behind my back, I check again to make sure I can easily grab the gun if I need it. Bullets won't kill an angel, but it might slow her down enough to let me reach the blade we've hidden in the living room. I'd prefer to have it on me instead of the gun, but we couldn't figure out a way to keep it secure without it touching against my skin.

I watch warily as she walks to the foot of the stairs. She's carrying a small, dark brown satchel.

"Finn." She peers up at me from the bottom of the steps.

"Muriel." I keep my tone casual, but all of my senses are on high alert.

"Corsun said you were in need of a little assistance." She pats the satchel. "Aren't you going to invite me in?"

Why is she here? Where is Corsun?

Stay on guard, Finn. Something's up.

I motion for her to come up the steps.

"Where's Corsun?"

She brushes past me to go inside. "Since you didn't show up with the witch yesterday, the magistratus is watching your known associates. We decided it would be best if I came in his place."

"You're the one changing the TODs?" I close the door behind her and lock it.

She twists her lips. "I'm the one here, aren't I?" She surveys the room. Her eyes come back to rest on me. "I must say, Finn, I don't think anyone expected this from you. You're full of surprises."

I ignore the remark. "Did you get the time of death changed?"

She shakes her head. "We tried, but it was too late to do anything. I have your new identities, though."

I keep my disappointment hidden. Staying on the run is

going to make life infinitely more complicated, especially since I'm sure Management will put a large bounty on my head and probably Chloe's, too.

Watching me, Muriel slowly moves toward the couch. She sets the satchel on the coffee table. I move closer as she takes two passports and two IDs out of the middle section, setting them down next to it. "Do you have the money?"

"I do." I wave my hand toward the gym bag on the couch. "Why are you doing this, Muriel?" I reach over and unzip it to show her the cash. It feels like we're negotiating a drug deal.

"Why am I helping you? Why do you think?" She smirks.

"Money?"

Something doesn't add up. She doesn't answer me. Instead, she makes a circle around the space we're standing in, casually walking behind me, then around the couch. I turn, watching her. She's searching for something, or maybe she's making sure I'm not setting her up. She pauses near the closed door to the bedroom and stares, but then continues back to where I'm standing.

"Breaking the rules for money seems like an odd thing for an angel to do," I reply.

My uneasy feeling continues to grow. A gnawing sensation fills my stomach, warning me that all is not as it seems. Muriel is a little too at ease. A little too collected. I try to remain calm on the outside, but inwardly, all my senses are on high alert. I silently curse. I should have had Chloe wait for me down at the lake and not in the next room.

She waves her hand, showing off a gold bracelet. "I like nice things. Money helps."

So much for that thing about angels having moral superiority.

"How do I know you won't send the magistratus for us once you have the money?"

"Well, it wouldn't be very good for business, would it?" She gives me a strange smile. "The passports and IDs have the names of people who have already passed. There are also birth certificates and social security cards. No one is going to look for you under these names. You can both ride off into the sunset to your happily ever after, with no one the wiser."

I reach down, picking up a passport from the coffee table. It has my picture, but the name reads Aaron Tolbot. The second passport has Chloe's picture and the name Chelsea Tolbot.

Interesting. I've somehow gone from getting a girlfriend to having a wife.

I move the gym bag off the couch and set it near the satchel. "Two hundred and fifty thousand, just like Corsun said."

"Pleasure doing business with you." She peers inside again, then zips it shut. She shifts the satchel closer to me. Turning toward the fireplace, she studies the picture above the mantle. "Do you still have the blade?"

"The blade?" I pause. Why is she asking about it? The hairs raise on the back of my neck. My gaze shifts over to the bedroom door, then back to Muriel. I hope Chloe is listening and getting ready to run.

"The one Chloe's attacker used when they tried to kill her." She looks over her shoulder at me.

"I do."

She lets out a breath as her shoulders relax. "Good." Her fingers run along the edge of the mantle. "If I can present it to the magistratus, I might get them to reverse Chloe's date of death the right way. You'd still have to answer for defying an order, but your girlfriend would be safe."

In the back of my mind, a little voice whispers a warning to me, but I can't quite understand what it's saying. The uneasy feeling grows some more. "Let's get this over with so we can both get on our way."

"Is the witch here?" Muriel ignores my request, turning to face me. "I'd like to meet her."

I shake my head. "No, only me." The little voice in my head gets louder. From the recesses of my mind, a question forms. "Muriel, how did you know about the blade?"

"What do you mean?"

"The blade. How did you know I got it away from Chloe's attacker?"

She waves her hand. "I guess Corsun told me."

"I didn't say anything to Corsun about the blade. I told him someone attacked Chloe. I never said how." I've stashed the blade a couple of feet from me, but I don't want to alert her to that fact. I keep my eyes trained on her.

"Oh, my mistake." The strange smile returns. "Someone else must have mentioned it." She turns toward the fireplace again.

I attempt to grab the blade from between the seat cushion and the back of the couch. When Muriel whirls back toward me this time, though, she's brandishing the iron fire poker from the stand by the hearth. Before I can react, she swings it, catching me near the wrist. It knocks the blade from my hand. The skin on my arm burns where the poker strikes, but I ignore the pain.

"You couldn't leave it alone, could you, Finn?" She points the poker at me. "All you had to do was let the witch die." She takes a step forward. "Do you know how much trouble you're in? I can still fix things, though. Give her to me. No one ever has to know what you did."

I raise my hands. I still have the gun. It won't kill her, but it will slow her down enough to let me retrieve the blade.

Keep her talking, Finn.

"I don't think so."

She takes another step toward me. "I was told you were a good little soldier. I thought you didn't break the rules." She cocks her head. "Well, except for that unfortunate incident with your supervisor and you disobeying an order to save that kid." Her grip on the handle of the poker tightens. "You're certainly an enigma, aren't you? It was almost finished. One more witch. That's all that was needed, but you had to ruin it, didn't you? You had to get in the way."

"You seriously believe you can overthrow Hell?"

She looks at me, surprised. "You figured it out." She raises an eyebrow. "I'm impressed."

"It wasn't hard." I take a small step back. "I don't understand why you would want to do something like that, though."

"Office politics." She adjusts her stance, repositioning her hands on the poker handle like it's the ninth inning in a baseball game and she's up to bat. "You know what they say, Finn. Better to reign in Hell than serve in Heaven." She takes another step toward me. "Tell the witch to come out."

"She's long gone, Muriel." I motion toward the back door. "She left as soon as you arrived. You'll never catch her."

She can't help it. She turns to look.

Reaching for the gun secured in my waistband, I don't hesitate. I point it in her direction and pull the trigger, then fire off the five remaining bullets in the cylinder—just for good measure. They all hit center mass.

And apparently, I heard wrong about angels and guns. It doesn't slow her down at all. It does absolutely nothing except make her mad. She swings the poker, hitting me hard on my right side. When she pulls back, it tears my shirt, searing my skin.

Shit!

I drop the empty gun. I try to get away from her, but I get tripped up on the leg of the coffee table. My foot twists, causing me to lose my balance. Falling backward, I land hard on my ass with my legs stuck out in front of me.

Smooth move. Idiot.

Muriel glances down at the bullet wounds in her midsection. The front of her white shirt becomes a bluish black. "You know, I really liked this shirt." She shakes her head in disappointment. "I'm going to enjoy killing you, Finn."

I scramble backward, trying to get farther away, but the rug I've landed on keeps me from gaining any traction. She changes her stance, swinging the poker while I shift out of the way. It grazes my right side. Towering over me, she raises the poker again, this time intending to ram it straight into my chest.

I move my leg to trip her, but before I can, a blue streak of jagged lightning surrounds her.

Muriel drops the poker. She tries to speak, but before she can get the words out, the room fills with a burst of bright white light. It's blinding. I look away and close my eyes.

I carefully open them again as an eerie silence creeps in. Muriel is gone. Chloe stands in her place.

She rushes over to me. "Are you okay?" She holds her hands out in front of her, studying them. "I swear I didn't mean to kill her. I was only trying to stop her from hurting you."

"Yeah, I'm good," I mutter. The burns are uncomfortable, but the only thing really hurt is my pride. My job was to protect her and she had to save me instead.

I struggle to my feet. "We need to get out of here." I pick the blade up off the floor. Unzipping the gym bag, I toss it and the empty gun inside along with our new identification, then sling it over my shoulder.

Chloe used her magic. Plus, she killed an angel. We're going to have angels and demons on top of us any minute.

"I'll get our stuff," Chloe offers.

I shake my head. "Leave it. We need to go. Now." I hold out my hand and she accepts it, but before we can take two steps, the door crashes open. Two demons burst in, followed by two angels. The magistratus. They usually come in pairs. Apparently, they didn't think one set was enough to apprehend me this time because they've sent them from both divisions.

This is bad. Really bad.

No one moves for a moment as we all stand and stare at each other. With a deep sigh, I drop the bag on the coffee table, then put my hands up. Chloe slowly follows my lead. I can tell she wants to use her magic again to get us away from them, but I shake my head as a warning not to try it. Magic won't work on the magistratus. It's over. They have her energy signature now. Even if she gets away, they can track her in an instant.

She shoots me a look. At first, I'm afraid she's going to ignore me, but she finally raises her hands up all the way.

The bigger and uglier of the two demons stares at me. A slow grin spreads over his face. "Well, well. If it isn't Aiden Finn. This is going to be fun."

Fuck.

A couple of hours pass. We're still at the cabin. I glance down at the shackles on my wrists. They're too tight, but I suspect this is intentional. Again, my reputation precedes me. Since I served time in Hell for trying to kill another demon, some of the other demons treat me like I'm an ex-felon, which I guess, technically, I am.

At least they let Chloe and I stay together, even though it's getting uncomfortable sitting here on the couch.

I turn my attention to the bigger demon magistratus, who keeps pacing back and forth in front of us. Over the years, I've tried to erase his yellow stringy hair, pale skin, pointy ears, and protruding forehead from my mind, but I recognize him, the same way he recognized me. He was one of the guards who tortured me while I was in Hell. Apparently, he's received a promotion since the last time I saw him. His name starts with an M.

Marid.

He's on his cellphone talking to someone higher up—or I guess it's lower down, since it's someone in Lower Management on the other end.

Meanwhile, the other demon—Preta, Marid called her—is one unhappy demon. She's done nothing but argue with the two angels since they arrived. The angels are here because Muriel is dead, Chloe is not dead, and she missed the ferry. The demons are here for me because I interfered with the natural order of things and Chloe is my reap and also not dead.

The problem is, I told them I kidnapped Chloe and killed Muriel. Chloe, however, has given them a different story. She says she made a run for it on her own and I tried to catch her. She also told them she killed Muriel.

Since the angels won't let them leave with Chloe, the demons don't know how to proceed. Demon magistratus are not the smartest of demons and they're stuck in their way of thinking, so they can't figure out what to do. This means both sides are waiting on their respective supervisors to show up.

Meanwhile, I've been keeping an eye on Chloe. She's taking all of this a little too well. I suspect she's in shock. I know it must have been hard enough for her to accept her boyfriend is a demon, but seeing two demons and two unhappy, identically dressed angels arguing back and forth with each other is a whole different level of surreal for her. Not to mention, she's probably wondering if she's going to die because she knows that's supposed to have happened already. Still, it bothers me that she hasn't said a word since they sat us down. Instead, she keeps staring at the bigger one as he walks back and forth. I suspect she wants to use her magic, but the shackles dampen her abilities. Even if she tries, nothing will happen.

Since the couch is growing increasingly uncomfortable, I consider asking the angels if they'll let Chloe get up and move around some. Before I get a chance, I hear a car coming up the driveway.

The four move over to the window and peer out. Chloe glances at me. I shrug.

There's the sound of car doors opening and slamming shut, followed by footsteps on the porch. One of the angels opens the door. Mr. Fitz stands there. Behind him is Jack.

Shit.

The higher-ranking angel magistratus and Marid step

out onto the porch and close the door behind them. I try to listen, but Chloe leans over toward me.

"Who are they?" she whispers.

"My supervisor, Jack, and an angel named Mr. Fitz from Upper Management."

"Silence," Preta snaps before I can say anything else.

The four stay out on the porch for another few minutes before the door reopens. Marid stalks back into the room. He angrily yanks my shackles toward him, pulling my elbows into a bind that hurts like hell, but I refrain from making any noise or letting him know I'm in pain.

To my surprise, he unlocks them. I keep my thoughts to myself as I rub my wrists. He turns to Chloe and unlocks her shackles as well. He tosses both sets to the female. Preta grunts, muttering something to him in an ancient demon language I'm barely familiar with, although if I'm not mistaken, she just insulted my mother. Marid makes a hissing noise. They both glare in our direction. Without another word, they turn and head out the door.

Mr. Fitz comes in and walks over to where we sit. "Finn, I've asked your supervisor to take you and Chloe home, or wherever you want to go for now, but stay there until we straighten this mess out." He rubs his hand across his chin as he looks over his shoulder to where Jack stands, talking to one of the angels.

"Did you get the photos?" I quietly ask.

"Yes, but I can't talk to you about it right now." He glances at the other angel standing close by.

"So, you're not going to—" I motion toward Chloe.

"I honestly can't say," he replies. "I've got to get back and talk to Upper Management. Lower Management, too. The board called a special meeting. Both sides." He gestures toward Jack. "He will let you know how it's going later tonight or by first thing in the morning."

"Chloe, go get our things, okay?" I motion toward the bedroom.

She purses her lips, and I can tell she wants to say something, but she does as I ask.

I wait until she's out of the room before I speak again. "She had nothing to do with any of this. Running away. Muriel. That was all me, okay?"

"For now, I just want you to go home and stay there, Finn." He ignores my comment. "Let us handle this from here on out." He gives me a pointed look.

Chloe reappears from the bedroom. She hands me my jacket. I reach down to pick up the gym bag off the coffee table. No one ever looked inside. *Interesting.* They don't know I have the blade.

I consider whether I should tell Mr. Fitz, but his phone rings. He digs it out of his pocket. "I've got to take this. We'll talk soon." With a nod, he dismisses me.

I offer Chloe my hand again, and she takes it as we walk out onto the porch. Jack doesn't say a word as we follow him to his car. I'm not sure what to do about Andrea's car, or about the cabin door the magistratus destroyed when they charged in. From the expression on Jack's face, I decide not to mention it.

I open the door for Chloe. After she gets into the backseat, I shut it and walk around to where Jack stands.

"Jack, look—" I start, but he holds up a hand, shaking his head. He doesn't want to hear a word from me.

He tosses me his keys. "Put your stuff in the trunk. I'll be back." He heads toward the cabin, then stops. He turns back with a look of disappointment on his face. "I don't know what you were thinking, Finn."

I don't reply. I put everything into the trunk, then slide into the backseat with Chloe. She's staring at the cabin, watching Jack. She hasn't spoken to me since she asked about Jack and Mr. Fitz, but there's something on her mind.

"What is it?" I wonder how I'm going to explain everything she's witnessed over the last few hours. Even though she's a witch and I know she's aware of the supernatural, I'm sure all this new information is overwhelming for her.

She pushes a strand of hair back. "So..." Her voice is serious, but I glimpse amusement in her eyes. "Aiden, huh?"

CHAPTER 18

October 23:

We spend the rest of Friday afternoon and evening at my place under house arrest, as Chloe calls it, while we wait to learn our fate. Jack finally calls to tell me the Board of Directors are still behind closed doors. He informs me he'll stop by in the morning, since he should have information by then.

The next morning, as promised, Jack arrives at 7:00. Right on the dot. He's in a considerably better mood than he was the last time we saw him. He's even brought a bag of doughnuts and is toting a drink tray containing two coffees and a tea. I'm hoping this is a good sign.

Chloe takes the tray from him and leads him into the kitchen. He sets the bag down on the island, then grabs a coffee and takes a seat at the counter. She thanks him for bringing breakfast. The two exchange pleasantries like it's an ordinary day. Meanwhile, I do my best not to pace. I'm too on edge to sit down. I need him to get this over with.

Chloe takes the tea for herself, then slides the tray with the second coffee over to me. She reaches into the bag for a doughnut. "My favorite kind." She gives Jack a smile, sliding up onto the stool across from him.

"Nice place you've got here, Finn," he says through a mouthful of doughnut.

"Thanks." I study him as I pick up the coffee. It's not normal for him to act this nice. It's either because he doesn't want to say anything in front of Chloe, or he has bad news. I stare hard at him, hoping he'll take the hint.

"Right." He swallows. "It took most of the night, but it looks like the board got almost everything sorted out. Since Muriel was manipulating the TODs, they've agreed to reset Chloe's time back to what it was originally, which I'm told is quite a few years from now." He glances at me. "Of course, not much we can do about the ones who already crossed over, though."

"What does that mean?" Chloe looks from him to me.

"They've reset your time of death. It's good news." I give her a smile. Not as good for the other witches. Dead is dead. But at least Chloe's safe. I let out a breath I didn't know I was holding.

"What about Finn?" Chloe takes the teabag out of her cup and sets it on the lid. Taking a sip, she makes a face. She reaches for the two packs of sugar and stirrer sitting in the middle of the tray.

Jack's lips form a thin line. He glances at me. "Lower Management wants to talk to you. You've piled up quite a few infractions again. You'll need to sit through a hearing or two. Standard stuff. Since you seem to be making a habit of this lately, I guess you're getting used to all of it by now," he says, adding a heavy dose of sarcasm to his voice. "I doubt you'll get any time on this one but expect a demotion. Plus, you'll probably end up on the graveyard shift for a while. A long, long while." He raises an eyebrow, indicating he doesn't want to hear a word of complaint from me.

I won't say it's fine, but I'm relieved. The graveyard shift sucks. Still, it sounds like I may get off easy compared to what I was expecting. I take a drink of coffee. "When do they want to talk to me?"

"Soon. They're hoping you can shed a little light on what Muriel was up to. They've already figured out she was the one responsible for murdering the witches you were telling us about at your hearing." He reaches into the bag for another doughnut. "Did she say why she did it?"

"She didn't have to. I had already figured it out." I give Jack a condensed version of what I learned about the seals and how each death created a key. I conveniently leave out the parts about visiting a church and sneaking into his office.

"Unbelievable." Jack shakes his head. "What did she think she was going to do when she unlocked all of them?"

"Kill the devil," Chloe answers before I can say anything. "She had a blade she stole from the museum where I work. She tried to kill Finn with it, too."

"Seriously? I didn't see anything in the report about her having a weapon." Jack looks at her in surprise. He turns his attention to me. "When the board finds this out, it could help your case, Finn." He rubs his chin. "It would help a lot if I could show the blade as evidence, though. Where did it end up? Do you have it?"

Chloe glances at me excitedly. We've kept it hidden from view with one of Chloe's spells since we got back. I was planning to put the blade in my safe, but Chloe's idea seemed better. Setting my coffee down, I walk into the living room to retrieve my gym bag. I return, placing it on the island in front of her. I give her a slight nod.

She puts her hands out and touches the bag. When I open it, the blade and my gun are visible inside, still sitting on top of the money. I raise an eyebrow. Her magic really is impressive. Chloe gives me a teasing smile, letting me know she's quite pleased with herself.

I take the blade out and set it on the island, but I block Jack's view of the gun or the money.

"The blade is silver," I warn him as he reaches for it. I take another sip of my coffee. It's got a funny taste, like it's over-brewed. I reach for the bag of doughnuts as my phone rings. Setting my coffee down, I dig the phone out of my pocket. It's Corsun. "I should take this," I say casually. I don't want Jack to know about Corsun's involvement in setting up the deal for the new TOD. I head to the bedroom to take the call in private.

"Hey, what's up?" I close the door.

"Heard you toasted Muriel last night. Management is losing its shit. Both sides. You stumbled onto something big." He hesitates. "You won't, uh, tell anyone—"

He's wondering if I plan to mention how he tried to help me. "No, you're good. I owe you one."

"You owe me more than one," he reminds me. He changes the subject. "But I still haven't figured out how Muriel fits into all of this. When you get a chance, you're going to have to fill me in."

I frown. "What do you mean? I thought Muriel was the one you contacted to set everything up. She said the magistratus were watching you, so she's the one who brought us the passports and fake IDs."

"It wasn't Muriel I contacted." He sounds confused. "They must have been working together," he says finally.

"What do you mean?"

Corsun hesitates. "I thought the less you knew, the

better. My contact wasn't Muriel, it was Jack. He's the one who was changing the TODs for the angels. The only way I knew about it is because a couple of guys in my office have been supplying him with clients. When I called and told him what you needed, he sounded surprised, but he told me he would handle everything." He takes a breath. "Shit, Finn, I'm sorry. I led them straight to you."

"He's here." My brain tries to comprehend what Corsun is telling me. It's like a jigsaw puzzle with pieces missing.

"What do you mean?" Corsun asks.

"Jack's here. At my place."

"Seriously?"

I'm not sure what game Jack is playing, but a sick feeling comes over me. *The blade.* I gave it to him. I was so relieved to know Chloe's TOD was reset, I let my guard down. Or was it actually reset?

I quickly pull up the Grim Reaper app. Chloe's file still shows as pending. It's also highlighted in red, meaning there's been a transportation issue. Below is a special notice of a new TOD. 7:31.

The exact time it shows on my phone.

More puzzle pieces slip into place.

The tea. How did Jack know Chloe drank tea?

I missed it earlier. He was the one in her apartment. Since his second aura is black like mine, the ski mask and outfit must have distorted it so I didn't realize her attacker was a demon instead of a human. Jack is extremely detail oriented. I'm guessing he checked out her apartment before the attack. That's how he knew Chloe prefers tea.

"He's going to kill her!" I yell into the phone as the last pieces fall into place. Dropping the phone, I yank open the door and run toward the kitchen.

I stop. She's standing next to the island, but something doesn't seem right. "Chloe?"

She looks at me, confused.

As I get closer, the scene playing out in front of me isn't making any sense. A brown puddle of spilled tea is on the floor near the island. Near it is an empty brown cup. Next to both is Chloe's body. Bile rises in my throat. Jack kneels over her, the blade in his hand. He hasn't touched Chloe's body yet, but it's clear what's about to happen.

No. No. No.

This isn't happening. It's a dream. I need to wake up. Please let me wake up.

Nothing happens.

This is real. I remain frozen to the spot.

Jack stares up at me. His expression is almost sympathetic. "It's okay, Finn. She didn't suffer." He gestures at the cup. "Hemlock. Poisonous to humans and witches, but it kills a witch almost instantly. Not a bad way to go. The cottage grounds were full of it."

"Why?" It's the only word I can get to come out of my mouth. I'm numb.

He stares at me like he thinks I should understand. "For the power, of course. Muriel and I were going to take over Hell, build an army, and then take over Heaven." He says it as if that explains everything. "Think about it, Finn. No more Management to answer to. She and I did the first one together to keep us both honest, then decided on four witches each." He circles the blade over Chloe's body. "It was going perfectly, but then you had to go and mess everything up. Guess it still worked out in the end, though. Once I have her heart, I can do the ritual and unlock the seals by myself." He gives me a bone-chilling smile.

I try to process what Jack is telling me. "You tried to kill me." Without thinking, I place my hand over the bandage under my shirt.

He gives a frustrated sigh. "Sorry about that. You've been so hung up on doing the right thing all these years. How was I supposed to know you would break the biggest rule of all over some witch?" He motions to the coffee cup I was drinking out of before Corsun called. "All you had to do today was finish your coffee. I didn't plan to kill you, Finn. You'd have slept through the whole thing."

I only drank about half, but I have no clue what he put in it. Whatever it was, it hasn't hit me yet. I turn my attention away from him and toward Chloe instead. She's not even in Stage One yet. She doesn't realize she's dead. This most likely seems like a bad dream to her. I keep hoping it is. Clearly, it's not.

"Chloe, go wait in the foyer for me." I use the gentlest voice I can.

She stares at her body, then at me. She blinks. "What?"

"Go wait in the foyer for me." I motion with my head toward the double doors.

The V between her brows forms as she tries to work out what's going on. She follows my instructions, but when she reaches for the doorknob, her hand passes through it. She turns back, a puzzled expression on her face. "It won't open."

Jack takes his eyes off me. He's watching Chloe.

This is good.

I take a step closer while he's not paying attention. His attention turns back to me. He twists the blade around in his hand, pointing it straight at me.

This is bad.

I put my hands up. "Come on, Jack, don't make her watch this." I turn my attention to Chloe. "Go right through the foyer doors, baby." I motion with my hand. "You don't have to open one. You can go straight through it."

She still doesn't grasp what's going on. She tilts her head to the side. "I love you, Finn."

"I love you, too." My heart lurches as the conversation I had with the Charge named Artie comes back to me. I should have told her sooner. Now, it's too late.

She takes one last look at me before walking straight through one of the doors.

I sigh, relieved. She won't see what happens next. I'm going to rip Jack apart.

"Well, wasn't that sweet?" Jack's voice drips with sarcasm. "I don't understand you, Finn." He levels his gaze at me as he stands.

I don't respond. My sole attention is on the blade. How do I get it away from him? He needs it to remove Chloe's heart. I don't intend to let that happen. I keep my hands up but take a small step toward him. "Why her, Jack? Why would you do this to me?"

"It wasn't personal. It was just business," he says with a casual shrug.

I glance down at Chloe's body and swallow. "I think you've made it personal, Jack."

"No, you're wrong." He points the blade at me. "You did this to yourself. You were told to follow the rules. I told you to do your job. I tried to warn you. But then, we had to postpone the last sacrifice because you decided to talk to Mr. Fitz again. Muriel was furious because we had to lay low for a few days." He shakes his head, thinking about it. "She had seen you at some benefit with the witch, so she decided to teach you a lesson by making your girlfriend a replacement for the one we were supposed to kill that day." He motions at Chloe. "I tried to tell Muriel. I told her I didn't think it was a good idea, but she could be very persuasive when she wanted something. I probably should thank you for doing me the favor of getting rid of her. You saved me the trouble of having to do it myself." He motions downward. "Besides, a witch? Seriously, Finn? What kind of demon are you?"

"Chloe. Her name is Chloe." I take a breath. "It's over, Jack."

He rolls his shoulders back, popping his neck. "I don't think so." He cocks his head to the side. "It doesn't have to be like this, you know. There are always other witches, if that's really your thing. You could join me. I could use a good right hand to help me lead. I know you're more than capable of the job."

"What would I get out of it?" I act like I'm considering it so I can take another step or two toward him, but my eyes betray me. He comes at me with the blade. I lunge at him, but I miscalculate the distance. The blade pierces the skin of my left shoulder. He yanks it back, then jabs it into my chest. It misses my heart by inches but slides in far enough to hit a rib.

Fuck!

This is the second—no, make that third—time he's stabbed me with this blade. The son of a bitch is going down. My eyes turn black, but his do, too. I lunge for the blade to knock it out of his hand. This time, he expects it. He moves his hand back, slashing me on the arm instead. It cuts deep. I throw my hand up to block him. The blade catches me on the wrist.

I didn't drink much of my coffee, but whatever was in it is taking effect and making me seriously off my game. I'm not reacting fast enough, and I feel like I'm off balance. I weave to the side, but he shifts and strikes me again. The blade pierces the lower side of my abdomen.. My mind is getting fuzzy, too. It keeps wandering to thoughts of Chloe, and it's about to get me killed.

Concentrate, Finn. Focus.

"Had enough?" Jack moves the blade from one hand to the other. He grins at me as if he's enjoying himself. "You don't have to mourn for her. I can end it for you. Put you out of your misery."

I ignore him, moving back a few steps. I keep one arm up, ready to block him. It forces him to take a couple of steps toward me. He shifts the blade in his hand again to get a better grip. Before he can strike, I catch his arm with my other hand, twisting it back before bringing my leg up. I slam into his kneecap with the heel of my boot. Tendons pop as his kneecap shatters. Jack drops the blade, crying out in pain, but he's not going down alone. He throws himself at me and we go down together.

I hit the floor hard, landing on my side. He falls next to me. My training from Iemon kicks in. The last thing you want to have happen in a fight is to end up on the ground battling for a weapon. I flip onto my stomach as we both scramble for the blade. I almost get to it first, but before I can grab it and get back up, he's on top of me. He tries to reach over me but can't get ahold of the blade either, so he pulls on my arm instead to stop me from reaching it. I roll over onto my back and try to knock him off of me.

His hands wrap around my throat and squeeze. I pull at his arms, but I can't get in the right position to unlock his grip. I change tactics. Stretching my arm over my head, I try again for the blade. It remains just out of reach.

Jack tightens his grip on my throat. He can't kill me by choking me, but I do need oxygen. Without air, I'll pass out. No telling what he'll do to me then.

I extend my hand up again as far as I can until I touch

the tip of the blade. It burns my fingers, but I hold on to it, anyway. Pulling it closer, I work my fingers up it until I can turn it around. As the darkness swirls around me, I grab the handle and pull my arm back toward me, raising the blade up. I jab it into Jack's heart with everything I've got left.

Jack hisses as the silver burns inside his chest, but his hands remain around my neck. At first, I believe I've missed his heart completely and merely punctured one of his lungs. He continues squeezing the last breath out of me until I have spots floating in front of my eyes, but then his brain catches up with the information that his heart is no longer beating. His grip loosens, and with one very startled look on his face, he drops dead on top of me.

Panting, I try to catch my breath as I stare up at the ceiling. Jack's weight pins me beneath him. It takes every ounce of my remaining energy to push him away. He falls next to me with a thud, the blade still stuck in his chest. It didn't get me in the heart, but it would appear Jack hit a major artery when he stabbed me in the abdomen. I glance down at my blood-soaked shirt. I have no way to stop the bleeding and I'm too weak to get help because I'm losing too much blood.

I'm going to die. Three thousand years and this is it. I close my eyes, wondering what happens when it's over. It's so seldom a demon dies; I don't have a clue. I do know I've never seen the soul of a Grim Reaper or demon board the ferry.

"Well, isn't this interesting?" Jack's voice cuts through the encroaching darkness.

I force my eyelids open to find Jack staring down at me. His soul is back on its feet and he's corporeal. A sick smile twists on his face. He's going to enjoy every single second of watching me die, and when my soul separates from my body, I guess we'll get to do this song and dance all over again.

He takes a step back as I struggle to sit up. Glancing down at all the blood I'm losing; I know my death is imminent. I continue pulling myself up into a sitting position as best I can, resting both of my hands on the floor.

Jack reaches down and pulls the blade out of his own body. No learning curve for him, either. I guess as a dead Grim Reaper, he can move objects without having to practice. He steps toward me but stops as the entire room begins to shake. We both hear howling in the distance.

He freezes.

The howling grows louder, bringing back a buried memory from thousands of years ago when I was a child. I know this sound. I've heard it before.

Hellhounds.

Three of them appear to my right. They're huge black beasts, baring their teeth and growling at us like rabid dogs. I've heard a Hellhound attack is a painful way to go. I hope I die quickly.

One springs toward me. Covering my face with my arms, I expect to feel it tear into me. Nothing happens, but then Jack screams. I open my eyes to find the first one knocking his soul down to the floor, then watch as the other two jump over me to join in.

They tear him apart like hyenas preying on a wildebeest. Jack screams until the end. It's barbaric to watch, but I can't look away. It only takes a minute or two until there's nothing left. The body next to me fades until it disappears completely.

The Hellhounds finish, then one whips around to face me. I'm next. I make no sudden movements as it growls.

You had a good run, Finn.

As it leaps toward me, something strange happens. The alpha hurls herself at the other hellhound and knocks it to the ground. She snaps at the other one, too. Her ears go back. The two growl at each other, then the other one backs off. The alpha approaches me.

I raise my hand to defend myself, but she only sniffs at me, touching the palm of my hand with her snout. I slowly move my fingers one by one, gently stroking the black fur beneath her chin. Whining, she puts her entire snout under my hand. I scratch her head. She whines again. There's something familiar about her, but I can't place what it is. I'm so tired, I can't think straight.

I can't fight this any longer. With a final pat to the Hellhound's head, I stop trying and give in. My last thoughts are of Chloe as I drift away into the welcome darkness.

CHAPTER 19

October (I think):

My entire body hurts. I take inventory of the pain. Shoulder, rib, arm, wrist, stomach. Even my fingers. Why am I in so much pain?

I try to open my eyes but can't quite do it. It feels like I'm wrapped in a nice, warm cocoon.

What happened to me? Where am I? Why can't I remember?

Far away in the darkness, there's whispering.

"Is that him?"

"It is."

"What's he doing up here?"

"It's not our place to know or ask questions."

"Leave him alone. He needs to rest."

Silence.

CHAPTER 20

STILL OCTOBER (MAYBE):

Fingers touch the top of one eyelid. They force it open. A burst of white light shines into my eye.

Shit. Stop it. You're blinding me.

They let go.

Thank you.

They repeat the process with my other eye.

Seriously?

The whispers start again.

"They're both black."

"It's normal for them."

"Really? It's weird."

"Yeah. I've never seen that before."

"Why isn't he waking up?"

"His body needs time to heal. Did you see how he was when they brought him in? It was bad."

"I still don't know why he's here."

"Me neither."

"You two again? Come on, let's go. Let him rest."

I go back into the darkness.

CHAPTER 21

October (possibly):

The darkness lifts. I can't muster the energy to open my eyes, but there's more whispering. It's louder this time.

"Where is it?" I know the voice but can't place it.

"Right next to him, on the bed."

That sounds like Corsun. Why is he here? Where am I? My eyes flutter open long enough to see Corsun talking to Andrea.

What the hell? Why is she here? Why are they both here together?

Maybe I'm dreaming.

The darkness returns.

CHAPTER 22

October? Not a clue:

"Is it still there?"

It's Andrea's voice again. I fight to open my eyes, but don't have the strength.

"Yeah, it hasn't left his side since they brought him back." Corsun again.

"What does it look like?"

"I don't know. Like a dog. Big. Black. Its eyes are red."

I want to ask what they're talking about, but my brain can't make the words come out of my mouth.

The darkness beckons.

CHAPTER 23

October 27:

Someone is washing my face. It's not entirely unpleasant, but it feels strange. I want to see what's going on. I force my eyes open. A giant black dog stares down at me. I close my eyes. I'm hallucinating. That's what this is. I wait for the darkness to come again, but nothing happens. I open one eye, then the other. The dog is still there. It barks at me, wagging its tail.

Maybe I'm not hallucinating. I slowly raise my hand to pat it on the head. Then, I notice the red eyes. A Hellhound? It barks again and licks my face. *Yeah, let's not do that anymore.* I pet it again, and it lays down on the bed next to me.

Bed?

Flashes of memory rush back to me. Running away with Chloe. Our night together at the cabin. Jack poisoning her. My fight with him after he killed her, then watching him get annihilated by the Hellhounds.

I survey my surroundings. Gray walls. Gray curtains. I'm in my bedroom, in my bed, yet I have no clue how I got here. I also don't understand why I have a Hellhound lying next to me, but that's low on my list of questions at the moment.

Corsun interrupts my observations as he walks into the bedroom. "Andrea, he's awake!" he hollers into the hall. *That sounds familiar.* He smiles. "Hey, mate."

I use the little energy I have to give him a small wave with a couple of fingers. I am so confused. Why is he here?

Andrea pops her head in the door. She flips on the light, blinding me. She switches it back off. "Sorry." She moves slowly over toward the lamp on the bedside table and turns it on instead. "Where is it?" she asks Corsun.

"It's still on the bed." He points toward the Hellhound.

Well, at least I'm not hallucinating.

The Hellhound keeps an eye on her until she steps away from the bed. "How are you feeling?"

"Like I got run over by a train." I try to swallow. "My throat's dry."

A glass of water with a straw in it appears in her hand. "Here." She doesn't come any closer, but slowly reaches over to give me the glass.

"What are you doing with a Hellhound?" Corsun asks.

I struggle to sit up enough to take a drink. "I'm not sure."

"Well, it is very protective of you." He motions to Andrea. "We didn't think it was going to let her take care of you, but it finally did. Brother, it hates the angels, though."

"Angels?" I take another sip of water. It hurts to swallow.

"They've been here off and on since they brought you back," Andrea informs me.

Back? I went somewhere? "Where have I been?"

Corsun shrugs. "We don't really know. I came over after

you called and told me Jack was here. Andrea arrived a short while later and then the Grim Reaper named Tyler showed up. After that, the magistratus, Mr. Fitz, and two more angels from Upper Management arrived. Not Management, Finn. Upper Management." He almost sounds impressed. "They argued about whose custody you were in."

That also sounds familiar.

"You were in bad shape at that point," Andrea says. "I tried to help, but you had lost a lot of blood."

I still haven't figured out why she's here. Andrea hates me. Maybe I'm dreaming.

"Anyway, the magistratus got a phone call from Down Under. They backed off, and the next thing we knew, you and the angels vanished into thin air." Corsun looks at me. "You were gone for about four days, then some other angels brought you back." He lowers his voice. "They had wings, Finn. Never seen that before. They left you here." He motions to the bed.

"But why are you here?" I ask Andrea. Her presence is stranger than the Hellhound sleeping next to me or finding out angels were taking care of me. *Well, almost.*

"Chloe made me promise to take care of you."

"Chloe?" For a moment, I want to believe she's still alive, but the expression on Andrea's face tells me differently. "What do you mean, Chloe made you promise?"

"After she died—" Andrea's voice breaks. She tries again. "Well, apparently, she told this Grim Reaper named Tyler she wouldn't leave unless she could talk to me first, so he brought her to the apartment. I couldn't see her, but he convinced me she was there. She told me she loved you and she wanted me to look after you. She made me promise I would."

That's my Chloe.

"Did she get on the ferry?" I ask.

Corson nods. "Tyler came here to see if there was anything he could do to help after he dropped her off. He said she fought it every step of the way, but the magistratus didn't give her a choice. They made her board the ferry." His face softens. "Sorry, mate."

Andrea takes the water glass from me. "You should rest. The angels said it's going to take you time to recover. Honestly, we didn't believe you were going to make it."

"We'll be in the living room if you need us." Corsun puts his hand on Andrea's back.

I narrow my eyes at him. He smirks and shrugs.

I don't want to think about the two of them together. I will my brain not to go there. Instead, I want to argue that I'm fine and can get up, but I don't have the energy to make my case. I decide I'll close my eyes for a few minutes, and then I'll get up.

The Hellhound places her paw on my arm.

Corsun and Andrea leave the room, shutting the door behind them.

Listening to the rhythmic sound of the Hellhound's panting, I drift off to sleep.

CHAPTER 24

October 29:

My recovery is slow. It's never taken this long for me to heal before. Almost an entire week has passed since I had my fight to the death with Jack and Chloe died. I still can't believe she's gone. I'm guessing I'm about a fourth of the way into Stage One. I'm also apparently in the denial stage as far as my injuries are concerned. Whenever I try to do anything, I wonder why it hurts. Andrea constantly has to remind me it's going to take a while for me to feel like my old self again, especially when I mention I have no energy.

Her demon research, which I suspect consists of Reddit and stories Corsun told her, has led her to believe I have silver poisoning, which is the equivalent of mercury poisoning in humans. She keeps telling me to give it time, but for me, simply making it from the living room back to my bedroom all by myself suddenly is a major achievement. She says it's normal after surviving multiple stabbings, but it's never taken me this long to heal before.

I confess, I don't know what I would do if Andrea wasn't here to help me, but I wouldn't dare tell her that.

She is temporarily staying in one of the guest bedrooms, which means Corsun now stays here almost all the time, too. This has led to a few awkward moments, such as me walking into the kitchen the other night to get a drink of water, only to find him digging around in the refrigerator without a stitch of clothing on—well, except for his socks.

At the moment, he is thankfully at work. This leaves only me, Andrea, and the Hellhound, which Andrea has named Bella. She enchanted a red collar, so humans and witches can see Bella when she wears it. Apparently, there's a glamor spell at work, too. While Corsun and I still see her as a large black Hellhound with red eyes, to everyone else, Bella looks like a Golden Retriever. An unusually large Golden Retriever, or so I'm told.

I'm just waking up from a nap on the couch when Andrea walks into the room with two bottles of Fat Tire. Her eyes are sad. She's melancholy again.

"I miss her, Finn." She sits down next to me on the couch and hands me a bottle.

"I miss her, too."

Andrea sighs. She holds the bottle up. "To Chloe."

We clink the bottles together. "To Chloe." We both take a drink. I finish my beer and close my eyes for a minute.

When I wake up again, the baking show is on. I've discovered Andrea is a fan, too. We watch it in silence for a while.

After she finishes the beer, she works on peeling the label off the bottle with her fingernail. "Will you get to visit her?"

"Visit?" I look over at her, confused.

She points upward. "Up there."

I suspect she's talking about Heaven, but I'm not sure. I

didn't think witches believed in Heaven and Hell. I wonder how many beers she's had while I was asleep.

"That's not the way it works," I reply. Plus, I don't think the angels are going to do me any favors. Not with the type of trouble I'm in.

"Well, it wouldn't hurt to ask. Or you could do the Grim Reaper thing and sneak in. Corsun told me about it."

For half a second, I wonder if I could. Andrea's a bad influence. Back to reality, I shake my head. "Demon, remember?"

"Maybe she's gone to Hell instead." She seems excited about the possibility. "You could see her then, right?"

I raise an eyebrow.

"Okay, yeah. I guess that would be bad."

You think?

"Are you sure you don't want to have a funeral service for her or do something to remember her on Samhain?"

She doesn't answer me. This is my second time approaching the subject. Instead of telling anyone Chloe passed, Andrea and Corsun simply arranged for it to look like she took a job somewhere else and moved out of town. My experience with my Charges tells me Andrea is a solid Stage One right now.

"Have you eaten anything today?" I change the subject. "I was thinking we could order a pizza."

"What kind?" she asks.

"Pepperoni?"

"Hawaiian?" she counters.

"I guess we could—" Before I can finish, she waves her hand. A pizza box appears on the coffee table. *Impressive.*

She smiles. "I'll get the plates."

"Why don't you just—" I bring my hand up to wave like

she did, but she's already bounced up from the couch and is on her way to the kitchen. *Okay.*

Bella looks up at me from her current spot on the floor. This witchcraft stuff is new to both of us.

I shrug, and Bella rests her head on her paws and goes back to sleep.

CHAPTER 25

October 31:

It's the last day of the month and it's warm outside. It's unusual for us to have weather like this at the end of October. The sun shining in through the window doesn't match my mood at all. I pull on a pair of gray sweatpants and a black T-shirt Andrea set out for me. When I make my way into the kitchen for breakfast, she tells me the good weather is a sign.

You may have heard on Halloween—or rather, Samhain, as Andrea prefers to call it—the veil between this world and the next is at its thinnest. What this means is that during this time, it's easier for those on this side to communicate with their loved ones on the other side, and vice versa. Sometimes, they may even make an appearance. I have occasionally seen this happen, but it requires a special ticket because it's the only day of the year the ferry captain allows return trips.

Andrea hopes Chloe will visit, but I'm not as optimistic. She's still adjusting to her existence on the other side, so it's not likely they'll give her a pass after she's only been there a little over a week. I also suspect she's enjoying spending time with her parents. I can't help but wonder, though, if she misses me as much as I miss her.

On the positive side, working as a Grim Reaper has its advantages. If Chloe shows up, I won't have any trouble seeing her. On the negative side, Andrea asks every hour or so if I've seen any sign of her.

The day stretches on. All remains quiet. I tell her and Corsun I can take care of myself, but he stays with me while Andrea goes out. When she returns, she has a pumpkin and a bag with a few other things she's purchased. She brings a package of Halloween cookies into the living room.

"Happy Samhain," she announces as she sets them on the coffee table.

"She's too cheerful today. I think she's in denial," Corsun says after she disappears back into the kitchen. He reaches for the cookies.

We sit in silence, watching a black and white horror movie about a mummy while we munch on cookies decorated with orange and purple frosting. They aren't bad for store-bought.

Suddenly, Bella howls like she's trying to raise the dead on her own. And by howling, I mean, it's amazing the windows don't shatter. It's an ear-splitting noise, a cross between an ambulance siren playing through an amplifier and hundreds of banshees singing off key. It wouldn't surprise me if a tsunami appears off the coastline. It's that loud.

Belatedly, Corsun and I discover Andrea walking around, smudging the place to get the negative energy out. Unfortunately, she failed to discuss this with me or Corsun first, or we could have stopped her. She has no way of knowing a demon's life force comes from negative energy.

The nausea I experience from her cleansing ritual is almost worse than what it was like during the church incident. It comes on quickly. Bella continues her dirge in the living room while Corsun takes off running for the bathroom. I barely make it to the kitchen sink before tossing up the remnants of my breakfast, lunch, and the Halloween cookies that followed afterward.

Corsun, Bella, and I escape into the elevator. As the door closes, Andrea hollers to us that she'll do some kind of reversal spell to fix things. Or, at least that's what I think she said. Okay, I have no clue what her plan is. She simply told us to stay gone for a couple of hours while she figures it out.

Regardless, I know I'm going to receive a nasty letter from the HOA concerning unacceptable noise levels. Adding to the fun, while there are no villagers with torches and pitchforks, there is an angry group of residents waiting for us when we reach the lobby. They all want to have their say about the noise. This is bad enough, but then a fire truck pulls up out front. Apparently, the smudge stick set the smoke detector off right after we left. A short while later, there's a message on my phone from the president of the HOA. He tells me to expect a fine for that, too.

Happy Halloween.

CHAPTER 26

November 8:

We survive Halloween, but there never was a sign from Chloe. I didn't expect one, but I guess on some level, even though I knew better, I was still hoping. A week goes by, and while I don't have much energy, I believe I'm finally on the mend. I don't feel like my old self, but life has settled into a new routine. Corsun is at work. Andrea is somewhere in the apartment doing whatever it is she does when she's not by my side, looking after me, and I'm dozing on and off again while something plays on tv. It was a game show when I turned the television on, and now it's an episode of *Law and Order.*

I listen to it with my eyes closed—okay, maybe I fell asleep again. I open them to find Andrea standing in front of the television, staring at me. I hit the mute button on the remote.

"There's an angel named Wallace here to see you. He's kind of a jerk." She studies my expression. "Do you want me to get rid of him?"

Like turning him into a toad or something? Yes, please. "No, it's okay. Show him in." I suspect this is about my hearing.

"What about..." She nods at Bella. "Should I put her in another room?"

"Yeah, but show him in first." I smirk. Let's have a little fun at Wallace's expense.

She narrows her eyes, but she can't hide her grin. She's gone for a minute before she comes back into the living room with Wallace trailing behind her.

Bella stays next to me on the couch, but as soon as she sees the angel, she growls, low and deep. Her eyes burn a bright red.

"Holy shi-sk-ka-bob." Wallace stops in his tracks. He takes a step back. "Is that a Hellhound?"

"It is," I reply casually, as if having one up on the couch with me is completely normal. I reach over to rub her behind the ears.

Wallace doesn't know what to do with himself. He continues to stay glued to the spot until Andrea can't stand it anymore and takes pity on him. She shoots me a look, telling me the joke is over. "Come on, Bella."

Bella glances at me. I pat her on top of the head, then motion for her to go with Andrea. She sighs as she crawls off the couch and follows her out of the room.

I can tell Wallace wants to ask why I have a Hellhound, but he refrains. "I've never seen one before," he says instead. He moves a little closer after he's sure Bella is locked away in the other room. "Nice place you've got here."

I know. "Thank you." *See, I can play nice.* I motion for him to have a seat.

Before I can respond, Andrea returns. She glares at

Wallace, then nods at me. "I'll be in my room. Holler if you need me for anything."

"I don't think she likes me," Wallace says once he's sure she's gone. He takes a seat in the chair across from me.

"She doesn't like anyone," I reply. Immediately, my thoughts turn to Chloe.

We both stare at the television even though the sound is turned off.

"How are you feeling?" he finally asks.

"Better."

"Good."

"Yeah."

More silence.

"Any pain?"

"Some. Not too bad."

"Good."

"Yeah."

His eyes settle on the television. "You like *Law and Order,* huh?"

"Yeah."

"Me, too."

This time, I turn my attention to him and blankly stare.

After a moment, he shifts uneasily in his chair. "So, Finn—" He pauses. "I think you and I may have gotten off on the wrong foot when we first met." He doesn't return the eye contact. "I believe I could have handled things better."

That's one way of putting it.

He realizes I'm not going to respond. "Since the Angel of Death division is going through some big restructuring like the Grim Reaper division is, I guess you know I'm filling in for Muriel until Upper Management decides on her replacement."

I think he wants to say something else, but he holds back.

"Someone might have mentioned it." *Interesting. I haven't heard a thing about it.* In fact, I haven't heard a word from Lower Management, or even Management. Corsun, who always knows everything about everybody, hasn't heard anything, either.

I bite my tongue. Wallace gets a promotion because I broke the rules and stopped a takeover attempt, but I've lost Chloe, and now, I'm most likely getting a one-way ticket back to the place I saved. Life certainly isn't fair, is it?

"They want me to coordinate with you to see when you feel you can come in to talk to Upper Management." He shifts in the chair again.

I raise an eyebrow. This means the angels are handling my hearing. I felt certain the demon magistratus would want to get their claws into me again. Last time I was in serious trouble, only Grim Reapers were involved, and they handled it all in house, so I only dealt with Lower Management.

Since the rule I broke is a big one and crosses over into both divisions, it appears the Grim Reaper division has washed their hands of me and plans to let the angels decide my fate. This means they will either extradite me after I'm sentenced to more time in Hell, or maybe they plan to annihilate me themselves, since this is my second major infraction and the biggest of them all.

Finn. You. Are. So. Screwed.

I'm honestly surprised they are giving me a choice when I can see them. If there's been that big of a shakeup in Management, there's probably been a delay with my paperwork.

I shrug. "Maybe by the end of the week?" I'm not sure

what difference it makes, but I guess it's better to set a time of my own choosing than have them come and drag me out of here.

"If you're up to it." Wallace gets out his phone. He taps out a text or two—or three. "How about Friday at, say, nine o'clock?" He glances up from his phone.

"Might as well." It gives me a few days to get my affairs in order.

He taps around a little more, then puts the phone back into the pocket of his jacket. "Finn." He hesitates. "No hard feelings about the hearing after the traffic accident, right? I hope we can put all that behind us."

"I believe we can do that," I lie. I never forgive or forget, but maybe he'll put in a good word for me. He is getting promoted because of me, after all.

He lets out a breath. "Good." He stands and puts out his hand. "If you need anything, don't hesitate to get in touch."

Shit. He wants to shake hands. I expect to get frostbite as our hands touch, but I only feel a mild coolness. He pulls out a business card from his coat pocket and gives it to me. "Seriously, if you need anything at all between now and then, call me." He nods at the card. "My personal cell number is on the back."

He appears sincere. Worried about me, even. Maybe I'm not going to Hell. Perhaps, he's heard something and it really is total annihilation instead. Maybe, on some level, the angel feels sorry for me. Since they're the ones handling my hearing, I probably don't have a prayer.

You know what I mean.

CHAPTER 27

November 12:

The next few days drag by and my apprehension builds. On Wednesday, Corsun informs me that Lower Management has told him he's not allowed to accompany me when I go to see Upper Management. They refuse to even discuss my case with him, stonewalling him every time he tries to get information.

It appears I'm completely on my own for this one.

Friday arrives. This is the day I will learn my fate. I say my goodbyes to Corsun, Andrea, and Bella. Of course, if I'm on my way to Hell, I may get to see Bella there, but my future existence is uncertain, so I put my affairs in order, as they say, because I have no clue what comes next.

I arrive at the Promenade Building shortly before 9:00. I'm still finding it odd the angels are letting me surrender on my own, but they've always done things differently.

I check in at the desk. The same bored guy is on duty again today. I don't have to show my license this time. He tries to make small talk while personally escorting me over to the area on the left. He gives me a big smile and tells me I shouldn't have long to wait.

Okay, that's a bit unsettling. Strange, even.

In less than five minutes, Wallace gets off an elevator. He comes over to the waiting area.

"Good morning, Finn." He gives me a bright smile. "Right this way." He motions toward the elevators with his hand as if I don't know where I'm going.

This is bad. Really bad. Counter Guy was polite, and Wallace has been nice to me twice now.

You are screwed, Finn.

I follow him into elevator B. He swipes a card over the elevator controls, then punches in a code. "I've only been on the Upper Management floor twice," he says as the elevator doors close. "Nice tie, by the way."

So. So. So. Screwed.

We ride the rest of the way in silence while Pharrell Williams belts out *Happy* from the speakers overhead. It's a relief when the doors finally open.

I expect to find security guards waiting, but there's only one lone young angel standing in the hallway to greet us as we get off the elevator. She looks nervous. Like most of the angels in Management that I met during my last hearing, she's dressed all in white. It's a sleeveless number. She's got dark hair almost the color of mine and freckles scattered across her nose, but her skin is pale. I bet she burns to a crisp if she gets any sun at all. As we get off the elevator, she sticks her hand out to shake mine. She comes up to me about mid chest. Her handshake isn't as icy cold as some of the other angels' hands I have had to shake, but I think it's because her palms are sweating. Or maybe it's mine.

"Hello, Mr. Finn," she addresses me before greeting Wallace. "Mr. Wallace, nice to see you again."

"You, too," he replies.

"I'll take it from here," she tells him.

His expression shows disappointment. *Sadist.*

"Of course." He takes a step back, putting his hand out for me to shake again. "Good luck."

"Thanks."

He gives me a pat on the arm and one last smile before getting back on the elevator. He presses a button, and I watch the doors close.

Did I say screwed? I'm fucked. So. So. Fucked.

"My name is Celeste." Now, she's smiling at me, too. "If you'll follow me right this way." She motions ahead with her hand.

The hallway walls are a soft blue color and the marble tile on the floor is a soft white. The layout of the office space looks a lot like it does for Management, but more upscale. There are other offices we pass, but they're much bigger and have more of an executive feel to them.

When we reach the end of the hall, she waves her hand toward a room on the right. It's a corner office containing two expensive office chairs facing a fancy-looking desk with an even more expensive-looking executive chair behind it. Both are in front of a large glass window. Another long glass window is on the left. From where I stand, whoever the office belongs to has an impressive view.

Celeste waves her hand once again. "If you'd like to have a seat, they should be ready for you soon." She gives me another smile. "Can I get you anything? Coffee? Tea? We have muffins in the breakroom. I could get you one."

I shake my head. I'm too nervous to think about drinking or eating anything. "I'm fine. Thanks."

She remains rooted in place, acting like she wants to say something more. Or maybe she's waiting for me to say something. After a moment, she gives up. "Okay, well, if you don't need anything, I'll get back to work, but I'm right outside the door if you change your mind." She motions behind her toward the hall.

"Thank you."

She gives me an odd look before retreating from the room. I wipe my hands on my pants as I take a seat in one of the chairs facing the desk. It's comfortably soft. If I had to make a guess, I'd say it's suede.

After about ten minutes, I get up and pace. Catching a glimpse out the window, I stop and stare. It seems a lot higher than twenty-five stories. Everything below looks so small. I'm so high up, I can see clouds at this level. The view is like a satellite image. If I didn't know better...

I shake the thought out of my mind. Like they would bring a demon this close to Up There.

I sit and take out my phone to distract myself. No service. Management has shut off my phone. Another sign of my impending doom.

Five more minutes pass. Celeste pops her head back in the door. She gives me another odd look. "Is something wrong with the chair?" She stares at the one behind the desk.

"Looks all right to me," I reply.

She bites her bottom lip, appearing puzzled, but says nothing else about the chair. "They wanted me to let you know it won't take much longer."

The longer the better, I guess.

Ten more minutes tick by. I wonder if this is some sort of angel torture technique. Maybe they've had a holdup with my arraignment papers, or maybe things take longer when they plan to end your existence. I don't know enough about angel protocol to know what's going on.

Celeste reappears. "Mr. Mason is ready to see you now. Please, follow me." She motions with her hand yet again, a gesture that keeps reminding me of Vanna White on *The Wheel of Fortune.*

We go back down the hall, past the same elevator I rode up on, and down another hallway to the other side of the building. There are fewer offices in this wing. They're much bigger than the office I was sitting in before. Celeste stops in front of one on the left. She does the thing with her hand for a fourth time. Inside the room, she does a half curtsy as I walk by her, then gives me yet another smile.

And people think demons are evil. I'm beginning to think all angels are sadists.

"Sorry for the wait." The angel behind the desk gestures for me to take a seat. I assume this is Mr. Mason. I thought they would have me in front of the entire board like they did at my last hearing, but maybe this is only a preliminary meeting.

"No problem," I reply, because what else am I going to say?

As I expected, he's dressed all in white, too. White shirt, white tie, white jacket, white pants, white shoes, and if that wasn't enough to alert me of his status, he's also got the telltale white vest like Mr. Fitz wore. Mr. Mason has one up on him, though—even his hair is white, the color of freshly fallen snow.

"It took the paperwork a little longer to get sorted out than we expected. It's antiquated, but we like to do things old, old school on this floor." He gestures toward a small pile of scrolls stacked on the left side of his desk. The desktop is clear glass, so everything in front of him appears to float in midair. Or maybe everything actually is. I resist the urge to reach my hand out and see.

Instead, I nod, although I don't know why he's telling me all this. "I noticed I couldn't get phone service up here." I'm not sure why I mention it, but I do. Nerves, I guess. My palms are sweating again. I rub them across my pants once more.

"They've probably already turned your old phone off." He swivels around in his chair toward a pale blue bookshelf behind him and picks up a small white box. Setting it on the desk, he opens it to reveal a new iPhone. It's gold. He presses the button to turn it on, making a face as he studies the apps. "Obviously, our tech support has a sense of humor. We can change it for you if you'd like."

He slides the phone over. In the spot where my Grim Reaper app used to be, there's now an app with a blue background and a pair of black angel wings.

"You're giving me a new phone?" I don't get the joke. I'm more confused than ever.

"Well, we are on a different network," he replies, as if that explains it. He sees my expression. "Of course, if you want to keep your old phone, we can reprogram it, but it's one of the perks that comes with the promotion." He unrolls the first scroll in the pile. "Now, this explains that they approved your transfer. We've never done this type of thing before, as you might imagine, so Upper Management thought we should document it this way—" He waves his hand across the scroll, then stops. His brow furrows as he studies me. "What's wrong?"

"I thought I was here because there were several... infractions I may have committed." I choose my words carefully. *You know, including confessing to killing one of your angels and messing with the Grand Plan of the Universe.*

Now, he's confused.

"What? No. Didn't someone from Lower Management go over all of this with you last week?" He shakes his head. "Heavens to Betsy. Well, I apologize." He picks up the white phone on his desk. "Get Celeste in here, pronto." He hangs up, faking a calm smile that I'm sure is for my benefit, even though he looks tense.

Celeste appears. "Yes, sir."

"Did you not explain everything when you showed Mr. Finn his office?"

"No, sir, I thought—"

My office? Suddenly, the question about the chair makes sense, but I'm still lost. Completely and totally lost.

"Oh, dear." Mr. Mason stares at me, embarrassed. "Obviously, someone dropped the ball somewhere." He dismisses Celeste with a nod, then rests his hands on the desk. "Yes, well, from the beginning, then. During our internal investigation, we discovered Muriel's entire division needed reorganizing, so there were quite a few dismissals. Apparently, it was the same in the Grim Reaper division." He studies me. "We're not exactly sure how far the corruption goes, or if we caught all of it, so we mutually agreed to restructure both divisions completely and also create a position so someone could look into things whenever we have a problem." He points his two index fingers at me. "That's where you come in. We've given you an AoD promotion to Level Fifteen."

"Me?" I lean back in my chair, suppressing the urge to burst out laughing. Instead, I stare at him with what I'm sure is a stupid expression. "I'm no angel."

Trust me, I realized it as soon as I said it.

Not to mention, Level Fifteen is Upper Management. Now, I understand why Wallace was so nice to me. At this level, I would outrank him.

Mr. Mason suppresses a smile. “Yes, we’re well aware of that, but we still believe you’re the right one for the job.” He moves the first scroll to the side, unfurling a second one so I can read it. It has the formal announcement of promotion to Angel of Death, Level Fifteen. “There were nine souls taken before their time and not one of our angels caught on that there was something amiss. In fact, you’re the only one who questioned any of it.” He lowers his voice. “Plus, you stopped a major takeover attempt, which would have affected all of us. I can’t imagine what would have happened.” He shudders, tapping his finger on a scroll. “The point is, Lower Management wasn’t too keen about forgiving you for your infractions.” He makes air quotes around the word *infractions*. “We—or more importantly, Mr. Fitz—intervened on your behalf and the Board approved your transfer. You could, of course, refuse, but I don’t think you would like Lower Management’s plans for you. I think if you give us a chance, you’ll find we’re more forgiving up here. We need you, and we hope you’ll accept.”

I’m in shock. “What exactly would I be doing?” I can’t believe I am considering this. Earlier, I thought I was toast. Now, I’m getting a transfer to the angel division and a promotion. I don’t even know what to say.

“Well, we need the new AoD recruits chosen and trained. We would want you to oversee that first, but we also want you to head up a bilateral task force to investigate ethereal misconduct on both our side and the demon side, too. Lower Management does agree with us about that.” He takes a breath. “As I said, it has become apparent the corruption was a lot more widespread than we first thought." Frowning, he unfurls more scrolls and begins going over the job duties.

I'm still not sure what to think, but I guess it beats the alternative.

"Questions?" he asks when he's finished.

"I can't think of any." *I have so many questions.*

He smiles. "Well, as your assistant, Celeste can answer them, if you do." He picks up a white feather, which I am certain was not on his desk a few seconds ago. He hands it to me, along with a small bottle of black ink. Turning the first scroll around where I can read it, he points at several different places for me to sign. "Now, we'll need to get your signature here, here, here, and here."

Bella is waiting at the elevator door in the foyer when I arrive back at my place. I don't even care when she jumps up, knocks me backward into the table, and licks the entire length of my face with one long stroke of her tongue. I'm just relieved I'm here.

Andrea comes through the foyer doors to see what all the commotion is about. She stands in front of me, stunned, then rushes toward me. She hugs me hard. Really hard. It's about a full minute before she releases me.

"We will never speak of this again," she warns me.

"Never," I agree.

We walk through the double doors together, Bella following in my footsteps.

"Hey, Sugar Bear, I found leftover spaghetti in the fridge —" Corsun walks out of the kitchen, holding a glass container in one hand and a fork in the other. “Finn, holy fuck! You’re back!” He moves in for an awkward hug that pins my arms to my side. He releases me, grabs my hand and pumps my arm in a handshake, gives me a fist bump, and then we’re back to the awkward hugging thing again before he finally releases me for a second time. A spaghetti noodle hangs from the corner of his mouth. He holds out the container. “Want some?”

I shake my head. “Are those my sweatpants?”

He’s gotten tomato sauce on them.

“Yeah, I didn’t think you’d need them anymore.” He glances down. “Oh, shit.” He puts the fork into the container and wipes at the spot with his hand. “I’m sure you can get that to wash right out.”

“Keep them.” I shake my head. I haven’t been gone a whole day and he’s already into my stuff.

“Tell us what happened.” Andrea shoos Corsun away, motioning for him to take the food back into the kitchen.

We all end up in the living room. Andrea pours drinks while I launch into my story. It takes about an hour to recount my day because Corsun keeps saying, “Holy shit!” over and over again, interrupting me.

“I don’t understand,” Andrea remarks. “How are you able to be up there? I thought you said you couldn’t enter Heaven.”

“Upper Management isn’t Heaven,” Corsun corrects her. “Upper Management, Lower Management, and everything in between are considered neutral ground.”

“Can you find out how Chloe is doing once you’re working up there?” she asks, hopeful.

I shake my head. “Completely different department.” Although, I confess, it’s already crossed my mind to try, but I don’t want to give Andrea false hope.

"Well, congratulations, mate. You live to fight another day." Corsun slaps me hard on the back. "This calls for a celebration!" He grins at me. "And this time, you really are buying dinner."

CHAPTER 28

November 25

Somehow, I survive my first week as an Angel of Death and although it's hard to believe, I'm closing in on the end of my second. I suspect my coworkers have already given up on the Angel of Death title, though. Despite my AoD15 promotion, I suspect most of them still consider me a Grim Reaper. I don't quite fit in, and frankly, I look hideous in pristine white, which is apparently what Upper Management prefers us to wear, although I've found nothing in the handbook they gave me to officially confirm this.

The problem is, I can't keep anything white clean.

On Tuesday, I caught the angel sitting directly across from me staring at the brown coffee spot on my white tie. He fixated on it the entire time we were in the meeting. Later, as we headed back to our offices, he even felt obligated to point it out to me in front of everyone else in the hall. And yet, they say demons are the ones hard to get along with.

~~**Who Moved My Halo: Angel of Death Training 101:**~~

~~*Trying a New Way of Doing Things; Following Team Etiquette Makes You a Team Player.*~~

The 7 Habits of Highly Effective Reapers: Grim Reaper Training 101: *Reframing the Situation When Dealing with Adversity.*

This morning, I'm back to wearing black. Black sports jacket, black button-up shirt, black pants, and black shoes. I also did away with the tie. No one has said anything about my wardrobe choice, but I think it's a relief to everyone, especially after I had the copier ink cartridge mishap on Monday.

Don't ask.

Thankfully, I get to go back into the field next week, even though I'll have an Angel of Death in training shadowing me.

Yay, me. Don't get me wrong. I don't totally hate the job. It's just that, unlike demons who get the Grim Reaper designation at birth, angels believe the Angel of Death job is a noble calling because positions are given as promotions. Since Muriel and Jack's coup attempt corrupted quite a few angels, I've spent most of the last week and the first three days of this one either interviewing potential candidates for the Angel of Death program, or I've been in meetings. Lots and lots and lots of meetings.

Today, I return to my office after the latest one to discover I have received a slap on the wrist in the form of an email after I used the word *fucked* in a staff meeting.

From: rthompson@angelsofdeath.org
Subject: Language
Date: November 18 14:32
To: afinn@angelsofdeath.org

Mr. Finn,

Mistakes happen. Beings get frustrated. Please note, we do not allow swearing on the premises. While we cannot control what occurs after hours, we do strongly encourage our team members to refrain from using profanity at all times. If you feel this is not possible, please select one or more of the allowed alternative expressions from our approved list of more suitable words that you will find listed below (also see attached).

Have a blessed day,

R. Thompson

Angel Resources, Upper Management

Suitable Words We Allow:

Fudge
Fudgesicles
Lucifer, Lilith, Beezlebub
Beezlebub on a biscuit
Sunday beaches
Son of a biscuit eater
Fiddlesticks
Gee wilikers
Balderdash
Hells bells and buckets of blood
Cow patties
Son of a gun
Oh, snap
Holy cow
Sugar
Merlin's beard
Sticky wicket
Good grief
Goodness gracious

H, E, double hockey sticks
Jiminy Cricket
Holy moly
Heavens to Betsy
Good Heavens
Bloomin' heck
Heaven help me/us

Well—fuck.

CHAPTER 29

November 26:

It's 4:25 in the afternoon. I am so ready to have this week over with. I've had another steady stream of Angel of Death candidates passing through my office, and all the names and faces have become one big blur. Mr. Mason wants the final list by the end of the day, so I've been doing interviews back-to-back with no breaks in between ever since I returned from lunch.

Pinching the bridge of my nose, I make a conscious effort to relax my shoulders. I swear, I've never talked to so many angels in my entire life.

"Is that all of them?" I ask hopefully as Celeste comes into my office.

Please say yes.

She gazes down at the floor. "Pretty much, sir—I mean, Finn."

We've been over the *sir* thing a few times, but she continues to either call me that or Mr. Finn. I'm not sure which is worse.

"What do you mean, pretty much?" I study her. She's

holding a folder behind her back. "There's still one candidate sitting out in the waiting area, but I suspect they were added to the list by mistake. Since it's so close to 5:00, I was going to tell them all the positions have been filled."

I almost tell her that, if that's the case, she can go ahead and put the file on top of the stack with the others who didn't make the cut, but now, she's got me curious. "Why do you think it's a mistake?"

She hesitates. "There's been some disciplinary issues. It's in their file." She brings it out from behind her back and drags a finger down the page. "They—well, the candidate keeps asking for a transfer to—" She casts her eyes downward.

I try to remember what's on the floor beneath us. I make a guess. "Accounting?"

She shakes her head, pointing at the floor. "Farther down. They want a transfer down there, sir." She fidgets. "To Hell, I mean." She points again. "The candidate keeps wanting angel resources to transfer them to Hell." She sounds horrified. "Why any angel would want to work for them..." Her voice trails off.

I raise an eyebrow. I know I intimidate her, but sometimes she makes it too easy. I decide to have some fun. "You don't enjoy working for me, Celeste?"

"What?" She considers what she's said. "That's not what I meant, sir." She stares at me, eyes wide. "I mean, Finn."

I give her a look. "What *did* you mean?"

"What? I mean—yes, I do. I like working for you a lot, Mr. Finn. You're different."

"Just Finn," I remind her. "How am I different?" I tent my hands on top of the desk. "Tell me."

Stop it, Finn. You're terrifying the girl.

"Finn. Well, you do things a lot differently than—" She waves her hand toward the door. "Them."

The angels.

"So, no complaints?"

"Yes, sir. I mean, no, sir. Mr. Finn. I mean—" Her entire face becomes a brilliant shade of red as she continues to flail about. "Cow patties," she mutters. "I'll shut up now."

I hide my smile. Glancing at my watch, it's 4:30. Mr. Mason wants the final list by 5:30 today at the latest. If Celeste leaves at 5:00 and the interview goes beyond that, it's me who will end up having to type it out on the keyboard. They did not cover typing skills in Grim Reaper Training 101, and I suck at it. This last candidate has me curious, though. I reach for the file. "Give me that, and send them in. You can leave at five o'clock."

She smiles. "Thank you, sir—er, Mr. Finn, I mean—" She places the file on the edge of the desk, watching me nervously as I pick it up. She takes a step back, does the half curtsy thing, then scampers out of my office.

This. This is your life now, Finn.

I lean back in my chair, tilt my head back, and close my eyes. It's been one long week.

"You can go right in." Celeste's voice rings out from the hallway.

I keep my eyes closed for a few more seconds. *Find your peaceful place, Finn. This is your last one. You can do it.*

"Finn?"

I'd know that voice anywhere.

My heart does a weird pitter patter. It skips a beat. My eyes snap open.

This isn't real. I'm asleep. I'm dreaming. That's what this is.

I close my eyes again and slowly reopen them. I blink.
Copper hair. The most stunning blue eyes I've ever seen.
Chloe stands in the doorway.
Holy Fudge.

Acknowledgments

What an incredible journey it has been to reach this point of having my book published. Even as I write this, I know I'm going to forget to acknowledge someone, so know that when I say I want to thank my family and friends who have supported me along the way, I mean you, even if I don't mention you by name.

Thank you to my agent, Leslie Truex, for championing my manuscript and helping to find it a home. I still smile whenever I think about how you told me you first read my story while you were traveling, and how you kept having to tell your husband why you were laughing out loud as you were reading it.

Thank you to the entire Blue Ridge Literary Agency community. Losing Dawn Dowdle, our illustrious leader, was hard, but the ongoing comradery and support we've continued to all give each other is amazing. I appreciate every one of you.

Thank you to Harbor Lane Books for taking a chance on a debut author, and showing me patience and understanding, even though I'm sure I occasionally make you want to pull your hair out or bang your head against a desk.

Thank you to my Beta Readers, especially Christine and Emma. Your invaluable input helped make my story into what it finally became.

Thank you to Adam and William (you will always be

'Pat' to me) for letting me bounce ideas off you, and for your advice and constructive criticism.

Thank you to my Literary Sisters (you know who you are) for the wonderful camaraderie, handholding, and occasional tough love.

Thank you to Anita, Lisa, and Wendy for the friendship and support. You have kept me sane throughout the writing process and gone above and beyond every time I needed talking off that proverbial cliff!

Thank you to Bill for putting up with my crazy dream of becoming a published author. Your love and support mean everything.

Thank you to everyone in the writing community who helped me along the way, and a special thanks to all of you who took a chance on me by buying and reading this book.

And—finally, thank you to Finn, my snarky Grim Reaper, who appeared one day and wouldn't leave me alone until I agreed to write his story. It's been an incredible experience and I look forward to continuing our relationship. I know. I know. You dictate...I type.

ABOUT THE AUTHOR

C.A. Kennedy is a fantasy romance and mystery author with a propensity for quirky characters and good stories with a 'gotcha' twist. Although she always considered herself a mystery writer, when a snarky demon grim reaper kept bugging her to tell his story, she knew she couldn't refuse. When she isn't writing or channeling her inner demon, you can find her spending time outdoors with her Golden Retriever, Murphy, and trying to stay in the good graces of her two cats, McGee and Tobias.

www.cakennedynovels.com

 facebook.com/CAKennedyAuthor

 instagram.com/cakennedyauthor

ABOUT THE PUBLISHER

Harbor Lane Books, LLC is a US-based independent, digital publisher of commercial fiction, non-fiction, and poetry.

Connect with Harbor Lane Books on their website www.harborlanebooks.com and TikTok, Instagram, Facebook, X (formerly known as Twitter), and Pinterest @harborlanebooks.

facebook.com/harborlanebooks
x.com/harborlanebooks
instagram.com/harborlanebooks

www.ingramcontent.com/pod-product-compliance
Lightning Source LLC
Chambersburg PA
CBHW021620030826
48979CB00034B/485
9781963705164